Praise for *The Serpents Trail* . . .

"Devotees of Henry's Alaska mysteries will be delighted to see sixty-three-year-old Maxie McNabb, the Winnebago-driving, free-spirited widow introduced in *Dead North,* starring in this gentle whodunit. . . . Cozy crime fans . . . will love to live vicariously through Maxie and Stretch in what promises to be a long and popular run of adventures."   —*Publishers Weekly*

"Another winner. . . . A fine series debut."   —*Booklist*

. . . and the "wonderfully evocative"* Jessie Arnold series

"Twice as vivid as Michener's natural Alaska, at about a thousandth the length."   —*The Washington Post Book World*

"The twists and turns keep you turning the pages . . . a thoroughly good read."   —*The Denver Post*

"Henry revels in the wilderness of Alaskan scenery and keeps the tension mounting. . . . A fine adventure."
—*The Cleveland Plain Dealer*

"This fast-paced page-turner will make the miles fly during any trip."   —*Boston Herald*

"[Henry's] descriptions of Alaska's wilderness make you want to take the next flight out, buy heavy sweaters, or at least curl up with an afghan, a cup of steaming hot chocolate, and the book."
—*The Phoenix Gazette*

"[Her] grasp of tense storytelling and strong characterization matches her with Sue Grafton. Give her a try—she'll challenge your powers of perception and deduction."
—*The Colorado Springs Gazette*

"Sue Henry is an agile writer . . . hard to put down."
—*The Charleston Post and Courier*

*The Baltimore Sun

THE
SERPENTS TRAIL

A MAXIE AND STRETCH MYSTERY

SUE HENRY

AN ONYX BOOK

ONYX

Published by New American Library, a division of
Penguin Group (USA) Inc., 375 Hudson Street,
New York, New York 10014, USA
Penguin Group (Canada), 10 Alcorn Avenue, Toronto,
Ontario M4V 3B2, Canada (a division of Pearson Penguin Canada Inc.)
Penguin Books Ltd., 80 Strand, London WC2R 0RL, England
Penguin Ireland, 25 St. Stephen's Green, Dublin 2,
Ireland (a division of Penguin Books Ltd.)
Penguin Group (Australia), 250 Camberwell Road, Camberwell, Victoria 3124,
Australia (a division of Pearson Australia Group Pty. Ltd.)
Penguin Books India Pvt. Ltd., 11 Community Centre, Panchsheel Park,
New Delhi - 110 017, India
Penguin Group (NZ), cnr. Airborne and Rosedale Roads, Albany,
Auckland 1310, New Zealand (a division of Pearson New Zealand Ltd.)
Penguin Books (South Africa) (Pty.) Ltd., 24 Sturdee Avenue,
Rosebank, Johannesburg 2196, South Africa

Penguin Books Ltd, Registered Offices: 80 Strand, London WC2R 0RL, England

Published by Onyx, an imprint of New American Library, a division of Penguin
Group (USA) Inc. Previously published in a New American Library edition.

First Onyx Printing, March 2005
10   9   8   7   6   5   4   3

Copyright © Sue Henry
All rights reserved

Map and author photo by Eric Henry at Art Forge Unlimited

 REGISTERED TRADEMARK—MARCA REGISTRADA

Printed in the United States of America

Acknowledgments

With sincere thanks to:

The people of Grand Junction, Colorado, who were so generous with their expertise, guidance, and hospitality, both long distance and in my visits to that fascinating area

Especially to:

Henrietta Hay—friend, mystery fan, and sports-car-driving liberal in a conservative town—whose weekly column in the local *Daily Sentinel* is its most popular feature. Happy ninetieth, Henrietta

The National Park Service at the Colorado National Monument, Superintendent Palma Wilson, and Ranger Todd Overbye

The Grand Junction Visitor and Convention Bureau

The Grand Junction Area Chamber of Commerce

Joe and Ellen Hopkins for their kind hospitality

Also to:

Claire Carmichael McNab, my expert on all things Aussie

My brother John Hall, the family geologist

My son Eric Henry of Art Forge Unlimited for the author photo and map

Maxye Henry of Motor Home Magazine

Fran Connors, Recreation Vehicle Industry Association

A&M RV Center, Anchorage, Alaska

High Country Gardens of Santa Fe, New Mexico, for information on plants for western gardens

For J. A. Jance,
who took the time to listen,
and encouraged the creation of this series

And for all the readers of *Dead North,*
who asked me to give
Maxie McNabb and her mini-dachshund, Stretch,
a book of their own

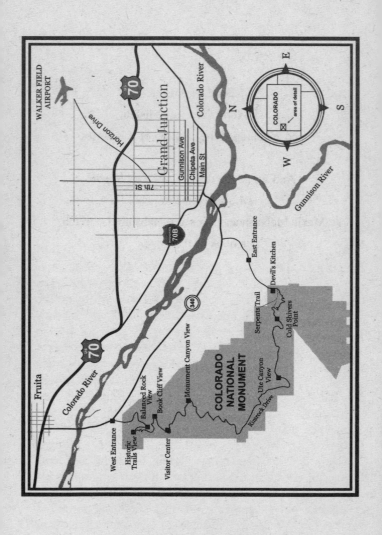

CHAPTER ONE

A PARTIALLY OPEN DOOR ALWAYS HAS A QUESTION IN IT.

At the end of a four-thousand-mile road trip, I stood on the back porch of Sarah Nunamaker's large Victorian house in the center of Grand Junction, Colorado, uneasily considering the half-open door that swung ever so slightly as the curious fingers of a dying breeze reached in under the sheltering roof to give it a tentative nudge. After robust and extended use of the heavy brass knocker on the front door had resulted in nothing but echoes and silence from within, I had made my way through a side garden and around to the backyard, glancing up at each window that I passed for evidence of occupation within. At well after eight o'clock in the dark of the mid-September evening, all of them showed nothing but the mottled reflection of a streetlight that filtered in between the curbside trees. Only one, a rear second-story pane, held a soft hint of illumination that crept through the lace curtains of a room I knew from past visits was Sarah's bedroom.

The discovery of the partially open back door had me

frowning in concern as I considered the situation. I knew that my arrival had been anticipated, so something was wrong. Had there been an unpredicted turn for the worse in Sarah's condition? Had she been transported to the local hospital? It would explain why there was no one to respond to my summons at the front door. The light that was barely visible in that upper room could have been left on in the rush that resulted from a medical emergency. But why that light and no other?

And why an open door if no one was at home?

It was later than I had expected to arrive in Grand Junction. But as I had driven the last few miles into town a late summer storm had swept in with a ferocity of wind, thunder, and lightning that had sent pedestrians lunging into doorways and dashing under trees for shelter from an unanticipated barrage of hail that preceded the tempest's primary thrust. For a few menacing minutes pearls of ice had rattled and rebounded from pavements and roofs before rolling into gutters where they were swirled away into storm drains by the five minutes of torrential rain that followed before they could melt. The sudden elemental assault had forced me to pull my Winnebago motor home off the road and wait it out. The clatter of hail playing the roof like a snare drum had roused my mini-dachshund, Stretch, from his nap in a basket that hung from the front of the passenger seat's backrest and set him barking defensively at the threat he couldn't identify.

"Cool it, you silly galah," I told him, reaching across to lay a calming hand on his head. "It's only noise that can't hurt us."

Even when caught out in one, I have always enjoyed the energy and abrupt force and crash of thunderstorms, which are not common where I live in Alaska. They are like grand music, with kettledrums and cymbals within a string and woodwind orchestra of falling, splashing water. My favorite exhibitions are the ones that occur at night, with lightning hurled like fireworks from the sky, immediately followed by the thunder's growl, exciting and stimulating to the senses.

This storm was not without welcome as it cooled and added humidity to the hot, dry air. The last few days of travel through Idaho, Utah, and finally into western Colorado had been warmer than I was used to in the far north, or had expected in the Lower 48 this late in the summer. Though the Winnebago has efficient air-conditioning, I hate the feeling of being sealed inside a box of any kind, moving or otherwise. I can't escape the feeling that eventually I may breathe all the oxygen out of the air and wind up gasping like a fish out of water. I feel the same way about hotels with unopenable windows, and avoid them if possible. So, I had dressed in a cool sleeveless blouse and my denim traveling skirt, and let the warm air blow in through open windows most of the time as we approached the high desert of the Colorado Plateau through Utah.

Over as abruptly as it had begun, in fifteen minutes the storm had moved away and the wind had died to a zephyr, leaving water gurgling down drains and the leaves and branches of trees bent with the weight of left-over rain they were shedding. The scent of ozone faded and that of damp vegetation and the rain evaporating from hot pavement drifted in as I made my way through half-remembered streets, finally locating Sarah's familiar address on Chipeta Avenue, a block south of Gunnison, in the center of town.

I was tired after the long trip. Still it had taken less time than usual for me to drive the highway from Alaska to

Colorado, because most days I had traveled farther than normal by spending longer hours on the road. On other trips down the Alaska Highway I had taken my time, stopping to enjoy visits to favorite places and people along the way. It is a journey of spectacular scenery in which I always take pleasure, and had done on this trip, though I had skipped several of my customary intermissions—a soak in Liard Hot Springs, an overnight with friends at Dawson Peaks Resort in Teslin, an always fascinating visit to the Jasper Rock Shop, a stop at the carousel by the riverbank in Missoula. In leaving Alaska, however, I had indulged myself a little by taking a favorite cutoff, rather than traveling straight down the Alaska Highway to the Canadian border crossing.

Eleven days earlier, before entering Canada, I had stood beside my thirty-foot Minnie Winnie motor home and gazed west into my home state from a turn-out at the highest point on the Top of the World Highway between Alaska and Dawson City in the Yukon Territory, 4,515 feet above sea level. Looking back across a hundred miles of ridge after purple-blue ridge of mountains that form the Alaska Range, I had wondered how long it would be before I would see them again.

My hair is thick and dark brown, with more and more silver each year. I wear it long enough to use a clip to fasten it high on the back of my head in a kind of twist that keeps it off my neck. As I stood there and appreciated the incredible view, the wind tugged several strands loose and blew them across my face. Noticing that silver, for a moment or two I wondered if it was still a good idea, at sixty-three years old, to be leaving all that was familiar and safe to take to the road again. I couldn't help smiling, however, as the satisfaction of pleasing no one but myself replaced the momentary hesitation. My smile widened and I felt like a child running away from home with an extra-large satchel full of all her favorite toys and snacks.

I love to drive, and there aren't that many roads in Alaska, where we climb into airplanes the way most of the world drives or catches a bus. It was, as ever, exhilarating to be traveling again, though my destination was more specific and less carefree than usual.

My short-legged mini-dachshund companion had trotted off to explore the rocks and weeds around the edge of the turnoff, his ears flapping slightly in the wind. He ignored my first "Come along, Stretch." Glad to be free of his leash, he asserted the independence of his breed by pretending he hadn't heard me and trotted a bit farther away.

"Come here, you," I told him firmly, taking a step in his direction. "Time to go if we want to get across the Yukon before the ferry stops running. I want dinner tonight in Dawson City—one I don't have to cook for myself."

He cocked his head to look back and make sure I was serious, then came padding back cheerfully enough and allowed himself to be lifted into the motor home and deposited in his padded basket. It raises him up for a comfortable view of the passing scenery, which he loves, so he immediately scrambled up to put his front feet on the edge, ready for whatever was coming next.

I hesitated long enough to move the hands of my watch an hour ahead, remembering that the time changes as you cross into Canada, then put the Winnebago in gear and drove back onto the well-maintained gravel width of the Top of the World. I made a quick stop a few minutes later at the border, to assure the friendly customs agent that I carried no contraband and would be passing straight through parts of Yukon Territory, British Columbia, and Alberta on my way down to the Old Country, as I at times refer to the forty-eight contiguous United States.

Crossing international borders always makes me cross my fingers as I tell one falsehood that would probably show up as a significant spike in a lie-detector test. When I bought the Winnebago and knew I would be once again traveling alone, I hired a trusted neighbor to build a secret sliding panel over a hidey-hole large enough to stash a shotgun with extra shells. This is definitely illegal if it is not declared, but as it makes me feel safer and, since it isn't a handgun, I commit the sin of omission with as innocent a smile as I can muster. They would have a devil of a time finding it, even if they knew it was somewhere aboard. Besides, who's going to search the motor home of a sixty-three-year-old grandmother anyway?

Just knowing that shotgun is there if I need it has made me feel better about flitting around by myself the last few years. Where you could miss more easily with a handgun, or have it taken from you, it seems to me that anyone bent on a break-in or assault should be rightfully reluctant to challenge an alarmed female senior citizen holding a shotgun in her unsteady hands. So, I showed the agent my passport with all five of my names on it—Nora Maxine Stillman Flanagan McNabb, which always makes them smile—and he, unsuspecting, waved us cheerfully across into Canada.

Though the journey would not be a leisurely one, and this side trip would take a bit longer than the usual Alaska Highway to Whitehorse route, where the two roads come together, I was glad that I had taken it, especially on such a clear day. It had let me take a departing look at a breathtaking part of the state that I love and will always return to, sooner or later.

The reason for my making the trip without unwarranted delay was a promise my old and dear friend, Sarah Nunamaker, and I had made long ago to always *be there* for each other. When Sarah, now terminally ill with a heart condition, had phoned and reminded me of that agreement, I had offered to fly there immediately. She had assured me it was not necessary—that I should bring the motor home in which I intended to spend the winter in New Mexico. I was relieved that there would be enough time to settle my mind about her approaching death before arriving, for highway travel always calms and revitalizes me. Concern had kept me heading steadily south, knowing time was limited and would sadly be less than either of us wished, and shorter for every day it took me to arrive.

"The doctors have promised me at least a couple of months, dear," she had told me. "Just come as soon as you safely can in that rolling house, and don't take chances. I'll be—fine until you get here."

Her tone had faltered on the last sentence and I, knowing her well, had sensed an odd hesitation in the assertion.

"What's wrong, Sarah? You might as well tell me."

There had been a significant silence from the other end of the line before she spoke again. I had waited it out with an uneasy feeling.

"Maxie, I need your help—as well as your smiling face—need you to figure some things out for me. But it's not telephone conversation and will keep till you get here. I . . ." Her words had faltered again and drifted to a halt. "Don't worry, or drive that thing too fast. It's not about my health. There are things I need to tell and show you. I need your advice on some important things—but they'll wait. Just come."

Two days later, I had the Winnebago serviced and stocked, the neighbor who cares for my house when I'm away notified, the post office advised to forward my mail, and drove away from Homer on the first leg of the long journey, to Anchorage and points east and south. Early afternoon of the second day of driving had brought me to this high Canadian border, where not quite seventy miles and a river crossing would put me into Dawson City.

I had enjoyed the previous winter in the Southwest and meant to spend this one in New Mexico. The previous June I had driven the long road north for the first time in two years to spend three months in my small house in Homer at the end of the road on the Kenai Peninsula.

It had been a satisfying summer at home tending my garden, spending long afternoons in the hammock on the deck that overlooks the glorious Kenai Mountains that frame Kachemak Bay, and renewing the relationship with my extensive library. There had been congenial evenings with old friends gathered around my large dining table to enjoy good food and wine seasoned with a gratifying abundance of conversation and laughter.

I had soaked in the pleasure of belonging and wandering the familiar rooms of the house built by my first husband, Joe. An early morning sun had caught fire in water droplets along each strand of a spider's web and gilded each blade of grass in the yard as I stood on the deck with my coffee mug warm between my hands. One memorable mid-August night I had laid aside a book and gone out to watch a full moon rise like a five-dollar gold piece that laid a gleaming path of reflection across the calm waters of the bay. Above it gossamer wisps of the aurora borealis had slowly coalesced into a glowing point directly overhead, then cast pulsing arms of light stained green and red and blue to the horizon on all sides in an enormous star. Through this unusual formation had fallen a shower of the annual Perseid meteors, tripling the natural extravagance. I had laid myself down in the hammock and watched in awe until the aurora faded and my eyelids grew heavy.

As always, I missed my late husband, Daniel. In the place we lived together, I find reminders of him everywhere, but five years have mellowed that specific grief from the sharp anguish of loss to a more lingering nostalgia. Remembrances of my second husband are welcome, for time has finally made memories more significant than absence.

"We had six fine years before you nicked off, you stubborn old Aussie coot," I said to him, fondly and aloud, a habit that I enjoy and have no intention of breaking. He is still good company.

Daniel McNabb, Australian expatriate, is not the only husband I have cherished and outlived, however. At forty-five, I scattered the ashes of Joe Flanagan, my high school sweetheart and first husband, into the waters of the bay, after he drowned in the storm that sank his commercial fishing boat. Meeting and marrying Daniel years later was a surprising gift when I least expected it and considered myself a confirmed widow. From him I picked up bits of Aussie slanguage that frequently slip in to enliven my speech and, though I sometimes confuse their meaning a bit, the sound and rhythm is familiar and comforting to me and to Stretch, who was originally his dog.

Alone again at sixty-three, I know I was lucky in both relationships, but have no inclination toward another. My independent spirit has finally won out over any desire for companionship.

Daniel's careful investments left me with no financial concerns. So I used some of the interest to buy a motor home, found a caretaker for my house in Homer, and took off to see parts of the world that, except during college years, I had missed by living in the far north. During the past summer, however, I stopped at a motor home show in Anchorage where I instantly fell in love with a Winnebago Minnie Winnie and traded in my Jayco for a new rig. It provides compact, comfortable room for us with hydraulically powered slide-outs for both the central space and bedroom, which gives me extra room when parked, and has enough storage for the limited cargo I find necessary for a snug existence on wheels.

I'm a reasonably practical person, old enough to have learned not to waste time on nonsense or things I can't control. I try to see the world and people around me as clearly as possible, good and bad, and keep my expectations at a realistic level. A sense of humor is important to me. I don't bother to impress anyone, or fool myself or others, but rather take what's positive, deal directly and as little as possible with the negative, and get on with it. Traveling and meeting new people have turned out very well. Sarah's request made me sad, and leaving Alaska sooner than I had planned confused a few things, but I wasn't sorry to get back to my nomadic lifestyle after a pleasant summer at home. Perhaps I've always been a gypsy in at least part of my heart.

So, headed down the Canadian side of the Top of the World Highway that snaked along the ridges until it dropped steeply down to meet the upper reaches of the Yukon River, I was definitely getting on with it. Part of my mind was concerned with reaching Colorado, for it wasn't like Sarah to be reluctant to talk about much of anything, at least with me. For the moment, putting whatever it was that my friend needed to share with me on hold, another part of me was delighted to be starting a trip on my own and relishing that feeling of playing hooky.

I made it to the ferry in good order and into Dawson City on the other side of the Yukon River. There, I found an RV park in the middle of that historic site of the Klondike Gold Rush, followed by a sustaining shot of Jameson's Irish before dinner at the Downtown Hotel on the corner of Second and Queen Streets, right where I expected it.

A week later I fibbed my way across the Canadian border again, this time into Montana, and three days after that I was a few miles outside Grand Junction, Colorado, when the storm forced me momentarily off the highway.

CHAPTER TWO

As I STOOD ON SARAH'S BACK PORCH, CONTEMPLATING the dark house and the open door, the breeze died into total stillness. Not a leaf moved in the aspen trees that had been ashimmer at the slightest breath of air from the end of Sarah's garden. Retreating to the bottom of the porch steps, I looked up to make certain there really was a light in that second-story window. There was. I also noticed that a few stars had appeared overhead. They seemed to drift across the sky in an illusion created in opposition to the clouds that were quickly breaking up to slide away over the surrounding cliffs and plateaus.

I now had two immediate questions: why the back door had been left ajar when other access to the house was closed and locked, and whether or not to go through it into the house in search of my friend Sarah. Where was she, after all? The situation made me uneasy enough to consider going back to the motor home to dig out my shotgun. I told myself not to allow paranoia to gain a hold on my thinking, and gathered resolve.

Crossing the porch to a window beside the open back

door, I cupped my hands around my eyes to close out residual light and peered into what I knew from prior visits was the kitchen. Beyond the dark contours of the table and ladder-back chairs of a breakfast nook, vague shapes of cupboards and the bulk of a refrigerator were silhouetted against a single beam from a streetlight that found its way through from the front of the house. All was shadows. Nothing moved.

Inside there would at least be a telephone through which to transmit my questions and concerns to someone, find answers, and determine a course of appropriate action. Making up my mind, I pulled the door wide open and, stepping into the kitchen, closed and locked it quietly behind me. I had forgotten that Sarah had refused to have her old-fashioned push-button switches replaced with newer ones, so it took a minute for me to identify the fixture that my fumbling fingers found beside the door. Adjusting mental expectations back several decades, I pushed the one at the top and the kitchen sprang to life in the light from a ceiling fixture.

It was a long corridor of a room, clean and orderly, with the tall, mossy-green cabinets of an earlier age reaching to the ceiling above pale yellow countertops. Modern laborsaving influence was revealed in a microwave that had been installed under a vent hood over the stove and a dishwasher with a heavy chopping-block top that stood on rollers where it had been pushed out of the way into a corner. The room smelled faintly of toast, onions, and a hauntingly familiar flowery scent that wasn't immediately identifiable but spoke to me of Sarah. The window behind the sink was open about an inch, enough to allow the dying breeze to gently stir a pair of green and yellow striped café curtains that I remembered.

Hesitating by the door, I listened carefully and,

though there was nothing but silence, there was an inexplicable atmosphere that made me feel, uneasily, that I might not be alone in the house. Something about the place didn't seem empty—some shift of air, a sound beyond my ability to hear inspired the sensation that someone else was present and listening. Ever practical, I shrugged off the impression as imagination, but it made me wary, so when I moved across the kitchen toward the door to the dark dining room on the opposite side, I moved with caution. Perhaps Sarah was home after all. She could be sleeping so soundly in that back room upstairs that she had not heard the racket I had made at the front door. But the feeling was unsettling just the same.

Passing the white porcelain sink, I noticed a single mug in one of its deep double sides and leaned close enough to examine it. A small amount of what appeared to be tea had pooled in the bottom and had not yet evaporated to a dry residue. Taking Grand Junction's late-summer, ninety-degree temperatures into account, it meant that someone had been in the house to set it there sometime earlier in the afternoon.

As I stood frowning down into the mug, from somewhere in the house above my head came a hint of muffled sound, like a quiet footstep on carpet. It was only a suggestion, almost a vibration in the air, but it caught my already edgy attention. Freezing in place, I listened intently to identify the location of any repetition, visualizing the arrangement of upstairs rooms that opened off a hallway at the top of stairs that went up from the vestibule inside the front door.

Almost convinced I had imagined it, or that the sound had filtered into my ears from somewhere outside, I tiptoed toward the door that led to the dining room, still listening. Within an arm's length of the door a board beneath the dark green tile of the floor squeaked a protest under my right foot. Response came instantly in several succeeding thumps that were definitely footsteps in the upper hall. Staring at the ceiling, as if it could become transparent and reveal the identity of the walker, I tracked the thuds across that ceiling to what I knew was the landing. They rapidly began to descend, creating a slight echo in the vestibule with its uncarpeted floor and high ceiling. Who was this? Sarah could not have moved so quickly.

"Hello," I called out, giving up the attempt at stealth and moving forward into the dark of the dining room. "Who's there?"

The only answer was an increase in the speed of the descending footsteps, muted by a carpet runner on the stairs.

Reaching to the right of the doorway I found nothing but an empty wall and quickly ran my hand along the left side in anxious search of another push-button switch. Instead, my wrist struck something that tipped over, rolled along some kind of shelf, and fell off to shatter with a crash into unseen fragments on the floor below. Too late I recalled that the switch was on the kitchen side and a sideboard hugged the dining room wall just inside the doorway on the other. It had contained a pair of ornate crystal vases. One of them, to my regret, was now history.

The sound of hurried footsteps reached the vestibule, and I heard the snap of a deadbolt being released before the front door was flung wide enough to thump against the wall and allow someone to dash through. I gave up on reaching back to the kitchen switch. Hoping the dining furniture had not been rearranged since my last visit, I moved forward around it and through another doorway into the living room, where I immediately stumbled over an ottoman, cracked an elbow on an end table in the process, regained my balance, and finally reached the vestibule—too late. The pounding feet made it across the wide front porch and down the front steps as I swore and felt my way through the dark to the now open front door.

I caught a glimpse of a running figure just disappearing around the rear of the motor home that I had parked on the street and heard Stretch begin to bark warnings at the person he believed had come too near his residence. Out of sight beyond the Winnebago, a car door slammed, an engine growled to life, and a dark vehicle of some small, economical variety sped away down the street, leaving no way to ascertain its make, license number, or the identity of the driver.

I stood watching, helpless, in the doorway, cradling my smarting right elbow in my left hand. There was a flash of brakes, and before the taillights vanished around the nearest corner, I noticed that one of them was a different color red than the other, as if it had been replaced sometime in the past.

If the open back door had held questions, the one in which I now stood held several more.

For a few frustrated minutes I stayed, looking out into the soft shadows of the calm summer night with a sense of unreality and confusion, and listened until Stretch stopped barking and dropped back out of sight in the motor home. It was very quiet. Somewhere in the dark beneath the shrubbery that surrounded the porch a cricket chirped—the sound as foreign to my Alaskan ears as the situation in which I unexpectedly found myself. A bit of breeze, reluctant to follow the vanished storm, sighed gently around a corner of the dark house to stir the leaves on the trees that lined the street and set a mosaic of shadows in motion on the front lawn. They were large shade trees—elms perhaps, or sycamores—well established and still green, their shape unfamiliar compared to the birch and spruce I was accustomed to at home.

There was light in a house diagonally across the street, and through a large front window I could see into a living room. A man relaxed there in a large chair, his feet propped on a hassock, watching a television set that was just out of sight to the right. Behind a thin curtain the changing patterns of light it created flickered in that unmistakable blue that nothing else creates. It seemed odd that he had heard none of the sounds that had occurred in the last few minutes, but I realized that none of them, even the crash of the shattered vase, had been loud enough to carry much beyond the walls of Sarah's house—definitely not across the street and through the window. For a second or two I felt unheard and invisible, as if none of it had really happened.

But I *was* there and, heard or not, the noises had all been very real. It was time to find out about that light in the rear bedroom. The complete lack of any other sound on the upper level now raised my concern for Sarah's welfare.

Turning, I closed the front door, shutting out the street and the night, and thumbed the button beside the front door. The resulting illumination of the vestibule brought reality back and left me blinking in the brightness as my eyes adjusted. The light that hung from the high ceiling on a long chain shone on the lower two-thirds of the stairs and the rail that accompanied them down to end in a curl of polished wood at the bottom. Slightly faded burgundy carpeting in an oriental pattern rippled its way up the tall flight, a few inches of similar wood visible at either edge. There was a dusty smell in the air as I started the climb, probably created by the pounding of the intruder's feet as he fled.

Who had he been, anyway? And why had he run? One hand on the rail, I hesitated slightly as a new thought crossed my mind. Had it been a *he*? I had seen the escaping figure only from behind. Could it have been a woman? I would not have bet on it either way.

It was dark at the top of the stairs, and once again I couldn't remember where to find a switch for the hallway. Far at the other end I could see a pale line of light leaking out from under a closed door on the left—Sarah's room. Carefully venturing forward, with no desire to cause another bumbling disaster similar to that of the vase in the dining room, I walked slowly down the center of the shadowed hall, noticing that, as remembered, it had four doors that faced each other across it in pairs. Three of them were open, but the interiors all were dark. The only evidence of light came from the one I had identified as Sarah's.

Reaching it, I turned the old-fashioned oval knob, pushed the door slowly open, and walked through it—into *chaos*.

CHAPTER THREE

THE ROOM WAS SARAH'S BEDROOM, AS I'D REMEMBERED. But, my friend, the soul of neatness, would never have allowed it to have fallen into the wild disarray I found.

Items of clothing lay everywhere, the contents of drawers that had been jerked from two chests and dumped onto the floor. The closet door gaped open and more wearables had been yanked from hangers and thrown out, shoes pitched after them. A round hatbox appeared to have been crushed underfoot with Sarah's favorite garden hat still inside, its straw brim broken as well A square blue box that had clearly held a cherished collection of photographs and letters was empty, all it had contained flung out to flutter down over the bright fabrics of dresses, slacks, and blouses.

Pictures in frames had been snatched from the walls and hurled across the room to land near an antique vanity that had been swept clear of lotions, perfumes, and other grooming items that lay, some broken, on the floor between it and the rear window. A book, facedown next to an overturned wastebasket, was minus the pages that had been ripped from between the covers. The bed had been stripped of linen and its mattress shoved aside to reveal the box springs underneath, both slashed open with some sharp blade. On a bedside table, a lamp with a beaded satin shade had been tipped over, probably when the drawer had been pulled out and upended. The telephone had been torn from the wall and lay halfway across the room, next to several plastic pill bottles and a box of facial tissues. Feathers from Sarah's prized down pillows covered everything, several still floating, disturbed by the wave of air I had caused in opening the door.

Aghast at the ruthless devastation and damage that confronted me, I stood in the doorway staring into the room. My first concern was to make sure that Sarah was not inside, but a quick glance reassured me of that. Except for the tangle of belongings, the room was empty. Anger quickly followed. I have never had patience for senseless acts of destruction, or those who perpetrate them. What could have inspired such a savage search? From all that was cast aside, whoever it had been must have been looking for something specific. Had he, or she, found it before I made my way in through the back door to interrupt the attempt? I hoped not, but if not, would this person return?

Leaving the door open, I wheeled and started quickly back down the hall, headed for the telephone that I knew from past visits stood below in an alcove off the living room that Sarah used as an office. It was past time for some answers. This was a situation for the police.

Law enforcement was exactly what I got, much sooner than expected. As I reached the top of the stairs there was a sudden thunderous pounding and someone shouting outside. I halted where I stood when the front door, which I had neglected to lock, crashed open, again

rebounding off the wall, and
stepped cautiously through it, ha
he called out, catching sight of me s

It was a toss-up which of us was n
stared at each other for a few seconds i
ment. Obviously, a sixty-something wo
what he had expected. Nor did I believe tha
wish for officers would cause one to materia
genie from a bottle.

"You call dispatch about a break-in?" he a
frowning in a combination of confusion and suspicio

With visions of a night in the local lockup, I was
supremely grateful that Sarah had insisted on providing
the name and phone numbers of her lawyer in one of our
last conversations. "No, I can't think of a reason you'd
need it, but it never hurts to be thorough, and you just
never know, do you?" she'd said.

Attorney Donald Westover answered his home telephone on the third ring, recognized me by name, and
arrived to reassure the police of my identity less than
half an hour after I was allowed to dial his number.

As we waited, the police had listened dubiously to
my account of having disturbed a prowler in Sarah's
house. An anonymous telephone tip had brought them,
without sirens. But the only person they had found
inside was a female senior citizen with a tale about an
unlocked back door—which they had checked and
found locked, thanks to me—claiming to have heard
and seen someone—whom she couldn't identify—making a hurried exit from upstairs, and a vehicle—for
which she had no make or license number—speed away
and disappear. As if that were not enough, they had
found me close to the turmoil of the upstairs bedroom. It
made sense even to me that they would react with suspi-

a hefty man in uniform
dgun drawn. "Police!"
tanding above him.
ore startled as we
silent astonish-
man was not
my simple
ize like a
ked,

l to consider me a

m straight with a
d me as Sarah's
nd gave me the
nsed that they
at I had not
hey accepted
n area with-
r who went
parts of the
...ak-in, they were soon gone,
...questions for Attorney Westover.

Those questions had waited that long, however, and would wait a few minutes more while I caught my breath. In Sarah's kitchen, I made each of us a mug of tea, and then sat down with this tall stranger at the breakfast table near the back window through which I had peered earlier.

"Now," I demanded. "Where is Sarah? Why isn't she here?"

When he hesitated, frowning, thick brows hiding his eyes as he glanced down at the mug he held between his hands, and sighed before answering, anxiety rushed in to replace concern. Refusing to allow free rein to my imagination, I sat quietly and waited, forcing my attention to what I could learn from a cursory assessment of Westover's appearance. How much could I count on him for the help I suspected I was about to need? Having come directly from home after office hours, he was dressed in a neat but casual shirt and jeans, without a jacket. It made him look younger than he would probably appear in a courtroom in the armor of a well-tailored suit and tie. With only the top of his head in view, I noticed that his hair was thinning slightly at the crown, and that he must have dressed in a hurry, for the right half of his collar was caught inside the neckband of his shirt. It made him seem younger still, and a little vulnerable.

Straightening to look at me, he lost the frown but retained a serious expression that told me something was very wrong with my friend.

"She's not . . ."

"No," he assured me. "Not yet. They took her to the hospital this morning. I saw her this afternoon, but she's not doing well, I'm afraid."

"What do you mean, she's not doing well? She was supposed to have weeks left. What happened?"

"They're not sure, but think something upset her enough to put too much stress on her heart. A visitor found her unconscious sometime before noon. She's regained a kind of consciousness, but is very confused and weak. She's been fading in and out and asking for you. I'm sorry, but I'd have to say she's just holding on and waiting for you to get here. Seems very determined to speak to you in her few semilucid moments—keeps asking for you."

I stared at him without really seeing, remembering Sarah's words on the phone: *I need your help. There are things I need to tell and show you—important things.* What could be so important that my friend would stubbornly refuse to die until she could convey it? As long as I had known Sarah I had at times been amused, at others frustrated, by my friend's intractable nature, though it came very close to my own. Now, whatever it was, only Sarah had the answers. Would she be able to communicate whatever it was that she felt was so essential?

"Then we're wasting time sitting here," I declared,

rising from my place at the table. "Will you drive me to the hospital, Mr. Westover?"

"Of course. But please call me Don."

I rinsed the tea mugs and left them in the sink with the one I had noticed earlier. There would be time to take care of them tomorrow.

Considering the warm conditions, I checked before leaving to be sure Stretch had plenty of water and that the doors of the motor home were securely locked.

"Will you stay in Sarah's house tonight?" Westover asked as he drove down quiet residential Chipeta Avenue and turned north on Seventh. "You can, you know. She expected that."

I considered and decided against it. "I think Stretch and I will both do better in our own space—particularly after tonight's nastiness. I'll back the Winnebago into the driveway at the side of the house where I've parked it before. I can hook up to electricity and water there. Do you have any thoughts on who it might have been in the house tonight—or what they could have been looking for?"

He shook his head, once again frowning. "Not a clue, but it worries me."

"How about what Sarah wants to tell me?"

"I don't know about that, either. But . . ."

He stopped, frowning again, and chewed on his lower lip for a thoughtful moment before he continued.

"You know Sarah, so you know she doesn't like loose ends. Before that first surgery, two years ago, she put all her affairs in order: revised her will, settled debts—all that sort of thing. She's kept it up to date since then, with advice from me. Hired an accountant I recommended and knew that she could trust. Gave him power of attorney to take care of her bills and taxes.

"About two weeks ago she called and asked me to come to the house because she wanted to make some changes in her will. Did she tell you that she had put your name in as executor?"

"No. I called her a couple of times from the road and she didn't mention it. And I don't understand it. Why me?"

"I asked, but she wouldn't say why. Just that it would be better that way. She was very definite about it. It was going to be Alan's job—you know, her son, Alan? It made sense, because there wasn't anyone else."

"I've met him a time or two, but I don't really know him." I neglected to say that I had never been particularly impressed with Alan the few times I had encountered him. "Does he know about this?"

"I assume she told him, but I don't know," he said, frowning again.

"And she didn't give you reasons for the changes at all?"

"I have to admit I pressured her a little, but she just smiled—you know that enigmatic, determined smile— and wouldn't give me any other reason. Just said she trusts you to do the right thing. She seemed concerned about something, but kept it to herself. Said you'd be able to take care of all of it."

I sighed, frowning now myself. The assumption seemed a large one. It would certainly be difficult if I found that Sarah wasn't able to communicate her intentions.

We came to North Avenue, a main east–west cross street, then Orchard, both of which I recognized from past visits. I considered what Westover had told me as I watched circles of illumination cast by the streetlights slide past along the tree-lined street. Green and leafy, the branches spread wide and sheltering in a way I always found unexpected.

Seventh Street rose gradually as he drove north, and we were soon pulling into the parking lot of St. Mary's Hospital, a large complex that stood like a fortress overlooking the residential area between it and the Colorado River, which flowed beyond the south side of the downtown area. As we walked from the parking lot to the entrance to the hospital, I recognized the sweet scent of honeysuckle blooming somewhere close on the grounds and was reminded that it was one of Sarah's favorites. I remembered her teaching me to gently tug the small trumpet-shaped blossoms from their stems and suck out the minute amount of sweetness they contained. The thought made me suddenly sad that that particular flower and fragrance would always be associated in memory with the friend I was about to lose.

Westover guided me straight to the intensive care unit for coronary patients where, though it was late, and considering the circumstances, I was allowed to see Sarah.

"Just you, and only for a few minutes," the nurse supervisor—a Miss Tolland, I learned from her badge—told me decisively.

"This was unexpected," I said. "What happened?"

"Are you immediate family?" the nurse asked.

Westover, who was listening, stepped in to explain that I was the executor of Sarah's estate—had her power of attorney, which meant I could be treated and informed as family.

"That's all right then. I'm sorry, but we really don't know exactly what happened—we're still waiting for some of the test results. You're right about it being unexpected. From the tests we have, the doctor thinks she had another minor heart attack, which wouldn't be unusual given her condition, but we're still waiting on more definitive word from the lab. You should talk to him tomorrow. For now, she's been asking for you, Mrs.

McNabb. So you can see her—briefly. She needs to rest, but I think she's awake and may know who you are."

She was—and she did.

Though the light in the room was dim to encourage shadows and sleep, Sarah's eyes blinked opened and she knew me immediately when I approached, leaving Westover to wait in the hall outside.

"Maxine," she said softly in recognition. "Where have you *been*, dear?"

Relieved at being recognized, I stepped to the bedside and reached to gently take her hand. "I'm here now, Sarah. I've been on the road, you know. How are you feeling?"

Sarah closed her eyes for a moment as she nodded and half smiled. "I'm just fine. But you're very late." Her eyes blinked open again and her tone changed to one that was weakly admonishing. "It's almost time for the party and we aren't dressed yet."

Party? Dressed yet?

Having assumed cognizance from recognition, it took me a second or two to shift gears and realize that, in her mind, Sarah was somewhere else—evidently somewhere in the past.

"Sarah," I reminded her quietly, "you're in a hospital now. I'm here from Alaska to help. You don't need to dress."

"I don't?"

"No. It's all right."

"Okay." Sarah smiled. "If you say so. Didn't want to get up anyway." She closed her eyes again, frowning in some kind of confused effort. "It was so dark," she murmured a moment later. "There was someone that I couldn't see."

Her eyes blinked wide and she looked straight at me with what seemed a sudden flash of awareness.

"Maxine," she said. Her grip tightened and she tugged at my hand. *"Listen now.* It's *very important."*

"Yes? I'm listening."

"It's not *right.* Will you fix it? *He's* not right. Not . . ." Her words trailed away and her hand relaxed in mine. "I can't remember," she said, shaking her head back and forth in annoyance.

"Who do you mean—*he*?" I asked, hoping to get Sarah back on track.

"He? I—I'm so tired."

There was silence and she seemed to have drifted off into sleep.

I glanced around and, through the interior glass window of the room, saw the nurse walking toward us—obviously about to put an end to the visit. Whatever it was Sarah needed to communicate, it would have to wait. I tried, gently, without waking her, to let go of the fingers Sarah had interlaced in mine.

"No," Sarah said, opening her eyes and gripping my hand. "Not yet. At the house, Maxine . . . I wrote it all down. You can read it."

It was a big house. "Where is it, Sarah?"

I heard the swish of the door opening behind me and the squeak of rubber-soled shoes as the nurse walked in.

Quickly, Sarah, I thought. *Tell me quickly.* But I waited without encouraging; afraid that to interrupt would challenge Sarah's tenuous train of thought.

The aggravated frown of realizing memory loss had returned to Sarah's face, but her grip on my hand was surprisingly strong and insistent.

"You—remember? We played Sardines?" she tried. "You know—where we hid? It *was* a party. Remember?" She slumped against the pillows that propped her up.

Sardines? It was a game I hadn't played for years—had almost forgotten—where one person hides and the rest hunt. When the hider is found, one simply crawls in and hides too, and the last one left is "It" for the next game. Sarah was rambling again and it was too late, I knew, to ask her to repeat—to clarify.

Miss Tolland arrived at my side, protective and authoritarian. "I'm sorry, Mrs. McNabb. You'll have to go now."

"I'll be back, Sarah, first thing tomorrow," I assured her. "You can tell me all about it then—okay?"

Eyes closed there was no indication that she had heard. Though her lips twitched as if she would speak again, not even a whisper escaped. Her limp fingers slid away without hindrance when I released her hand.

CHAPTER FOUR

ALL EVIDENCE OF POLICE PRESENCE HAD VANISHED when Westover returned me to Sarah's Chipeta Avenue house. A good look around told us all was quiet and peaceful. The television watcher directly across the street had evidently gone off to bed, for the room where I had noticed him was as dark as the rest of his residence.

Assuring Westover I would meet him at his office the next afternoon after seeing Sarah in the morning, I watched him drive away and vanish around the same street corner the trespasser had turned earlier. Dropping the set of keys he had given me into the deep pocket of my denim skirt, I decided not to go back into Sarah's house. Walking briskly back to the Winnebago, I unlocked and carefully backed it into the driveway along the side of the house. There it took only a few minutes to retrieve the lines that were stored in an outer compartment and connect them to an exterior outlet and faucet on the house, providing electricity and water to the motor home. Earlier in the day, knowing there would be no hookup at Sarah's, I had emptied the holding tanks for gray water—from shower and sink—and black water—sewage—so there was no need for attention to either.

Stretch greeted me enthusiastically when I stepped back inside through the coach door, locking it behind me. Tail wagging and short legs pattering close, not about to let me out of his sight lest I disappear again, he accompanied me as I closed the blinds and curtains, converting the interior into the snug and private space that is part of what I appreciate about a motor home. When I had finished with the few chores that would enable me to stay where I was for the time being, I dropped onto the comfortable sofa and lifted him onto my knees. Giving him my full attention, I stroked his silky reddish-brown ears indulgently and scratched under his chin, a favored spot.

"So, you missed me, did you? You're a good and patient bitser, you are—if a bit wacko."

He leaned contentedly against my hands and gave my wrists appreciative licks when he could reach them. Wriggling over on my lap, he presented his stomach for consideration.

"Impenitent hooligan. Okay, I won't go walkabout anymore tonight. Ready for a snack, then?"

Recognizing those words, he rolled over to right himself, allowed me to lower him to the floor, and trotted off to wait expectantly by the drawer in the galley where he knew the dog biscuits were stored.

Giving him his two customary bedtime treats, I reached for a pair of glasses from an overhead cupboard and filled one with ice and cold water from the small refrigerator. Into the other I poured a shot of Jameson, set them both on the dinette table, and slid onto one of the benches that faced each other from either side. Sipping the whiskey, I followed it up with a swallow of ice water and a sigh of relief. Except for the cooling effect of the rain, it had been a day of unaccustomed heat. The cold water was so satisfying that I quickly drained the glass and went back to refill it before settling again.

In the quiet comfort of my familiar house-on-wheels, I considered the events of the day and the unexpected situations I had found upon arrival. Briefly, I wondered about the person I had surprised in Sarah's house, and felt disgust and resentment at the turmoil of the upstairs room. But it was Sarah's sudden hospitalization that was most troublesome.

A time or two during the long drive from Alaska I had allowed myself to consider that, because of Sarah's heart condition, I was about to lose one of my oldest and dearest friends. Anticipating that we would have several weeks of the enjoyment of each other's company and time to develop a mutual level of acceptance, that I would be able to make the passing easier for Sarah, I had set it aside. Now, as the new reality of the circumstances and their inevitable result swept over me, I put both elbows on the table and dropped my head into my hands as a wave of grief and anger filled my eyes with tears. It wasn't fair. But a lot of things aren't, I tried to remind myself. It didn't help much.

Sarah and I had been friends since our freshman year in Seattle, when we found ourselves roommates in a University of Washington dormitory. Though I have developed many friendships through the years, none have been closer, or as enduring. Those four undergraduate years cemented our relationship into something nearer a sisterhood than a friendship. Though weeks, even months, have at times gone by without contact, when we were separated by distance and occupied with busy lives and raising families, the thread of connection had continued true and deep, allowing us to pick up where we left off, as if there had been no time lost. Time had never been a part of the equation.

"We are each other's memories," Sarah had told me once with a smile. "What I forget, you remember, and vice versa. You have one half and I have the other."

Knowing that all I'd soon have was memories, I wondered sadly how I would cope with losing her half of them. I retrieved a tissue from a pocket to wipe my eyes and blow my nose, glancing down at Stretch, who had come to stand looking up at me, puzzled. I seldom allow tears—try to be practical and optimistic.

Enough, I told myself sternly. There were many other things to be concerned about. Sarah was still alive and needed me. I would deal with mourning later. We might—just might—have a little time, if she could recover from this setback.

One of the things that concerned me was that it might not be possible now for Sarah to communicate the *important things* she had mentioned on the phone— things she had clearly felt a need to share. Not prone to exaggeration, Sarah would not have said they were important if they weren't. Were those things connected to the reason Sarah had changed her will and made me the executor? It was a surprising and odd alteration. Her son, Alan, was a much more likely choice for that job. For that matter, I suddenly wondered, where *was* Alan? He had his own place and it was, of course, possible that in arriving after visiting hours I had missed him at the hospital. Don Westover would know, and I wished I had remembered to ask him. Considering use of my cell phone to find out, I glanced first at my watch. It was already too late to disturb the attorney again on this night. I would have to wait until the next day.

It would all have to wait until morning, I decided, finishing the last of the Jameson, then the ice water.

"What do you think, lovie?" I asked Stretch.

He had curled up under the table, muzzle comfortingly resting on my right foot. At the sound of my voice, he stood up, padded into view, and cocked his head to look up at me questioningly.

"Yes, it's you I'm yabbering at, as usual," I told him, leaning to give him a pat. "Time to go out before bed, you think?"

Another phrase that he recognized inspired him to pad across and wait by the coach door, looking back over his shoulder. *Well?* he seemed to say.

Amused and glad to have him for company, I found a flashlight and went to open the door. We stepped out together and walked around to the backyard, where, after a bit of what he considered the essential exploration of any new place, Stretch made his selection and piddled at the base of a tall lilac near the house.

In less than ten minutes, we were both back inside and I had tossed aside the quilt that covered my bed in the rear of the Winnebago. The rain had cooled the air, but it would still be too warm a night to require much in the way of covers. I dislike the constant sound of the air-conditioning, and opted for cracking open a couple of windows and starting a quiet fan in the galley to keep the air moving. Changing into my lightest nightgown, I brushed my teeth and washed my face before turning out the lights and finding a comfortable position in the bed. Stretch came to lie down beside it in his padded basket, where in just a bit I could hear him snoring softly in the dark. In minutes we were both asleep.

When the lights had been out and nothing had been heard from the motor home for over an hour, a dark human shape stepped out from behind a large tree near the back fence of Sarah's yard. Moving cautiously across the grass between the tree and the porch, shadow among shadows, this figure silently climbed the steps, testing each one, reached to the back door handle and found it locked, as expected.

A key was retrieved from a pocket, inserted carefully into the lock, and slowly turned, allowing the door to be quietly opened and closed as the figure slipped into the kitchen that Maxie had entered earlier. A shielded beam of light preceded progress through the house, but there was no one to see. A few soft scrapings and shiftings would only have been evident to someone listening very closely, but there was no one to hear.

An hour before daylight, the back door silently opened and the figure slipped out again, using the key to lock it before flitting quickly across to leave the yard through a gate in the back fence. Left behind, as well, was another question in the doorway, though it was now securely closed and would remain so for the time being.

I was up with the sun and making a mental list of things to be done as I filled the coffeemaker and set it to burbling cheerfully while I dressed. First on the list was transportation. I would need a car in which to get around and the easiest place to rent one was the local airport. As soon as I had fed breakfast to Stretch and myself, I used my cell phone to call a taxi and had the driver take me straight there.

The area north of the city, around the Walker Field Airport, was a sudden reminder that the trees lining the streets of Grand Junction were the result of a need for shade in desert country, which the local juniper and pinion pine did not provide. Its residents have planted most of the elm, cottonwood, and other large trees in the central area. The airport, on the other hand, lies in surroundings that are closer to how original settlers found them: an arid land of few trees, and grasses that are briefly green in spring, but which summer annually toasts to a sun-burned tan. Above this area, to the north, rises the high rippling wall of the Book Cliffs, so named because John Wesley Powell, explorer of the Colorado River, thought they resembled the edges of bound volumes on a library shelf—a concept I have always found appealing.

Grand Junction lies on the western edge of the state, where the Gunnison River joins the Colorado for its long run across the Colorado Plateau, which includes the Grand Canyon, then on down to empty into the Gulf of Mexico. Between the Rocky Mountains to the east and the Great Basin to the west the Colorado Plateau encompasses a huge part of Utah, Colorado, Arizona, and New Mexico. It is a country carved directly from the stone foundation of the earth by centuries of wind, ice, and water escaping to lower altitudes and, bit by bit, wearing away the rock and sculpting spectacular cuts, canyons, mesas, turrets, arches, and other indescribable formations. Erosion of sedimentary stone by what became the Colorado River cut a canyon that left the Book Cliffs standing more than a thousand feet above the valley floor and far from the current course of the river. Framing Grand Junction to the north, they remain, gradually crumbling into dust, pebbles, and rocks that pile up and flare out in graceful forty-five-degree angle-of-repose skirts of debris at their bases.

The previous day's storm had hidden the cliffs in curtains of rain and hail as I drove into town. Now I hesitated just enough to take a long look at them before heading into the airport terminal. There is something hauntingly attractive about the stark lines and glorious red, brown, purple, and blue hues of this country and that of the rest of the plateau to the southwest. The basic horizontal shapes and lines bare of trees always remind me of Alaska's far north, especially during the frozen months of the year above the Arctic Circle, though there are few of the reddish colors there. The blues and purples of the cliffs, however, are similar in tone to the shadows cast by the thin winter sun into the lee of snowdrifts and low rolling hills.

It took only a few minutes and a credit card at the Hertz counter to rent a compact car that would easily serve my purposes in getting around the local area. From the clerk, I also obtained a detailed street map of Grand Junction and took time before leaving to have her point out the location of Don Westover's office near the downtown area.

Getting to the hospital was simple. The short trip took me southwest on Horizon Drive, which soon angled left into Seventh Street near the hospital. I was eager to visit Sarah, hoping she would be more lucid after a night's rest.

Pulling into the St. Mary's parking lot, I found my way through the reception area and hallways to the cardiac intensive care unit, where I was startled to see the same nurse raise her head from behind the counter. *Must be about to go off shift,* I thought.

Seeing me coming, Miss Tolland stepped out to intercept me with a concerned look.

"Mrs. McNabb, right?" she asked.

"Yes, how is Sarah doing this morning?"

The nurse's expression deepened to a combination of sympathy and reluctance that told me everything I didn't want to know.

"I'm so sorry, Mrs. McNabb. We did everything we could. She died in her sleep about five this morning. We had no way to reach you."

For a long minute, I simply stared at her without moving and didn't realize there were tears on my face until the nurse held out a box of tissue that she reached behind the counter to obtain. I took one automatically and used it to wipe my eyes. It was such a shock that I couldn't think for the enormous sense of loss that all but took my breath. Like a wooden puppet, I reached toward her with one hand.

"What happened? She was supposed to have more time."

Miss Tolland nodded, sadly. "I know. But sometimes it's like that—unexpected. At least it was peaceful and may have saved her a bad time later, you know? She may have just given up."

Suddenly it was all I could do to swallow my flash of anger at what seemed a gratuitously patronizing statement. *How would you know?* I wanted to say, but didn't. *Sarah was a fighter. She wouldn't have given up to save herself* anything *later.*

"Where is she," I asked instead, straightening my shoulders and resolving that, for the moment at least, there was nothing to be but practical.

"They've already taken her down. I tried to call her son, but no one answered the number he left us. Will you contact him, or should I keep trying?"

Where was *Alan?* I wondered again, focusing my annoyance on his absence, then realized it wasn't really Alan or the nurse with whom I was angry—and I *was* angry. That would have to wait until later as well.

"I don't know. You'll have to keep trying."

"There was someone else here to visit Mrs. Nunamaker," the nurse remembered thoughtfully. "A tall, older man. Didn't give his name, but asked if someone would be in this morning. When I told him you had said you would, he asked where he could wait. He may still be in the lounge. There." She pointed in the direction from which I had come. "Would you like me to check?"

"No," I told her. "I'll go. Thank you."

It was something to do, though I couldn't imagine who the *someone* could be—probably someone local that I wouldn't know or want to see just then.

I couldn't have been more wrong—or more surprised at the identity of the tall man who unfolded himself from a low chair as I stepped into the lounge.

"Maxie?" The rumble of his kindly bass voice was memorable and instantly familiar, though I hadn't heard it in years. He held out both hands as he stepped toward me.

"*Ed?* Ed Norris? Oh, Eddy, you darlin' man."

He swept me into a bear hug and I burst into a veritable flood of unexpected and uncharacteristic tears.

CHAPTER FIVE

"WHERE DID YOU SPRING FROM? HOW DID YOU KNOW?" I asked Ed Norris, stepping back out of his sympathetic hug of greeting and quickly wiping away my tears again with the now soggy tissue.

"Came in from Portland on an early plane. No one answered my knock at her house, so I hunted up a neighbor, who told me she'd been hospitalized yesterday. Didn't know she was gone until I found my way here. Guess I should have expected to find you wherever I found Sarah," he said, smiling a bit ruefully.

We stood looking silently at each other for a moment as our mutual loss and the past came sweeping in a wave of nostalgia.

For me, as for Sarah, Ed Norris had always been irrevocably linked to our memories of youthful college days in Seattle. One of six or eight of us who had grouped together socially, he had fallen deeply in love with Sarah during his junior and her sophomore year. To complicate matters, though she had not reciprocated, I unfortunately had, by falling for him at the same time. Thinking neither of them knew of my fascination, I casually pretended not to care. For a few months, until I realized it was merely an infatuation, the situation had been an unspoken, agonizing secret. Eventually I recognized that my true affection lay with my high school sweetheart, Joe Flanagan, who, happily for us both, later became my first husband. Meanwhile, except for her few dates with Ed, Sarah and I had gone everywhere, done everything, together, discouraging his inclination to be more than friends, keeping all three of our relationships on an even keel.

I had long since lost track of Ed—knew he had eventually married, moved to somewhere in Oregon, then divorced, if memory served me. As we stood staring at each other in that hospital lounge, I suddenly recalled that Sarah had once or twice mentioned him, so they must have kept in touch, at least infrequently. Couldn't have been too important if she had never told me about it, though.

Age had added a few smile crinkles around his eyes and mouth, and two deep frown lines between his brows, but I would have recognized him anywhere. At a couple of inches over six feet, he was almost as thin as ever, perhaps a bit thicker through the waist. His dark hair was streaked with gray. Those beautiful blue eyes seemed somewhat faded, but they held the familiar gleam of humor that I remembered, under lashes still so long they were almost girlish. *I've at least always had good taste,* I thought in wry amusement.

He had glanced toward the nursing station, thoughts turning back to Sarah's death, and spoke thickly, tears welling when he looked back again. "I didn't get here in time, did I? She's really gone, Maxie, and it's a smaller world without her in it."

I wondered how he had known Sarah was so ill. Time to ask.

"How did you . . ."

"Are you . . ."

We both chimed in at the same time—stopped, each waiting for the other.

"Oh, hell. Let's get out of here," he suggested, turning abruptly to retrieve a suitcase next to the lounge chair in which he had been sitting. "There's nothing for us here now."

Bag in one hand, my elbow firmly in the other, focused on escape, he hustled me through the corridors and out the front door. There I learned that he was without transportation, having taken a taxi from the airport to Sarah's, then to the hospital. In my rental car, we headed out of the parking lot.

"Where to?"

"I don't care," he shrugged. "Anywhere else, I guess. There'll surely be a service of some kind, so I'll find a place to stay and get some transportation of my own. Not just now, though. Have you eaten? I could use some breakfast. Coffee on the plane was abysmal—if you could call it coffee."

I had eaten, but assured him I could tolerate more caffeine, so I took a left out of the lot and headed for Horizon Drive, where I recalled a collection of both hotels and coffee shops.

Ed leaned back against the headrest and closed his eyes.

"Where's Alan?" he asked without opening them.

"I don't know. The nurse said she hadn't been able to reach him."

He sighed, shook his head in what appeared to be discouragement, and sat up again. "That kid! I don't understand why he thinks the world, or Sarah, owes him something. He's disappointed and taken advantage of her for years. He'll be forty-four in November. Time he grew up and took responsibility for himself."

Clearly, Ed and Sarah *had* stayed more closely in touch than I realized. Casual holiday cards would have been my guess. Learning that they had seen each other enough over the years for Ed to be familiar with her son was a surprise. I kept my interest to myself, my eyes on the road, and asked about Alan instead.

"You and he don't get along, I take it."

"Not so you'd notice," Ed told me, scowling at the windshield. "The times I've stopped to see Sarah, he made a concerted effort to stay away, which didn't hurt my feelings any."

Having never been particularly fond of Alan's self-indulgent personality myself, I understood what he meant. His assessment seemed a bit strong, even for a close friend, but I decided that it could be the shock of Sarah's passing that exaggerated his contempt and let it lie with no further questions—for the moment.

Halfway along Horizon Drive, we found Coco's, a bakery and restaurant next door to a Holiday Inn, which simplified Ed's need for a place to stay. He went in to register while I parked, found a table in a corner of the bakery next to a window, and ordered coffee for both of us. While I waited, I decided to call Don Westover and cancel our afternoon meeting, feeling no inclination to review Sarah's will at the moment. It could wait at least another day.

When I reached him at his office his voice on the line

held a note of sadness along with relief at hearing from me. I cut short his commiserations by canceling the appointment, to which he agreed.

"I tried to call you earlier. The hospital told me you already know about Sarah. I'm sorry, Maxie, there's a complication. The hospital called just after you left there to say that they need you to sign permission for a postmortem. Can you go back?"

A postmortem?

"Why? She died in the hospital. Not at home. Isn't that unusual?"

"They want to make sure of the cause of death, because it happened sooner than expected. I don't know exactly why. The doctor is concerned with covering all the bases, I think. Anyway, they seem to feel it's necessary and there's no reason to refuse, is there?"

None that I could think of. Sarah's untimely departure was something I'd like to know more about myself. I agreed to go back. We rescheduled our meeting for the following morning, when he said we could discuss arrangements for her burial.

"Are you sure it's my signature they need?" I asked before hanging up, thinking perhaps it should be Alan's responsibility.

There was a distinct and uneasy hesitation before Westover said, "Not according to what Sarah told me she wanted. She was very specific that you should take care of everything, including any decisions relating to her medical condition, or arrangements after she died."

"Does he know that?"

"I'm not sure. Haven't heard from him for a day or two. But the hospital knows you're legally responsible and won't allow him to make decisions. So it's up to you. Okay?"

"Of course, but . . ."

"Good. I'll call and let them know you'll be back soon. It'll be fine, Maxie. We'll talk tomorrow. The postmortem will give us an extra day to make sure all the arrangements are satisfactory."

Why in the world would Sarah make me responsible for everything that would result from her death? I wondered, as I walked back to the table, where I found Ed Norris already giving his order for lunch to a short blond waitress with an out-of-date hairdo.

"It's closer to noon than breakfast, so I changed my mind. Sure you don't want anything?"

"No, thanks," I told him, feeling no appetite whatsoever. "Just coffee."

"Something else wrong?" he asked, noticing my frown of concern as I sat down.

I explained the situation and my assigned part in it, including the need to return to the hospital.

He nodded. "Makes sense. She knew Alan would resent being responsible for any of it—probably make a hash of it as usual. Where is he anyway? That attorney have any idea?"

I assured him Westover had not. But it *was* a question that needed answering—among others.

I am pretty much of a live-and-let-live sort. Forging ahead to find answers to questions like the one held by the open back door of Sarah's house the night before had presented me with an unexpected difficulty or two in the past. I had an apprehensive feeling that answering those that were beginning to surface in my mind might be another such situation and could take some careful handling. There was something disturbing about the unexpectedness of Sarah's death, the idea of a postmortem, and knowing that she had, for some reason, felt it better for me than for Alan to be in charge of making decisions for her; something that needed serious answers—if I could find them.

I kept Ed company until he had finished his sandwich and cup of soup, then arranged to meet him for dinner that evening, dropped him off at the airport to rent his own wheels, and returned to the hospital to sign the papers for the postmortem. That done, I headed back to my rig next to the house on Chipeta Avenue, with a quick stop for a few supplies at a nearby Albertsons grocery that I remembered from other visits to Grand Junction.

Stretch had spent the morning alone in the Winnebago and met me enthusiastically at the side door—all wiggles and wags. He is a good traveler and a real character, affectionate and remarkably patient, while maintaining an independent and adventurous spirit that's much larger than he is.

All in all, I would rather have a dog than a cat. You never really own a cat. Cats just don't seem to give a damn. Years before the arrival of Stretch, a silky Seal Point Himalayan once owned me. I mean that Samantha allowed me the regality of her presence in the house—an exercise in her aloofness and my humility at best. At the opposite end of the companionship spectrum is my dachshund—bless him.

Wiping the licks he gave me from my face, I put away the groceries and decided we could both use a good walk. Time to myself without other people for some uninterrupted thinking wouldn't hurt, either. Later, before meeting Ed, I intended to see about cleaning up the chaos of Sarah's bedroom upstairs and taking a quick inventory of the rest of the contents of the house.

A glance at the thermometer before leaving told me that the noon temperature was once again inching into the mid-nineties, so I was glad for the shade from the trees that lined the street between it and the sidewalk as we walked slowly east along Chipeta for several blocks. With Stretch tugging on his leash to explore every unfamiliar smell he came to along the way, I enjoyed the yards and houses that we strolled past. The architecture of communities in the Lower 48 is always different than that of Alaska, where nothing has as much longevity or tradition. Grand Junction was no exception, especially in that older and central part of town, where many of the houses were historic. They were an assortment of styles: some Victorian, like Sarah's; others, bungalows, or Tudors with steep roofs that framed their doors and narrow porches. The yards were rich with well-established shrubs and large trees, many surrounded with late summer flowers in orderly beds and low hedges trimmed to rectangular correctness. There were even a few topiaries.

They reminded me that Sarah's grandfather had been responsible for the lovely house, full of antiques and family heirlooms that she had inherited from her father. That grandfather had come to Grand Junction in the early days of the twentieth century, married the daughter of an influential doctor, and found a lot on which to build the large Victorian just off what was now historic Seventh Street. He had become an important figure in the city's growth and success, active in its civic and social circles. His fortune had been made as a prominent orchard owner, earning him a position as a member of the board of the Grand Valley Fruit Growers Association. His son had succeeded to his father's standing and was also involved in community service to the extent of serving a term as mayor. He had added both vineyards and a winery to the orchards he inherited. I had no idea how much Sarah had received from her father, but had no doubt it was a considerable amount.

At the end of the fourth block, Stretch and I turned north on a side street that led us to Gunnison, across which lay a large park, green with expansive lawn under more huge trees. I found a place under one of them, sat down in the shade, and let Stretch off his leash for a free run, knowing he wouldn't wander out of sight. Aside from a car or two passing along Gunnison and the hum of other traffic in the distance, it was quiet and peaceful. Sarah and I had walked there in the past, so it was a familiar place where I felt more at home thinking about her.

Ed was right. As I sat there quietly, barely aware of the sounds of the city around me, the world *did* seem much smaller without her in it. She had been my dependable friend for so long I couldn't yet feel she was gone, probably wouldn't for some time to come. Her absence would settle in gradually, as the death of a handful of other, less treasured friends had for me. At sixty-three, I had reached an age where I should expect to lose people that I knew and cared about more and more often. One at a time, folks I had met, liked, and come to count on would go, leaving sudden emptiness in place of presence.

Sarah was not the first, but for me she had been the best, and was the most grievous loss apart from my Joe and Daniel. No one else had known me so long or so well. There was now no one left who could remember me as a girl. It felt like a piece of my life had vanished with her, and it had. I had a few photos in an album or two to remind me that I had once been young enough to whisper in the university library instead of studying, gossip about flirtations and romances, borrow each other's clothes, walk in the rain, and lavishly fill days with laughter and companionship. How could we possibly have been so brand-new and trusting—so far from the realization that we wouldn't live forever?

Feeling older than I had the day before, I leaned back to watch a cloud drift slowly across the blue of the afternoon sky and wondered again what it was that my friend had wanted to tell me. Her few confused words from the night before came back into my mind.

It was so dark, she had said. *There was someone that I couldn't see.* Then, *It's not right. Will you fix it?* He's *not right.*

But she hadn't said who she meant by *he*.

Stretch, finally tired of exploring, came back to lie down at my side, muzzle on paws, panting slightly, even in the shade, at the unaccustomed heat.

Sarah had mentioned something about Sardines, the game we had sometimes played in college and, once or twice, after. I wasn't sorry she had seemed to think she was back in those long past days, for they had been happy ones for the most part. I would like to have been sure that she knew I was there for her at the end, but I had to smile, remembering that silly game. Once we had even been "It" together—had hidden in a closet. "You know—where we hid?" she had asked. Had she remembered that particular time, too?

It had been a large closet in someone's house in Seattle. Not large enough for the whole group to climb in together as, one by one, they searched, found, and packed in to join us in hiding. In the crush of bodies, someone had been shoved against the closet's back wall and dislodged a panel that fell open, exposing another closet in the bedroom next door. We had tumbled through the opening in a tangle, the resulting crash and our laughter giving away our hiding place to those still searching.

I smiled, remembering that the incident had sparked Sarah's interest in secret spaces of all kinds. She had begun a collection of puzzle boxes with trick ways of opening them, and found a book in the library that described how to build secret compartments in desks, chests of drawers, and other furniture. It taught us how to hide small items behind electrical switch plates, moldings, even floorboards of a room. We had played games with the ideas; removed and replaced baseboards to create hiding places for our diaries and jewelry, found or created spaces to leave messages for each other in innocent, everyday items—an umbrella handle, a hollowed-out book. Our secret games had inspired the creation of the space that hid the shotgun in my Winnebago. In my house in Alaska I had a puzzle box in which she had once sent me a birthday gift, refusing to provide a clue as to how it could be opened. It had taken me days to finally learn the solution to the riddle and retrieve the earrings she had placed inside. I still sometimes wore them.

At the house, Maxine. I wrote it all down. You can read it, Sarah had murmured the night before as Nurse Tolland walked in.

Did she still have that penchant for secrets? Could she have hidden what she said she had written? It would be—*would have been,* I thought sadly, remembering to change the tense—very like her.

There was a note taped to the motor home door when I returned, and the snarl of a lawn mower coming from the backyard.

Please stop next door and see me when you come back, the note said, and was signed Doris Chapman, who I remembered was Sarah's neighbor. I slipped it into a pocket as I walked between my rig and the house to see who was at work in the yard. Alan maybe? Finally?

But it wasn't Sarah's son.

A short, olive-skinned man not much younger than I am was guiding the mower in an ever-diminishing rectangle on one side of a walk that led to a garden shed with an open door. He turned a corner and, seeing me coming toward him, shut off the engine, took off the billed cap he was wearing, and wiped perspiration from his forehead as he watched me approach. It was a gesture that reminded me of someone tugging a forelock in deference, but he raised his chin, straightened his shoulders, and gave me a direct look that told me he was confident of himself and his right to be where he was, doing what he was doing.

"Hello. I'm Maxie McNabb, a friend of Sarah's." I held out a hand, which he did not hesitate to take.

"And I," he told me with dignity, "am To*mas*, the once-a-week gardener."

He gave his name a Spanish stress on the last syllable and "once-a-week gardener" the formality of a title. I smiled and an instant twinkle appeared in his dark eyes as we both appreciated this small bit of humor without comment.

I'm going to like this man, I thought.

"Missus Nunamaker is not at home," he said—a statement with an implied question in it.

"No," I told him, realized it was the first time I must tell someone about Sarah's passing, and my throat constricted over a lump as I swallowed hard. "Mrs. Nunamaker died at the hospital early this morning."

"Oooh!" The twinkle vanished and his face fell into lines of distress. "So soon?"

I nodded.

"I am very sorry," he said, his precise English taking on a more south-of-the-border accent in his concern. "You were her good friend, yes? I remember her saying your name before. Is there something I can do for you, Missus McNabb?"

"Maxie, please. Just Maxie." I assured him there was not.

"Then," he said with a sharp, determined nod of his head as he replaced his cap, "I will make her yard as clean and beautiful as it is possible."

I left him aggressively attacking the rest of the lawn and went to see Doris Chapman, the next-door neighbor—another person to whom I expected I must carry bad news.

CHAPTER SIX

DORIS CHAPMAN CAME OUT ONTO THE PORCH AND stood waiting and rubbing her hands together as I crossed the lawn between the two houses and went up her front steps. Though almost as wide as she was tall, she seemed a little thinner and older than when I had last seen her. She had always reminded me of one of those toys that bounce back up when you push them over.

"I've already heard about Sarah—from the hospital," she said and reached out to pull me down into a generous hug. "I've been checking every few hours. I'm so sorry. She's been a good friend and neighbor. I'll miss her every single day."

I had forgotten that Doris was the demonstrative, grandmotherly sort but, though the hug was not unwelcome, I had a feeling she needed it more than I did.

"Come in. Come in, please."

She ushered me into the living room of her much smaller house, which was crowded with knickknacks on small tables and crocheted antimacassars on the arms and back of each of three overstuffed chairs. Family pictures crowded most of the wall space and overflowed onto the mantel in silver frames.

"Now wait right there. I have something for you," she said, disappearing through a doorway. She returned almost immediately with a casserole dish in one hand, a loaf of warm home-baked bread in the other, both of which she pressed upon me.

"Oh, you shouldn't . . ." I began, but she didn't let me finish.

"You must eat, and it's just a small thing. I wanted to *do* something."

It was what women of her age, one generation older than mine, had learned was proper. When there is a death in a family, people want to do something. Providing food for the living was that something and I was evidently now the closest person to Sarah's family that she could find. It would have hurt her feelings to refuse her offerings and I had, at times, done the same myself for others in similar situations.

"It's very good of you, Doris. Thank you," I told her simply and let it be. I *did* have to eat something, sometime, after all, and the smell of that freshly baked bread was irresistible.

She asked about plans for a funeral and nodded when I told her I would let her know after my meeting with Don Westover the next morning.

"Did you bring that other man with you?" she asked. "I was making the tamale pie when I saw him go in the back door this morning."

"I came alone. When did you see him?"

"About ten o'clock—after you left and before the gardener arrived."

That made it clear she did not mean To*mas*.

"Was it Sarah's son, Alan?"

She frowned. "Oh, no. I haven't seen him for several

days. No, this man had dark hair, and wore sunglasses. I don't remember seeing him before. That's why I thought he must have come with you."

If not Alan, then who? Had the intruder from the night before returned?

"Did you see him leave?"

She said she hadn't, though I suspected that very little happened next door of which Doris was not aware.

"But earlier there was that woman who's been taking care of Sarah."

Woman? I started to ask, then just nodded, assuming it must have been the nurse Westover had mentioned. I should have asked.

Thanking her again, I took the casserole home to the Winnebago, put it in the refrigerator, and poured myself a glass of iced tea. Buttering a generous slice of the still warm bread, I sat down at the dinette table to consider whether or not to call the police before going into Sarah's house. If it was the intruder, perhaps I should. Calling would be better than getting out the shotgun— which, I must admit, crossed my mind. On the other hand, would an intruder still be inside hours later? Probably not.

Stretch had deposited himself at my feet and was watching the bread go from hand to mouth with a silent longing that was not quite begging, so I absentmindedly tore off a bite and gave it to him. I don't usually let him have people-food and never when he begs—except for popcorn, which he loves and I can't bear to eat without sharing. There is nothing you can imagine that is quite as soulful as the eyes of a mini-dachshund staring up at the popcorn bowl to inspire an unendurable case of guilt.

The sound of the lawn mower stopped and I suddenly remembered Tomas in the backyard. *He* could come with me into the house. Decision made, I left Stretch in the Minnie and went to request the once-a-week gardener's assistance.

As I had the night before, we went in the back door. One by one we searched every room, even the basement, which we reached via a stairway behind a door in the kitchen. Chivalry is not dead. Tomas gallantly insisted on leading the way, a pair of pruning shears in one hand with which to do battle if necessary. I thought of Don Quixote as I followed along behind, but kept a straight face.

It was evident that the whole house had been searched.

All the doors to the upstairs rooms were now open, as were their closets, though I wondered if that might have been the result of the previous night's police investigation. Sarah's bedroom remained as chaotic as I had found it the night before, but did not appear to have been touched again. Other evidence of the search concerned me, however.

The desk in an alcove off the living room that Sarah had used as an office had clearly been ransacked. All the drawers gaped open and some of the contents had been tossed out onto the floor. One drawer deep enough to hold files had been emptied and particular attention paid to searching them individually as the contents had been dropped into a pile on the carpet by someone who must have been sitting in the desk chair.

Volumes from a bookcase in the alcove, as well as one in the living room, had been pulled from their shelves and cast onto the floor. Pictures all over the house were askew on the walls.

Storage shelves in the basement had been disturbed too; tools, paint, and supplies shoved aside, boxes moved onto the cement floor. A light had been left burning in a side room that had once been used to store coal before the furnace was replaced with one that consumed natural gas.

Tomas was bewildered and disgusted by the invasion. "Who would do such things?" he demanded, tone sharp with indignation. "Missus Sarah was such a nice lady."

I had no answers for him. But I did have a pretty solid idea that this *intruder* was not an ordinary burglar looking for odd items of value. This was a disturbance with a particular goal in mind. Whoever it was had been hunting specifically and I had an uneasy feeling it might have something to do with the *important things* Sarah had wanted to tell me—with which she had said she needed my help.

Oh, Sarah, I thought, *there are so many ways to miss you.*

Finding no one threatening in the house, Tomas went back to his yard work, and I, deciding not to phone the police, began the process of clearing up the mess. Perhaps I could learn something that would tell me what the object of the hunt had been by reversing the destructive process. With the house empty, the perpetrator had obviously had time to complete his search. He was gone, so either he had found what he was looking for, or now must believe it was not to be found in the house. If he had found it, there was no use looking. But, as I began to sort out the papers from Sarah's desk, I wondered about that.

At the house, Maxine. I wrote it all down. You can read it, Sarah had said. Going back to my thoughts in the park about her love of secret hiding places, I considered the possibility that she had one, or more, somewhere in the house and had used it, or them, to hide what she said she had written down. The idea made her mention of that game of Sardines more understandable. It had taken me days to solve the riddle of my birthday puzzle box. If she had created some, could I find her hiding places in less? It was worth a try. Where to start?

I looked around the alcove in which I sat with a new objective. The desk itself, of course, was one possibility. The drawers hung open, but only two of them had been removed, though all the contents had either been sorted through or tossed out. Carefully, one by one, I pulled the drawers free of the desk and turned them over to see if there might be an envelope taped to the underside. There was not. One of the lower ones, however—where the angle made it almost impossible to discern by any-one sitting in the desk chair—had been shortened a cou-ple of inches in the back by moving the rear edge forward to accommodate the addition of a narrow box that could be opened only if the drawer was removed and turned around.

Except for a single key that didn't seem to fit anything, the box was empty, but it told me that I was not searching in vain. I put it back, then sat on my heels where I had knelt on the floor to gain a purchase on the drawers, and chuckled in satisfaction. At some time during her occu-pancy of the house she had been up to her old tricks.

Clever Sarah.

Rewarded, I was encouraged to go over the desk from top to bottom, knowing there were other ways to create hiding places within it. Rapping knuckles over all the flat surfaces, I found no hollow spaces that could not be accounted for in its basic construction. None of the joints were moveable, nor would any of the decorative molding on this antique piece move, slide, or swivel. Under the large center drawer at the top I found several paper clips, a grocery receipt, and an eraser from some vanished pencil—all of which had probably slipped behind it by accident over the years. The chair held no secrets, either.

The bookcases in the alcove and living room were next. Standing back, I examined the balance and con-

formity of their structure. It was easy to see that the
large set of living room shelves—now minus the books,
thanks to the intruder—held no possibility of hidden
spaces. It was very plainly made, the frame and shelves
of equal width and depth. I moved back to visually
inspect the shelves next to the desk. These were of a different design, heavily decorated with carved panels
around the frame and across the front. Examining them
carefully, I noticed that the decoration on one of them
seemed slightly wider than the rest, extending a little
below the shelf.

Ah-hah!

Taking a huge step forward over the pile of books on
the floor, I laid one hand over, one under, that middle
shelf. A two-inch disparity that held my palms apart was
revealed. No shelf would reasonably or innocently be
made that thick.

"All right," I said to the empty room. "How does this
one work, Sarah?"

The decorative panel did not slide out of the way, nor
was it hinged to lift up, as I half expected. Switching on
a gooseneck lamp on the desk, I aimed it at the bookcase and once again dropped to my knees to look
closely. Could there be a latch of some kind hidden in
the scrollwork of the carved wood? Like a Braille
reader, I worked my fingers across it, with no results.
Tugging at the piece was also unsuccessful. It was
solidly attached to the rest of the case.

Frustrated, I used one of Daniel's oaths: "Bloody
hell!"

The answer was there. I knew it *had* to be there.

At sixty-three my knees tend to seize up periodically
when I've been down on them too long. I have been
known to crawl away from weeding a flower bed, with
Stretch padding along at my side, until I can find a rake

or a fence to use as a prop. Those knees determined that this was another such time, so, pushing a couple of the fallen volumes out of the way on the floor, I leaned a hand against that carved middle shelf to help pull myself back to my feet.

There was a click, and I felt the panel loosen under my fingers. Released by the pressure, it swung easily away.

So simple—so efficient.

Good going, Sarah.

Within the narrow cavity behind the decorative panel lay a few pages neatly held together with a large paper clip. The handwriting on the first page was familiar. I had seen it many times through the years in cards and letters from my Colorado friend. Under the pages lay three sealed envelopes with names neatly written across them: *Ed Norris, Alan Nunamaker,* and *Jamie Stover.*

Who, I wondered, was *Jamie Stover*? The envelopes were heavy enough to contain more than one page—perhaps two or three. Not meant for me to open, though I was inquisitive enough to consider it. I tend to lay, if not all, then, most of my cards on the table and appreciate the same from others. If she had named me executor of her affairs, wouldn't Sarah have expected me to know what was inside these communications? Would I, if they were mine? I decided not. They might be her personal good-byes to those three people—Stover included, whoever he might be. It remained to be seen if Westover could identify him. Still curious, but reassured of my own reliability, I laid the envelopes aside with only a lingering glance.

Sitting down at the desk, I thumbed quickly through the pages. On top was what appeared to be the first few lines of a handwritten draft letter. The lines were full of words crossed out, some replaced, by Sarah's editing. It seemed she had struggled to accurately communicate her thoughts and feelings, and had given up, perhaps intending to finish it later. Behind the draft were four other pages that I recognized as family group sheets and pedigree charts, partially filled in with names, dates, and places. Some of the names I recognized as belonging to Sarah's family, but many were unfamiliar. The contents of the spaces on the last page had been filled in on a typewriter and I didn't recognize any of the names at first glance.

Sarah, to my knowledge, had never been particularly interested in genealogy, but it seemed she must have developed a fairly recent interest.

I went back to the first page and read through those few lines in the draft of the letter she had started to write in ink.

> My Dear
>
> ~~A very strange worrisome~~ An unsettling thing ~~happened to me~~ has recently come to my attention, as it is something that may turn out to be important to ~~you, as well as to me~~ us and, because of my condition, especially to you, ~~in the near future~~ very soon. Because I may not be able to ~~follow through~~ discover the truth or ~~a solution~~ resolve this confusion and, if not, I hope, you ~~may~~ will be able to ~~complete~~ do both.
>
> One at a time, a few days ago I received two horrid pages ~~by~~ through the mail from someone who did not identify himself, or herself, nor was there a return address, though it was postmarked in Salt Lake, Utah.
>
> I believe that . . .

The draft stopped abruptly at that point and the rest was blank, except for the letters—"FHL"—*and* a phone number—"*801-240-2331*"—scrawled in pencil toward the bottom of one of the group sheets in Sarah's handwriting, along with a name—"*Wilson.*"

I sat staring at the pages in concern and confusion. The subject had clearly been something that seriously troubled Sarah. Evidence of that was all over the page, in corrections and deletions as well as her choice of words.

What and who could have caused her distress? I could see nothing frightening about the sheets of genealogy and there were four of them, not two. So where were the two *horrid pages* she had referred to? And who was *Wilson*, the person who must be at the other end of that phone number?

I considered for a second or two, then picked up the receiver of the phone that sat on the desk and dialed the number. It rang once and was picked up by an automated answering machine. A man's voice told me "Thank you for calling the Family History Library of the Church of Jesus Christ of Latter-day Saints. If you would like our hours of operation, press one. If you have questions about records or research for the United States and Canada, press two. If you have questions about records or research for the British Isles, press three. For other questions, press four. For Family Search, press five." It then instructed me that I could press zero, or wait on line, for a real person. I waited. When a woman came on line, I asked if there was a person there named Wilson and was told he was not in, but would be on the day after tomorrow. Would I like to leave a message? I refused, told her I would call back, thanked her, and hung up, not knowing what else I could ask that would make any sense. But I now knew two things: to whom

the number belonged and that someone named Wilson
at that number might be able to help me if I could figure
out what to ask him.

Rather than pursue any more of the puzzle, I thoughtfully laid the pages and the envelopes on the desk to
take with me to the Winnebago, then went back to work
and finished clearing up the mess left by whoever had
attacked Sarah's desk and bookcases. It was possible
that Don Westover would have answers to my questions
and could enlighten me at our meeting the following
morning. Meanwhile, just in case the intruder made
another attempt, those envelopes and pages would be
safe with me in a place that wouldn't be found, even if
my rig were searched.

As I finished replacing the last book on a living room
shelf, the phone rang on Sarah's desk. I hesitated a
moment, but then answered it to find Ed Norris on the
other end of the line.

"Tried your cell phone," he said, causing me to realize
that I had left it in the motor home. "It's cooling off outdoors. Would you like to take a drive before dinner—get
out of town for a bit?"

I would, indeed, and he agreed to pick me up at five.

Deciding I would confront the chaos of the upstairs
bedroom and other parts of the house the next day, I
took the papers I had recovered, and went out the back
door to find that Tomas had already vanished but, true to
his word, had mowed, swept, pruned, and cleared everything as if a funeral for Sarah would be held right there
on her own property. Not a weed, fallen leaf, or faded
blossom remained to spoil the splendor of that yard.

Hiding the papers and envelopes in the space in the
Winnebago that held my shotgun, I closed it up again.
Then I retrieved clean clothes and my shower kit, and
went up to Sarah's upstairs bathroom, where I took a

long cool shower that improved not only my cleanliness, but also my disposition. I seldom use the shower in the motor home, for there are almost always facilities available in the RV parks I visit and using them allows me to empty the gray water holding tank less often.

After Ed's suggested drive, I had a favorite restaurant of Sarah's in mind—Gladstone's on Twelfth Avenue, a comfortable and welcoming place with a more than acceptable menu. A Jameson and water would also be appreciated. Meanwhile, I refused further search or speculation and spent the remains of the afternoon with Stretch, who was feeling—and rightfully—neglected. Once again missing Sarah, and confused over what I had found, I could do with his unconditional appreciation of my company as well.

I did not, however, intend to hand over the envelope I had found with Ed's name on it until I'd had a chance to talk with Westover about all three of them, the family group sheets, and the draft of Sarah's letter with its reference to the two pages that appeared to be missing. It had waited this long, it could wait another day.

There was a long silence after the shower stopped running, the sound of the woman's feet had gone down the stairs, and the back door had been closed and locked. Then the metal latch made only a soft click as a door was opened in the upstairs hallway and a figure stepped out into the late afternoon shadows to stand listening, cautiously, to be certain of its singular presence in the house. A trickle of sweat ran down the forehead into an eyebrow and the hem of an oversized T-shirt was lifted to absorb it. Assured it was alone, the figure moved slowly, barefooted to the bathroom, where a thin stream of water was allowed to run into cupped hands that several times carried it to the thirsty mouth and splashed it over face and arms. They were quickly dried on the damp towel the woman had left hanging by the tub, which was used to wipe out the sink as well, and carefully hung back as it had been.

Refreshed, the figure slipped noiselessly down the stairs and through the rooms to the kitchen, where a bottle of juice was retrieved from the refrigerator and taken to a comfortable chair in the living room that faced a window overlooking the motor home now parked near the house. For a long time there was nothing but waiting and watching, until a car with a man at the wheel pulled up at the front curb and the woman locked the Winnebago and went to join him, with the dog on a leash trotting beside her.

CHAPTER SEVEN

TRUE TO HIS WORD, ED APPEARED PROMPTLY AT FIVE o'clock, as the shadows from the trees were lengthening across Chipeta Avenue. As the afternoon grew later, I had turned off the air conditioner and opened the doors and windows of the Winnebago to let a bit of breeze blow through. In the shade of Sarah's two-story house it was cool enough so that I could have left Stretch in the rig while I was away. But, deciding he had spent enough time alone in the last—could it possibly be only twenty-four hours?—I took him along. He would be happier to ride along with his humans.

The car's air conditioner, on full blast, had cooled the interior, and as I slid into the passenger seat, Ed handed me a tall paper cup full of iced lemonade.

"Oh, you dear man," I told him gratefully.

"Thank some fast-food emporium on Horizon Drive," he said smiling at me. "I figured the temperature would be pretty warm for you since your blood must be thick from all that Alaskan cold weather."

He was right. Even in the long days of summer it was

never so hot in Alaska. But, noticing that he had set the air conditioner to recycle, I lowered the window on my side a half-inch to let in some fresh air, so I wouldn't feel we were depleting the oxygen with each breath.

"Where are we going?" I asked as Ed turned right and headed north.

"Thought it might be nice to drive up to the Monument," he told me. "It was something Sarah liked to do late in the day. That okay with you?"

"Sure."

The day had been such a tangle of sadness, not to mention the confusion that littered Sarah's house, that I was glad to leave it all for a space and focus my attention on something else for perspective. I am so used to driving my own wheels that, be it car or motor home, it always feels strange to be relegated to the passenger seat of a vehicle. I can't seem to stop analyzing my way through traffic and completely trust whoever is behind the wheel to take us wherever we're going without incident. This had been strongly reinforced by my husband Daniel, who hated driving under any circumstance and was inclined to leave it all to me. This had filled me with relief, as he was a self-admitted horrendous driver.

I had been to the Colorado National Monument more than once before, but not for several seasons and the last visit had been in spring. It would be different with sun-dried grasses instead of early green. Late afternoon shadows spreading to define the rock formations of the plateau above the Grand Valley would be pleasant and we could look down at Grand Junction from the west side of the Colorado River.

"Good," said Ed. "Then we're off. How was your afternoon?"

I was about to tell him of my discovery in Sarah's secret bookcase space, but hesitated, something telling me to wait until I knew more about that letter and the envelopes; remembering my thought that the letter might have been meant for someone other than Alan— even possibly, Ed. The idea seemed a little ridiculous. What could he have to do with it? But I held my tongue and told him instead about the second break-in.

"You didn't call the police?" he asked, when I had finished relating the tale of my search of the house with Tomas. "Why not?"

"Everything had been thoroughly searched, so I doubt whoever it was will be back," I told him, wondering if I had been remiss in not making that phone call and to excite neighborhood gossip by bringing officers swooping in again on Chipeta Avenue. "I'd be willing to bet that if he didn't find what he was looking for, by now he must think it isn't there to be found."

"So, you think he was looking for something specific?"

"I got that impression from the way it was searched."

Ed was silent for a few minutes, thinking as he turned off Seventh and we were shortly starting up Horizon.

"What if he comes back?" he asked, frowning in concern. "Are you planning to move into the house? Or will you stay in that motor home of yours?"

"Stay in the Winnebago, I think. I'm very fond of this new rig and I like sleeping in my own bed. Stretch will be more comfortable there, too—in a place he's used to."

Ed was silent and thoughtful for a minute or two longer, then his scowl was replaced by a grin as he glanced over his shoulder at my dachshund, who was standing with both front feet on the narrow windowsill so he could watch what we were passing. "Tell me about this ferocious beast of yours," he said. "Seems like good company."

So I told him about Stretch being Daniel's dog to begin with and how it had taken him a few weeks to totally accept me as part of the immediate family when Dan and I married. "When he stopped barking every time I came in the door, I knew we were on the right track."

"How old is he?"

"He'll be seven in May and will probably be around for another five or six years, maybe more. That's about average for the breed."

"He must have missed Daniel, when he died."

"We both did." I thought back to that sad time and how Stretch and I had been comfort for each other.

"For weeks, he would start out the night sleeping in his basket. Then, sometime after midnight, I would wake to hear him whining beside my bed. I'd reach down and lift him up so he could crawl under a blanket I kept for him there and cuddle up next to me."

That warmth in the dark had been more than welcome and cemented our relationship as we both worked our way through the grief of losing Dan. I recalled how Stretch had seemed to know things were not right in my world, either, and was often solicitous during that time. He still was at times, if I was sick or sad for some reason. But now he usually slept in his own bed.

"Too high for him to jump up?" Ed asked.

"Yes, with those short legs he needs a lift. I'm particularly careful to lift him down. It's not good for a dachshund's back to jump down from any height. They tend to have disc problems—that long shape doesn't provide as much support for the spine as other kinds of dogs have. He's very quick, though. I wasn't prompt enough when he decided to launch himself a couple of feet from my porch into a wading pool, but it never seemed to hurt him and he finds it irresistible, don't you lovie?" I addressed Stretch, who, instinctively knowing he was the subject of conversation, had determined to be the physical focus of it as well and come clambering forward between the front seats. I lifted him into my lap, where he gave my nose a lick of thanks and, paws on the armrest of the passenger door, resumed his out-the-window watching.

Ed reached across to give him a pat. "Good dog."

The disdainful glance Stretch cast back at him said clearly, "You expected anything else?"

Partway along Horizon Drive, Ed turned onto Highway I-70 and picked up speed, so it took us only a few minutes to arrive at Fruita, a smaller community a few miles northwest of Grand Junction. There, we turned off and headed toward the west entrance to the Colorado National Monument. Most locals simply refer to it as the Monument, and I agree that it's less of a mouthful.

As he pulled up at the kiosk at the west entrance to this national park, Ed reached for the wallet he had tossed onto the dashboard and I noticed that the card he removed and handed to the attendant was not an annual pass to all the national parks, as is the one I've renewed and carried every year since I began my travels. It was annual, all right, and current, but specific to the Colorado National Monument. I wondered why, considering that he wasn't a resident who might like frequent access to this local park.

"How long has it been since you saw Sarah, Ed?" I asked him, as we drove away from the kiosk.

There was a hesitation before he answered and it seemed to me that his attention to the gentle curves in the road as it began to climb upward was just a shade too vigilant. He cleared his throat, and said in a carefully casual voice, "I saw her once last spring on my way through from a meeting in Denver."

The sidelong glance he cast in my direction told me he was gauging my reaction to this statement.

"Cost you less to buy a temporary pass," I suggested. "Only five bucks a week."

"Oh, I just like to support the national parks," he told me, still paying more than required attention to the road ahead, as it began to wind its way up. "This annual pass for the Monument was only fifteen dollars for a year."

To me it seemed another indication that he had, perhaps, been here to see Sarah more often than he was willing to admit, but I kept my questions to myself, assuming he would say more if he wanted me to know.

Sarah's husband, Bill Nunamaker, had died several years before I lost my Daniel, and she had been alone since. Perhaps sometime in that interim she and Ed had found each other again and been, as the old term says, "keeping company." It could have happened, especially considering the history of his affection for Sarah during those college years. Though back then she and I had made little of my temporary crush on Ed, the memory of that somewhat awkward fascination might have made her reticent to mention to me that they were seeing each other again. It might even be making Ed uncomfortable now. Even graying and bearing the documentation of our years in form and face, somewhere inside we are all twenty years old, I thought, amused, and decided once again to let it go. Instead of asking questions, I turned to consider the scenery as we began to drive by some of the colorful sandstone and shale that forms the cliffs and ledges of the Monument.

The twenty-three-mile Rim Rock Drive we were about to travel climbs more than 1,700 feet—from approximately 4,200 feet above sea level in the Colorado River's Grand Valley to about 5,800 feet as it snakes along the edge of the plateau, with the highest point on the drive at 6,640 feet. Sagebrush abundantly populates the lower elevations with puffs of silvery gray-green, interspersed with stiffer and more irregular branches of ragged saltbush. Rolling my window all the way down, I caught a hint of the pungent scent of sage warmed by the sun, which I have always loved. In a sudden flash of motion, a cottontail rabbit ran across the pavement in front of us. As it bounced out of sight through the brush, it exposed the white tail that gave it its name.

The road at first rose gradually between buttes on both sides, slipping in and out of the late afternoon shadows on the curves until we reached a loop to the right that headed almost back the direction from which we had come. Looking up, I was able to get a view of a huge, almost oval piece of pink sandstone that had once been a part of a cliff behind it. Erosion had worn away the connection between the two and finally left this rock improbably balanced atop its base, looking as if it would topple at the slightest whisper of a breeze. Another loop, to the left this time, and the road climbed more steeply as we passed through two short tunnels before reaching a pullout with space for parking, beyond which a path led to the edge of the high plateau we had now reached.

Ed pulled in and the three of us got out to follow the path to an area where we could look down into the canyon. Though it had cooled off appreciably, the sun was still warm on my back as I stood leaning against a chest-high barrier and found myself looking over the face of a cliff that dropped straight off practically under my feet, giving me a slightly dizzy feeling.

I'm not acrophobic, but it would have been a long vertical fall to the road we had recently traveled below. We were so high that I found myself looking down at a raven that was soaring in circles near the cliff face, much to the displeasure of a number of smaller birds. White-throated swifts, well-named for their speed in the air, spun and twisted in aerial acrobatics around the larger, darker bird, and the air was full of their shrill twittering cries as they joined forces in an attempt to chase it away. Slightly smaller swallows had joined the seemingly frantic effort, their plumage flashing a metallic green as they flitted out of the shadow of the cliff into the sunshine.

Stretch suddenly interrupted our concentration by deciding to yap at a green and yellow collared lizard that skittered from atop a boulder into a crack in the rock. I shushed his barking, and we went back to watching the drama below as the raven stubbornly continued to fly loops and circles in the air, evading concerted attacks. Finally, enough of the smaller birds gathered to drive the bigger bird off, and it glided away to some other part of the Monument.

"I know people like that," Ed commented with a grin from where he was leaning both forearms on the barrier to watch. "Coast along, refusing to give up until they're given what-for by an overwhelming majority."

I turned to find that inveterate explorer Stretch had wandered away again, off the path this time, and was growling at something I couldn't see in the brush. Stepping over to see what he was harassing, I froze at a sudden buzz from a flat piece of pink sandstone near a yucca plant. The sinister rattle revealed the coiled snake that Stretch had interrupted as it was catching the last warmth of the afternoon sun. Its forked tongue darted from the mouth of a triangular head to taste the enemy threat and the tail was a blur of motion. It was not large—uncoiled, would probably have been less than two feet—and did not exhibit what I remembered from pictures as dark diamond-shaped patterns on western rattlers. Instead the blotches on its back were a faded reddish color.

This was an unfamiliar confrontation for Stretch and, not inclined to retreat, especially when an opponent is close to his size, he was standing his ground almost within striking distance. Dachshunds were originally bred for hunting small game and are tenacious in pursuit. True to his breed, Stretch was stubbornly, fearlessly challenging the serpent.

Before my heart stopped completely, or he could attack, I snatched him up and out of danger, which he let me know he resented by struggling to be put down again as I stepped back to watch the snake uncoil and slither away. Returning to the path, I held Stretch so tightly he whined.

The whole drama had taken only a minute or two.

"Did I hear a rattler?" Ed asked, catching up.

I nodded and kept a firm hold on Stretch until we were back in the car. "Dumb! I never even thought about snakes," I said, when I had caught my breath. "We don't have snakes in Alaska, but I should have remembered that down here they do and put him on his leash."

I have no phobia about snakes; just a healthy respect and caution, not always knowing which ones may be poisonous. Spiders and creeping bugs, however—especially those with hard carapaces and scratchy feet—make my skin crawl, as I told Ed.

"Good," he said, with a shiver that hunched his shoulders. "I can't stand snakes. I'll take care of the spiders and bugs. You're in charge of snakes."

I realized that, typically, I had been more frightened after than during the incident. Thinking how quickly I could have lost Stretch made me feel a little sick. For the rest of the day I kept him close on his leash. Though I stayed on the paths, I saw the potential for snakes everywhere—crooked sticks appeared to slither, I imagined that I saw serpents coiled in shadows and shied away from cracks in rocks.

We drove on, soon coming to a place where, without leaving the car, we could look out across the width of the Grand Valley to the Book Cliffs I had seen on my way into the airport terminal that morning. Not limited to framing the eastern side of the valley, I knew that they extended in a huge, sweeping, sinuous S curve for two hundred and fifty miles—all the way to Price, Utah—for I had driven those miles on my way into Grand Junction, with their folds in the distance. In the brightness of the setting sun, the broad layers of different types of stone that formed the cliffs and lined the horizon were a spectacular rainbow from the warm side of the color spectrum—reds, golds, magentas—separated by vertical folds of deep purple-blue shadow.

In September, most of the crush of tourists that crowd the Monument during the summer months has gone, especially families who need to tuck their children back into school for another year. Though the road along the rim is open around the clock, at that late afternoon hour there were fewer people enjoying its views and we had not encountered a great deal of traffic. So we were both unpleasantly surprised when, as Ed was about to pull back onto Rim Rock Drive, a horn suddenly blared a warning from the right and a small dark car sped past, going much faster than was allowed on this winding, thirty-five-mile-an-hour road with its many blind corners and pullouts busy with people paying more attention to the views than to oncoming vehicles. Jamming on the brake, Ed tossed us both abruptly forward against our seat belts. "Where the hell did he come from?" he demanded angrily. "Are you okay?"

I assured him I was, scooped Stretch from where he had tumbled to the floor at my feet, and, after a moment or two to regroup, Ed cautiously resumed our drive—grumbling under his breath about inconsiderate idiots and reckless drivers.

We passed an attractive visitor center, now closed for the day, and continued on along the winding road, our attention drawn back to the fantastic effects of wind and water and ice on sandstone.

Throughout the Monument are magnificent standing stones carved over measureless eons of time from solid walls between the canyons. Many of these monoliths have been given descriptive names: Organ Pipe, Kissing Couple, Coke Ovens, and Independence Monument, for instance. The area is also a geologist's dream in terms of fossils and, in the very shadow of the Monument, rich yields of the bones of dinosaurs and smaller early mammals have been found. Looking down on the canyons and monoliths it was the rock itself that inspired my awe in the variety of its colors and textures. In the glow of the late afternoon sun, the brilliant reds seemed to have an inner light, contrasted against the buffs, purplish grays, and creams that were once the mud and sand deposits of streams, left behind when the water vanished to be transformed over time into the present metamorphic state.

As the day lengthened, we drove on around the long curve of the Monument, stopping a couple of times—once to gaze into the enormous sweeping reaches of Ute Canyon, named for people who once inhabited large areas of what would become Utah and Colorado. Though we saw none, deep in the canyons these people left evidence of their presence in the artwork they inscribed or painted on the rock, often scenes of hunters on horseback shooting bison. An earlier Fremont people had also depicted human figures, but these are distinctively elongated with broad shoulders, some holding shields and wearing jewelry or sashes. Some of the artwork is scratched or pecked into a dark coating on the rock known as desert varnish, a phenomenon of arid regions formed by minerals that over time leach out of the sandstone and run slowly down over stable rock surfaces in a red to black coating that makes the rock look wet or varnished. When mostly manganese is present, the varnish is black, but it grows redder when more iron oxide is part of the mixture.

From one of the highest walls a golden eagle, larger than any of the hawks, launched itself and dove into the bottom of the canyon in a quest for dinner—perhaps a cottontail, like the one I had seen earlier. I could imagine some poor bunny dashing frantically for cover in the brush, or under an overhanging stone.

We had seen many small rodents in the shelter of rocks, where they prefer to make their dens, shelter from predators, raise their young, and hibernate in the winter. Several varieties of chipmunks and ground squirrels were much in evidence and drove Stretch frantic with the desire to abandon his leash and chase after them. Yanking at the end of his tether, he barked ferociously at one saucy squirrel that hesitated briefly atop the low wall of a pullout, seeming to taunt him with an awareness of his limitation.

It was good to get away from Grand Junction and into an unpopulated area. Though with cars passing and parking in the pullouts where people came and went frequently, it was not the same kind of wilderness I am used to in Alaska, but there were no houses, or traffic lights, or the congestion and hum of collective humanity. And there *were* wild animals, birds, and plants in their natural habitat.

A mule deer stepped out of cover as we passed and, startled by our moving vehicle, bounded back into hiding. Juniper, which grows in twisted, complex shapes, exuded its sharp scent into the air when I crushed one of its dusty-blue berries between my fingers. The pinion pines were full of dull-blue jays the size of robins, busily collecting the late-summer cones for their seeds.

The sun went down and traffic thinned as other visitors departed and we progressed along the drive toward the east exit near Grand Junction. We passed the East Glade Park Road turnoff on the right, the pullout for Cold Shivers Point on the left, and there was a short semistraight stretch just ahead before a curve to the left that began a series of sharp turns that would take us down from the plateau. I could see that the right-hand side of that stretch was protected from a drop-off by a neatly built stone wall about eighteen inches high, when something bumped us hard from behind.

"What the hell is this idiot doing?" Ed asked in alarm and annoyance, knuckles white as he clutched the wheel.

I had started to turn to look back when we were hit again and the dark hood of another car swung out and came into view in the left rear window. Accelerating till it was alongside, it swerved into us, forcing our car to the right, wheels off onto the sandy shoulder between the pavement and that low stone barrier. The car rocked violently as Ed tried to force both cars back onto the pavement and was shoved again by the other driver, against the wall this time, and suddenly I was looking down—a long, long way down. At least a hundred feet below me I could see the road we would have been traveling in another few minutes and had no desire to reach by this shortcut.

"Hold on, Maxie," Ed yelled.

I had, as usual, fastened my seat belt. Ed, I suddenly noticed, had neglected to buckle his, but there was no time to correct that oversight. He was shouting and struggling to pull away as the other vehicle maintained contact with ours in a clear attempt to force us over the edge.

I had shoved Stretch off my lap and onto the floor on the passenger side, where the swerving rolled him over onto his back. With visions of Thelma and Louise, and a long silent drop into the canyon in my mind, I braced both my hands against the dashboard and ducked my head. Tires squealing in protest at the extremity of Ed's defensive maneuvers, I felt the tires on the left leave the ground and there were long terrifying screams of metal against stone as everything seemed to happen at once and, at the same time, in infinitely slow motion. The tires thumped back down again, jarring us, and there was a loud report on Ed's side as the exterior mirror snapped off, caught by some part of the other car as its driver gave up and pulled past and away from us. Toward the front of our car there was a crunch of impact, as its rear fender struck us for the last time, broke free, and was gone.

As Ed swung away from the stone guardrail and braked to a stop in the road, everything was exceedingly silent, except for Stretch whining at my feet. I sat up and, before laying a comforting hand on his head, took a look at the small dark vehicle that braked before disappearing around the curve a short distance ahead of us.

One taillight was a different color red than the other.

I recognized that particular configuration as one I had seen before—on the car that had turned a corner and vanished before I could get a look at the driver—in Chipeta Avenue, the night I had arrived and surprised an intruder searching Sarah's house.

CHAPTER EIGHT

IT WAS ALMOST NINE O'CLOCK BEFORE WE WERE finally ushered into a booth at Gladstone's restaurant and had ordered a couple of stiff drinks—Jameson for me, a double martini for Ed—to assist in the settling of our nerves before dinner.

Making sure that the car was still drivable, we had eased our way along to a small pullout a short distance ahead that had parking space for no more than four or five cars at most. There we flagged down a passing motorist who called the park service emergency number for us on his cell phone. It wasn't long until lanky park ranger Stanley arrived and climbed out of his pickup to express concern and take our report of the incident.

While we waited, I had examined Stretch carefully for injury and found him shaken, but thankfully whole. For a few minutes directly after the accident, frightened by the noise and violent motion of the car, he had curled shivering in my lap. Allowed out on his leash, he was soon back to his normal examination of new surroundings, including an attempt to chase a pair of ground squirrels that immediately ran off in opposite directions, leaving him torn by frustrated indecision.

"What is this pullout?" I asked Ed, wanting to talk about something else—anything but our close call.

"The beginning of the Serpents Trail," Ed told me, still pale and unsettled. "The early settlers needed a road for people with farms and ranches to get down to Grand Junction, so they built one. Now it's just a hiking trail that goes down to the road again near the Devil's Kitchen picnic area."

Hiking would certainly be better and more fun than driving, I thought—if driving included whoever it was who had tried to force us off the road. That car had disappeared so rapidly that neither of us had been able to identify the make or get a license number.

"But I'd be willing to bet it was the same car that almost hit us earlier, as we left the Book Cliffs viewpoint," Ed told the ranger, who was scribbling details on a clipboard report. "He must have pulled over and waited for us to come along."

At the time of that earlier incident I hadn't noticed the discrepancy in the color of the taillights, but the driver had been accelerating, not applying his brakes, so they hadn't lit up. It could have been the same vehicle. I couldn't be sure.

"And you didn't get a look at the driver?"

"Ah—nope." Ed glanced away to watch a jay flutter onto a branch of nearby pinion pine, then shook his head and frowned. "He was going too fast and I was too busy to do anything but try to keep from going over the edge."

There was something odd in the way he denied recognition of the driver that made me suspect that he was holding back.

Before I could examine that thought, the ranger turned to me for confirmation.

"I had my head down," I told him. "If we were going over the edge, I had no desire to watch it happen. If the windows broke, I didn't want glass flying into my face."

He nodded and told us, in an apologetic tone, that considering our inability to identify our assailant, and without more evidence, there was slim chance they'd be able to locate him. "Not that we won't try, of course, but it may have been a tourist smart enough to leave the area. We might get lucky, though, and find him locally. He left some black paint on your rear fender, but it's not much to go on—a lot of cars are black—and no one else witnessed the accident."

"He left his passenger side mirror," I hastened to inform him. "We found it, along with the one from our driver's side, in the road back there."

"Mirrors project from a vehicle—probably hit each other," he said. "Impossible to match up unless—maybe until—we find the vehicle. Like having the bullet that shot somebody—but no gun to match it."

He turned back to Ed, whose hands, I noticed, were still trembling slightly.

"My report will help you in settling insurance claims with the rental company. It'll establish that you were the victim of a hit-and-run. The passenger's side of the car, where you scraped along the wall, is pretty much of a mess. The black paint on the driver's side shows that this accident was clearly not your fault—without it as proof someone hit you it would have been iffy."

I thought it was anything but an *accident*. But why would anyone try to deliberately run us off the road in a place where, except for luck and Ed's skillful driving, we might easily have gone over that wall into the depths of the canyon? We would probably have bounced off a couple of rocks and come down on the road below, scaring some motorist half to death. It didn't make sense.

But, then, neither did a few other things in the last two days that seemed now to be less coincidence and more threat. The mental list left me puzzled.

It did make sense that I should drive us down from the Monument and back to Grand Junction. When I suggested as much—Ed's shaky hands in mind—he agreed to ride shotgun, we traded places, and with Stretch riding once more in the backseat, proceeded slowly in the partially wrecked car. Leaving the parking space at the top of the Serpents Trail, a bit farther on we passed the Devil's Kitchen with its picnic area, and from there it wasn't far to the east entrance. The ranger at the kiosk gave us a sharp look upon seeing the damage to the car, but allowed us to proceed when he knew we had reported the accident. I had a few ideas of how the rental agency would react when they got a good look at the smashed passenger's side, for the lower half of it was crushed and deeply gouged from the encounter with the rock retaining wall. The door would open—I had been able to get out through it—but it refused to close tightly, so, glad the weather was warm, we traveled with the wind whistling in around our knees.

From the park's entrance it was only a few minutes' drive back into Grand Junction where we parked at Gladstone's and received more attention from a patron on his way in.

"What happened?" he asked, hesitating to take a good look.

"Hit-and-run driver," Ed told him.

"Whew!" he said before walking on, shaking his head.

I enjoy Jameson enough so that I never gulp it, feeling it deserves to be savored and appreciated, never spoiled with too much, too fast. While I was alternately sipping it and a glass of ice water, Ed tossed down his double martini as if it were painkiller and quickly ordered another. Though he had regained his normal coloring and was no longer looking pinched and pale around the mouth, the scowl on his face now appeared more concerned than shocked and angry. Something was bothering him.

Time to clear the air, I decided.

"Ed?"

No answer.

"Ed!"

Startled, he dismissed his reverie and blinked his attention toward me. "Sorry."

"What's going on, Ed? You're worried about something. What aren't you telling me?"

"Like what?" he asked, carefully setting the martini glass gently, soundlessly down on the surface of the table in front of him.

"Like—if I knew, I wouldn't be asking, would I?"

He gave me a long, silent look, considering my question.

My thoughts went back to his odd behavior during the ranger's questioning and how I had felt he was being less than truthful.

"You recognized the driver of that car, didn't you?"

He stared at me, eyes narrowing. "Why would you say that?"

"Because I'm not stupid. Did you?"

He said nothing, glanced away toward the bar on his left, and I knew he was about to repeat the falsehood he had told to the park ranger.

"Don't lie to me, Ed. I might have gone over that cliff with you, you know. I think I've got a right to the truth. Who was it?"

He heaved a great sigh and, nodding to the waiter who set his new drink on the table and collected the empty glass before turning away, took a sip before pre-varicating.

"I don't know. I thought I might have recognized him, but it all happened so damn fast."

I wasn't about to let him get away with that.

"Who did you think it *might have been*?"

He stared at me, cheek muscles tightening as he gritted his teeth, still reluctant to spit it out.

"*Who?* Damn it, Ed! Who did you think it *was*?"

"All right—if you *have* to know. I thought it was—Alan, that's who."

"*Alan?* Sarah's son, Alan?"

My incredulity deepened his frown and straightened his spine in resentment at my lack of confidence in the statement.

"Yes—Alan," he snapped.

The idea staggered me.

"What gave you . . . ? Why . . . ? How can you think it was Alan?"

Ed looked away again, considering answers, his brows nearly meeting over his nose with the depth of his frown.

"It's very complicated, Maxie. There are things you don't know—about me—and about Sarah."

Ah—now we were getting to the heart of the question.

"So I'd guess it's about time you told me, don't you think?"

"Well, to begin with, Sarah and I've been seeing each other."

"I'd already figured that out."

"You had?"

How dumb did he think I was, for lord's sake?

"Of course. For starts, why else would you be stopping through here often enough to have an annual pass for the Monument? How long have you been seeing each other again?"

"Since shortly after Bill died."

"And what does that have to do with this? I know you don't care much for Alan, but could he possibly think you're trying to take his father's place and resent you enough to try to kill you—and me along with you, by the way?"

The idea struck me as far-fetched in the extreme. I finished my drink and drained the ice water as well.

"Another?" Ed asked.

"No, thanks. I'm starving, let's order. But you haven't answered my question."

He handed me one of the menus left handy by the waiter, who had gone past the booth twice, glancing over to see if we were ready, but not about to interrupt our intense conversation.

Good man.

"You're making the wrong assumption. It's possible that just the opposite is true," Ed blurted out suddenly, dropping the menu and leaning forward with both elbows on it, in a sincere attempt to convince me of what he was about to say. "If I'm right, Alan is my son. And he's convinced that I abandoned him. And I don't dislike Alan—he hates *me*. I think he's spoiled and resentful, but he's my son."

There are times when you are certain that the person speaking to you has completely misplaced his marbles. As I leaned away in reaction I felt confident—in this particular restaurant booth, after a hair-raising afternoon experience that immediately followed the death of my best friend—this was one of those times and Ed had lost his. I stared at him with no idea how to respond. The idea was so preposterous that, for the moment, it defied rational thought. *You've gone 'round the twist,* my darlin' Aussie, Daniel, would have told Ed. I almost said it for him.

"What do you mean, 'if you're right'?" I finally got out.

"Well, I don't have proof. Sarah would never confirm it for me."

"I'm sure she *would've* denied such an outrageous idea. It's not true," I told him flatly.

"She wouldn't deny it, either. When I demanded to know, she'd just smile and change the subject."

I had to put a stop to his nonsense somehow.

"Look, Ed," I told him. "He couldn't be your son. I happen to know—if you don't—that after Sarah and Bill were married and found they couldn't have children of their own, Alan was adopted—when he was three."

"I know that's what she always said, but . . ." He retreated into thought and we sat silently staring at each other with a world of constrained information between us.

The conversation was breaking new ground for me—raising questions about things I had been confident that I knew concerning Sarah. For Ed to even consider that Alan might be his son, he and Sarah had to have been much closer than I had ever suspected during our college days forty-plus years earlier. I remembered that she had dated him several times that I had assumed from her behavior were nothing but casual. We had told each other just about everything back then. If they hadn't been as innocent as they appeared, why hadn't she told me? Because she suspected I might still care about Ed? But that couldn't be true. I had no doubt she had known when I recovered from my momentary infatuation. Some of her dates with Ed had occurred after Joe and I were happily engaged.

I was still considering when the waiter materialized from behind me, ready to take our order. Distracted, I ordered a small steak and salad without further examination of the menu. Ed asked for something I didn't catch, which later turned out to be some kind of pasta, and the young man slipped away as if relieved to escape the tense atmosphere of our booth.

It was growing late, the windows were high and few, and it suddenly seemed very dark in the restaurant's subdued lighting. I stared across at Ed, who took another sip of his drink and set it back down in front of him, carefully observing the glass and not meeting my eyes.

"Look—" he started, just as I chimed in, "Why would you—"

We both stopped, waiting for the other.

He nodded at me. "You first."

"Okay. Why would you believe such a thing?"

He leaned forward again with a sigh.

"That's part of what you don't know," he told me. "Alan is forty-three years old."

"Is he that old?" Was I?

"He was forty-three last November. Do you remember when Sarah took a fall quarter off at the beginning of her junior year?"

I thought back. "Yes—she stayed home to work. I roomed alone that quarter and she came back in January."

"She *told* you she stayed out to work. She was three months pregnant when she left in June for the summer." He paused and ducked his head as he swallowed hard. "She didn't tell me, either. I found out later," he finished quietly.

The statement rocked me, though I had felt it coming. How could I not have known? But was it true? It was. Somehow I knew it was. I remembered Sarah's attitude when she had returned to school—despondent at times, almost manic at others. A couple of times I had heard her quiet crying in the night. Her grades had slipped from her normal As and Bs to Cs—the lowest, an En-

glish class that she should have aced. She had floated
the idea of quitting, but we had talked her out of it and
the next quarter she had seemed her old self again, aca-
demically and otherwise. Trouble at home, was all she
had said in explanation, and I had assumed it the answer
to her moods, for her mother *had* been ill.

"So, she . . . ?"

"Had the child and put it up for adoption," he nodded.
"But I think, when she and Bill decided to adopt, that
she had kept track of, or located, Alan somehow. How
she got him back, I have no idea. She would never talk
about it."

Oh, Sarah, I thought sadly, *you were too clever by
half. Why didn't you tell me? Why didn't I suspect? I'm
so sorry.*

And what, I wondered, still staring at Ed, did it all
matter now—or have to do with events of the last
twenty-four hours? There were now even more things I
didn't know that made me decidedly—and for good reason, as it later turned out—uneasy.

CHAPTER NINE

I SLEPT LATE THE FOLLOWING MORNING, RISING JUST IN time to ready myself for the scheduled visit to Attorney Donald Westover's office at nine o'clock.

After dinner with Ed Norris, I had returned to the Winnebago with relief that lasted at least as long as his battered rental vehicle was in sight before it turned the corner of Chipeta onto Seventh. When I switched off the lights and went to bed, my mind was still revolving like a carousel with unanswered questions and speculations. After an hour of similar, but physical, revolving in my bed, I gave up, got up, and made myself a cup of tea.

From the hiding space where I had stashed them, I retrieved the envelopes and pages I had found in the hidey-hole of Sarah's bookcase and spread them out on the table. Between sips of tea, I examined them, for a second time sorely tempted to open those three sealed envelopes, but once again resisting the impulse and shoving them to one side. Who, I wondered again in the process, was Jamie Stover?

The family history sheets told me nothing more than they had at first assessment.

It struck me suddenly that what I had found did not square with what Sarah had said in the hospital.

At the house, Maxine . . . I wrote it all down. You can read it, she had told me, then mentally wandered off to that silly childhood game.

Nothing in the pages I held fit that wrote-it-all-down description, did it? Unless it lay within one or all of the three envelopes that were not addressed to me. From her words I had had the impression that she had written whatever it was expressly for *me*. If so, that had to mean I hadn't found it yet.

I am not normally inclined toward late-night activity—or getting up absurdly early, for that matter. Some people are crack-of-dawn sorts—up with, or before, the sun. Of course, for the winter half of the year in Alaska this comes very late in the morning and means they get up facing several hours of darkness. The other half of the year is the opposite—in June the sun rises as early as three-thirty and sets as late as ten-thirty. This means that those who go to bed early have it still shining brightly in their windows. On the Fourth of July, we have to wait until almost midnight if we want to be able to see our fireworks. Other people are night owls, whatever the amount of light or darkness. We all learn to live with it, though it bothers some more than others at both times of the year.

I belong to neither crowd in particular. If I can't sleep I find something to do until I can, or until I resolve the issue that is keeping me awake. Answers to the questions that were keeping me awake just then might be in what Sarah had written to me—if I could find it. So the thing to do seemed to be to go and look again.

Not bothering to fully dress, I pulled on a pair of sweatpants and a T-shirt, took a flashlight and the keys Westover had provided, and went around to the back of the house, Stretch trotting along companionably.

Unlocking the back door, I went in, used the push-button switch to turn on the lights, and carefully locked the door again behind me. No surprises tonight, thank you.

The kitchen looked the same as it had the night before. Nothing had been disturbed, though the silverware drawer was slightly open. Then I noticed that the three mugs I had left in the sink had been washed and left to dry on a towel. Had I washed them without thinking? I didn't remember doing so, but I periodically do everyday jobs almost automatically when I'm considering something entirely different—keeping my hands busy when my brain has gone somewhere else. Who, besides me, could it have been? No self-respecting burglar would do household chores.

Crossing the room, I turned on the dining room light, careful this time to use caution in locating the switch without knocking over another vase—though it was a bit like locking the proverbial barn door, I thought, ruefully remembering the crystal shards I had swept up earlier that afternoon.

There are many types of hiding places, as Sarah and I had learned in our game of secrets so many years ago. Part of the idea is to suit the hiding place to the thing you want hidden. The more value—and not necessarily monetary value—the item has, the more important the security of the hiding place becomes. Anybody can stash money: in a sugar bowl, wrapped like hamburger in the freezer, or in a sock under a mattress—easy places where any burglar would look. Another part of the idea is to consider what type of searcher may be hunting for what you want to hide. A quick in-and-out thief, for instance, wouldn't trouble with the kind of search that could be mounted by a professional law enforcement team that was trained to take a place apart. You couldn't call Sarah and me really *trained*, but we had probably learned more in our games than most people. She was always better than I was at this sort of thing and would probably have borne that in mind in hiding something for me to find, so it should be in a place she knew I would be able to figure out.

Glancing around the dining room, I quickly resolved that it would be low on Sarah's possible choices of a serious stash. It would be more likely that she would hide anything she had written to me in a place where she, and I, could reach it easily. Lately, given her illness, that could mean somewhere on the second story—in her bedroom, or one of the others down the hall, perhaps. I went up, deciding to start with the most feasible, and work my way through those rooms hoping one would prove productive.

Two-thirds of the way up the long flight that rose from the vestibule, Stretch tired of the effort, stopped, and sat down. I scooped him up and carried him to the top, where I set him down in the hallway, reminding myself that it would be wise to carry him back down. He padded after me along the hall and into Sarah's bedroom, where I switched on the light and stared in astonishment.

The room that had been strewn with the results of the ransacking it had received was now almost normal.

The slashed mattress had been heaved back onto the springs and used to hold some of the clothes that had not been hung back in the closet. Personal items that had been scattered across the floor had been put there along with pill bottles, pictures, and the telephone. The bedside lamp and shade had been straightened and all the scattered photographs and letters collected and arranged neatly in the blue box. In the wastebasket, which had been placed by the door, things too damaged to save had been deposited—a book and its pages, broken glass from a perfume bottle, the crushed hat box and hat. Feathers from the ruined pillows still lay around the room and a few floated when I cracked a window to let in some fresh air against the still pungent scent of spilled perfume, but the space was orderly again.

Someone had come in while I was away and cleaned it. Did Sarah have a cleaning woman I didn't know about? Was that who Doris had seen going into the house? That couldn't be right, for she had told me she had seen a woman in the yard *before* I left.

Whoever it had been, it was enough for me to gratefully turn to my search without the effort of organizing.

Recalling Sarah's comments about the game of Sardines, I went first to the closet, remembering the back wall that we had fallen through into another room. Shoving the clothing that had been replaced aside, I began to go over the inside of it almost inch by inch, keeping in mind what I was looking for: the pages of a letter, possibly folded in an envelope like the three I had found in the bookcase. First I proceeded to go over the back wall of the closet to make sure it wasn't falsely backed up to a matching closet in the room next door. It was not. I then inspected the sides for hollow spaces. These were solid, but upon careful examination of the molding that ran along the bottom of one side wall, I found a moveable section, behind which lay a black box about five inches wide by twelve long and three inches deep.

In this box were several smaller boxes that held Sarah's most valuable, or treasured, jewelry: pearls inherited from her mother, a pair of diamond earrings, an antique jade ring and matching bracelet, a child-sized locket on a small gold chain, and a few more odd bits. In one blue cardboard box I found a pin that I remembered sending her for a birthday years earlier—two female figures constructed of beads and wire, holding hands, one dressed in purple, one in blue, one with hair as dark as mine had once been, one as blond as a young Sarah. Worth little, it had reminded me—and reminded me now—of what she had said about the two of us back then: "We are sunshine and shadow, positive and negative—opposites—and better together than apart. Everything is better with contrast."

Suddenly loss swept over me again and the image of the pin in my fingers swam in my tears. Swiping at my eyes with the back of one hand, I gave myself a mental shake. The pin had meant something only to the two of us. Unwilling to leave it to Alan, or whoever, I slipped it into the pocket of my sweats, refused to feel guilty over the petty theft, and returned the rest of the jewelry to the larger box. The space was empty of anything else, so I slid the box back inside and replaced the moveable molding for safekeeping.

The remaining parts of the closet yielded nothing, but it was heartening to know I was evidently on the right track. She had continued her old habit of creating hiding places. I simply had to find one that held the communication she had mentioned writing.

From the door of the closet, I looked around the bedroom for any other hiding place. The lamp with the beaded pink satin shade caught my eye and I picked it up to take a look at the base, but it was small and had room for nothing letter-sized to be inserted into the hollow brass from underneath. The dressing table held no hidden spaces. The rest of the moldings were all solid.

I turned my search to the hallway and the three other rooms along it.

As I glanced at their open doors, deciding where to go next, I noticed a narrow door in the shadows at the far end of the hall. A linen closet? Opening it, I found a steep flight of steps that led upward—access to an attic Tomas and I had missed in our search that afternoon. A switch inside the stairwell turned on a dim light somewhere overhead that shone on the steps and allowed me to climb them without using my flashlight, Stretch tucked under my arm.

The residue of the day's heat grew as I went up the narrow stairs and the smell of dry dust filled my nose. The space into which I stepped was cross-shaped and as large as the house was wide, with dormered windows at each of three ends, stairway at the fourth. The flooring was made of unpainted wooden planks laid down and nailed to the joists that formed a partial ceiling for the rooms below. The space was full of the accumulation of years, as I had half expected. At one end two stacks of boxes that had been piled atop each other near a chair with a broken back. One of the piles had evidently fallen over, scattering an assortment of papers and other unidentifiable objects onto the floor. A baby-buggy, old picture frames, three floor lamps—only one with a shade, bent—and two old trunks inhabited another corner. A third section held skis, two sleds, and a torn umbrella. A pair of ice skates and several tennis rackets hung from nails in a rafter, along with a guitar without strings and a battered, tarnished bugle. Everything was covered with a layer of dust—almost everything, anyway. As I stood there at the top of the stairs, I could see a scuffle of footprints that led across to that fallen pile of boxes and another to the trunks.

Still holding Stretch, who was now wriggling to be

put down, I used the flashlight to examine the prints more closely before allowing dachshund paws to muddle them. There were two distinct sizes and types. Flat-soled shoes had made the ones to the boxes, on large, probably male feet—and recently. I could see that these also went across to the trunks and mixed with them were smaller prints with a patterned tread—not running shoes, but something with a rubber sole. Did either of these belong to the intruder I had startled? Were there two intruders? A police officer? Not the latter, I thought. An officer looking for a burglar would not have found it necessary to cross to that pile of boxes in order to see that no one lurked in the attic.

I put Stretch down and he immediately padded across and began his assessment with a sniff at the edge of a quilt that had been folded and laid over one of the trunks. Leaving him to it, I followed the larger footprints to the toppled tower of boxes. Four of them, banker's boxes with separate lids, had fallen from the initial pile of five. The top two had spilled part of their contents into the dust on the rough wooden floor—old records, from the look of them, along with the sort of items you toss in with them and neglect to sort out later—pencils, a box of paper clips, a roll of Scotch tape, a plastic box of pushpins. I flipped quickly through the cascade of pages and bits of paper on the floor as I righted the box and replaced them. There was nothing but the sort of thing everyone saves to calculate their taxes: bills, receipts, file folders. Each of the five boxes contained two or three years' worth of the same kind of thing. I piled them back up and checked the other pile, with the same result. Short of sorting through each and every item in all ten of those boxes, there was no way I could learn if Sarah had used them to hide what she had meant for me. It didn't seem likely that she would have wanted me to go to so much trouble, or leave her writing open to any searcher determined to go through every page. Deciding to take a stab at them later, if I didn't find what I was searching for elsewhere, I turned to the trunks that Stretch had been investigating.

"Hey, galah. You find anything I should know about?"

He trotted over for a pat, then lay down.

"No luck, huh?"

Muzzle on paws, he watched me without comment from those irresistible liquid-coffee eyes and the next time I looked he had gone to sleep. It was, I realized, with a yawn and a glance at my watch, growing very late.

I removed the quilt from the trunk and found a pillow under it with a clean pillowcase. Neither of these items belonged in the attic. Both were in good shape, not dusty, and should have resided with the rest of the linen downstairs. Sarah had taken good care of the quilts she made and this, I recognized, was one of them. The pillowcase was slightly creased, as if someone had slept on it lately. Didn't make sense with at least four beds directly below the attic and three of them unoccupied before Sarah had been taken to the hospital. I laid them in the baby-buggy and considered the trunk.

It was unlocked and full to the brim with clothing carefully preserved in plastic or between layers of tissue paper. On top I found Sarah's wedding dress in its original box and remembered her looking remarkably pale in all that white satin and lace, her mother's pearls around her neck, creamy roses and lily of the valley in her hands. "I look like a damn ghost," she had remarked as we waited together for the wedding music to begin, and her father had chided her for swearing in a church. As maid of honor, I had worn moss green and held that bouquet for her while she pledged herself to Bill and they exchanged rings. Even "obey" was part of the ceremony back then, I thought with an amused smile of memory. As if *anyone* could ever require Sarah to *obey* if she disagreed with an idea in question.

Returning the cover to the box, I laid the dress aside and searched the rest of the trunk's contents, though I knew there would be nothing there to solve my dilemma. I had a similar trunk at home in my basement and neither of us would have thought it a worthy hiding place for anything really important—too easy.

There was nothing to find in the other trunk, either, though I dutifully looked through its collection of memorabilia—dried corsages, high school and college annuals, photographs, programs from formal dances—and made a quick appraisal of the rest of the attic. Was I fooling myself? Had Sarah only imagined that she wrote something for me? I didn't think so. There were still those other rooms just below to be searched, possibly the basement.

Not tonight. I decided, resolved to finish the task in tomorrow's daylight, woke Stretch by picking him up, went down both flights of stairs, and locked the back door on my way out. Finding my way back to my bed in the Winnebago, I went almost instantly to sleep, not to wake until I had to hurry to arrive in downtown Grand Junction for my appointment with Don Westover.

CHAPTER TEN

IT WOULD HAVE BEEN A FIVE-MINUTE DRIVE TO DON Westover's office had I not miscalculated the two hundredth block of Sixth Avenue and wound up traveling the four blocks of Main Street to find my way back. This was not an unpleasant mistake, for Main Street slows traffic by winding crookedly back and forth between areas of parking, trees, shrubbery, and a plethora of tempting shops and cafes. For those who stroll its sidewalks it is also an outdoor sculpture gallery thanks to Grand Junction's Art on the Corner program. Catching glimpses from a moving vehicle is decidedly unsatisfactory, but I did see a humorous representation of a locomotive welded of rusted found objects, a graceful dancer balanced on one bronze foot, and a buffalo made entirely of chrome, and vowed to go back and see what else was displayed in the mottled shade along the street. Already late, however, I turned north on Sixth, found a parking space on Rood Avenue, and, clipping Stretch's leash to his collar, hurried us both around the corner and up the stairs to Westover's second-floor office.

A secretary in a striped blouse looked up as I came through the door and greeted us. Red-framed glasses on a chain around her neck swung as she rose and came around her desk smiling a welcome.

"Hi," she said. "I'm June. You must be Mrs. McNabb."

"And this is Stretch."

Her smile widened at the name—a not uncommon reaction—and, bending, she gave him a pat. "Hi Stretch."

Knowing an admirer when he found one, he wagged his tail and licked her hand before she straightened to tell me, "Mr. Westover is ready for you. This way."

Interesting, I couldn't help thinking, that secretaries are often known by their first names, while some of their bosses remain Mr. or Mrs. If it was okay with her, who was I to object?

She rapped gently on the door to the right of her desk, waited till she heard a response from within, and leaned through to announce, "Mrs. McNabb to see you, Don—and Stretch."

Don? Well! That would teach me to make assumptions about other people's office relationships, wouldn't it? I've always liked the fact that Rocky Mountain people can be as professional as anyone, but most seldom fuss about it, or make judgments based on the casual approach they usually employ.

Don Westover met us just inside the door with another welcome. For this second meeting he was more professionally dressed in shirt and tie, and I saw a suit jacket draped over the back of his office chair.

"There you are. I was beginning to wonder if you were lost."

"Almost." I related my brief tour of Main Street as I took the chair he indicated in front of his desk and gratefully accepted the coffee he offered. Stretch lay down at my feet as usual.

"Everything okay at Sarah's?" he asked, back in his chair behind the desk.

I told him about the second intrusion the day before and how Tomas the gardener had accompanied me in making sure the trespasser was no longer lurking in the house. What was now old news to me was not to him and he questioned me about it with concern lowering his eyebrows.

"You should at least report it to the police," he suggested when I had answered his questions. He couldn't know that my nod meant only that I had heard him, so when he took it for agreement I didn't enlighten him with my opinion. But those two sets of footprints in the attic did cross my mind.

He opened the file that lay before him on his desk and took out a list.

"Before I show you the will and the papers you will need," he said, "I should make sure that we are on the same page on exactly what an executor is required to do to carry out the provisions and instructions. And, if you want to be picky, the term for a female is 'executrix.' "

I couldn't resist. "Does using that term make the job any easier or different?"

"No, of course not." He grinned.

"Then I won't be picky," I told him. "I always thought aviatrix might be rather dashing, but executor is fine."

If he could be Don to his secretary, I could be executor.

"Okay. Now, because Sarah started this a couple of years ago and anticipated a lot of things concerning her estate, it's very clean and this is going to be much easier for you than for a lot of executors. She made a complete inventory of all her assets and has kept it up to date. It's pretty straightforward—the orchards, vineyard and winery, the house, its contents, and whatever will remain in the bank accounts in her name after paying any remaining bills, federal and state income and estate taxes. She has no outstanding debts, except her last hospital bills and whatever utilities are owed for the house. The accountant I mentioned to you the other night will take care of those. You'll need to see him for final totals, but not just yet. You are aware that this is a significant estate, I imagine. Somewhere in the neighborhood of three and a half million."

Astonishing! Though I had known Sarah was well-off, it was more than I had imagined. That figure did, however, include the house, its antique contents, and both businesses.

Westover went on.

"She made all her own arrangements for what she called a gathering and her cremation with the Callahan-Edfast Mortuary. It's already paid for, but you'll need to visit and find out what those arrangements are, then set the date and time."

How like Sarah, I thought. Not only had she figured out how to diminish the decision-making burden for someone else—me, evidently—but, by making her own *arrangements* she guaranteed things would be done the way she wanted when she wasn't there to make sure.

With a half smile, I turned back to what Westover was saying.

"She had a life insurance policy and an investment or two that all name her son Alan as beneficiary, so those should go directly to him without going through probate. In fact, what is subject to probate is very simply defined and Sarah and I have it all set up. We will only have to file the proper paperwork, which I have ready for you to sign—petition to open probate and admit the will, that sort of thing. When the time is right, you can notify the beneficiaries, of course, and transfer the allocations of the inheritance.

"There are only a couple of things that we need to—"

He paused in midsentence and turned his attention from me to the door of his office and the sudden sound of a loud voice filtering through it from the area of reception outside. Stretch stood up, attention also focused.

"I'm sorry, but you can't—"

"Watch me!"

Almost immediately the door flew forcefully open, rebounded from the wall with a crash, and a muscular man stomped in, looking back over his shoulder at June, who was on her feet and indignantly protesting his interruption.

He turned to where we sat at Westover's desk and strode across to stand next to me and glare at us. "What the hell is going on here?" he shouted, fists clinched.

Stretch growled. He may be small but, when he decides I need protection, sometimes thinks he's a Doberman pinscher.

"Good morning to you, too, Alan," Westover said in a level voice. He remained in his chair, keeping the desk between them, and not offering the warm greeting he had afforded me. "I didn't expect you until our appointment this afternoon."

"And meanwhile you and *her* screw up and steal what belongs to me? What is this shit? *I'm* supposed to take care of what my mother left."

"No, Alan, you're not. Your mother left specific instructions that Mrs. McNabb was to execute her estate."

"Right!" Sarah's son cast a contemptuous glance in my direction, as he demanded, "Since when?"

"Since two weeks ago, when she had me come to the

house and make a few changes to her will. She didn't tell you?"

"She did *not*! And I don't believe it. Besides, if she did, she wasn't in her right mind and you know it. Whatever's going on here is illegal and I'm not going to stand for it."

"I assure you there's nothing at all illegal, Alan. Stop yelling, sit down, and I'll explain it to you. I was going to anyway, when you came in—later. Your mother was perfectly rational and there are witnesses to that fact."

"*You* are full of shit!" Alan barked, pointing an accusing finger at Don Westover. "You won't get away with this. I'll make sure you don't. And *you*," he said, turning toward me, "have no right to have anything to do with this. So don't get in my way. You understand?"

At this insult, Stretch, who was now tugging at the end of the leash I had shortened to keep him close, snarled a warning, and, had I let him, would have launched himself at whatever he could reach of this threat.

Alan glanced down at him, curled a disdainful lip, wheeled, and abruptly left the office as angrily as he had entered it, leaving a void of silence in his wake.

Stretch sat down, proudly assuming responsibility for ridding us of menace.

"I'm sorry, Don," June apologized from the open door. "There was no stopping him."

Westover sent a sympathetic look in her direction and sighed.

"Don't worry about it. I don't believe in martyrs, so you did well to stay out of his way. Are you all right?"

She nodded and closed the door.

The two of us sat staring silently at each other for a long moment.

"Well," he said finally. "Maybe this isn't going to be

quite as simple as I hoped. Sarah was afraid he'd make a fuss, but she made sure he can't do anything and will, eventually, have to accept her decisions. I had just hoped it would go better."

When we had finished discussing what my responsibilities would be, I signed the necessary papers, and he gave me a copy of Sarah's will, her inventory of assets, and a short list of the final arrangements she had wanted and already made. "I've got to be in court in half an hour, so you can read them for yourself," he suggested. "If you have any questions, call me."

Finished for the time being, I asked for just an additional minute or two of his time and took out the papers and envelopes I had brought along. I told him briefly exactly how and where I had found them and the jewelry that I had put back where Sarah had hidden it for safekeeping. Then I mentioned my conviction that somewhere in the house was a letter she had written to me that I hadn't yet located.

He took the envelopes, agreed they shouldn't be opened, and offered to keep them in his safe until it was time to gather the beneficiaries of Sarah's estate together for the distribution of her assets. He questioned the name Jamie Stover on the third envelope.

"Do you know this person?"

"No. I thought maybe you did."

"Never heard of him," he frowned, laying it down. "Alan, of course, we know—possibly too well. Ed Norris is an old—ah—friend of hers."

"I know Ed," I said, assuring him that I knew about the relationship between Ed and Sarah. "He's here. Showed up at the hospital yesterday morning. We talked last night—after someone ran us off the road up on the Monument."

Then I had to explain about the accident and Ed's take on the identity of the other driver.

"Good God!" he said when I had finished. "And you're sure you're okay?"

I assured him that, except for a bruise from my shoulder hitting the door frame, I was.

"And he really thought it was Alan?"

"Yes, he really did. And from what I just saw of Alan, it might have been."

"Good lord! This gets more and more complicated. What's wrong with that kid?"

He laid the envelopes with the will and the rest of the legal papers, and thumbed quickly through the draft letter, family group sheets, and pedigree charts that had been partially filled in with names, dates, and places of birth and death. "Strange," he said, finally laying them down. "The letter she was trying to write doesn't really tell much except that she was concerned about something she didn't make clear. There's nothing in the group sheets that she ever mentioned to me. But Sarah evidently felt the draft letter was important enough to keep with the rest of these pages *and* those envelopes. Maybe it has something to do with what she was trying to tell you and she finished it later. If you find it, or anything else about it, give a holler, okay? I've got to run."

He asked June to make copies of the letter and pages for me and keep the originals in a file with the sealed envelopes. Folding the copies to a size I could carry in my bag, I wondered again about that "FHL," the phone number, and the name "Wilson" written in pencil on the bottom of the typed family group sheet, and copied it before handing it back to June. Perhaps I would call again when Mr. Wilson was available.

Leaving Westover's office, I half expected Alan to be

lying in wait for me outside with more invective, but thankfully saw nothing of him.

The whole question of Alan's anger and resentment worried me. Could he really think that either Sarah or I would be unfair to him in terms of the inheritance, or was there some other cause for it? I wished I had had more contact with both Sarah and her son when he was growing up. It would have been helpful to have had our children play together, get to know each other, and for me to know more about Alan. It did not make sense to think that Sarah had been anything but a good and caring mother to any child, adopted or not, but I knew that he had always been a study in contradiction. Though he could be a happy, sunny child, he had a quick temper and could change moods without warning, as if a small dark personal cloud had floated in over his head to release lightning and angry thunder. I longed to be able to go to Sarah for a long talk about Alan—for help in understanding his resentful and unwarranted behavior in Westover's office.

Feeling frustrated and insufficient, I decided to ignore the whole situation and take a little time out to recharge my personal batteries. As I was only a little over a block away, I left my rental car where it was and went to take that look at Main Street I had promised myself. Perhaps I could find an early lunch in the process, having skipped breakfast in the rush to keep my appointment.

Stretch trotted contentedly along at my side on his leash as I took in the shopping opportunities that lined the sidewalks. They were many and attractive. Books, gifts, clothing, jewelry, flowers, toys, even office supplies were part of what was available and tempting to those casually sauntering along beneath the trees. Low brick walls enclosed planters full of shrubs and flowering plants, and among them were the sculptures—some incorporating fountains, so the sound of falling water, as well as the many small birds twittering in the trees made a pleasant background music. Benches were available for the weary, or those who simply wanted to enjoy the surroundings sitting down.

Several cafés and restaurants had outdoor tables and chairs for patrons. I picked one about halfway along and ordered a sandwich and iced tea, which I enjoyed while watching pedestrian and automotive traffic flow past and refusing to speculate about Alan's behavior.

It was a pleasant break, making up for what Alan had turned into a rather disturbing morning. How was I to know the whole equation was about to change again?

CHAPTER ELEVEN

AFTER LUNCH—AND BUYING A SET OF CUPBOARD HANdles shaped like oak leaves from a gift shop I couldn't resist—I went back to the car, intending to return to my home-on-wheels and read Sarah's will before finishing the search of her house. The car had been sitting in the sun and was boiling hot inside, so I turned on the air-conditioning and let it run for five minutes, while I walked back to a travel agency in the next block and picked up several brochures on New Mexico, where I intended to spend the winter months.

When I came back the interior of the car was cooler, so I risked it. Still, I could barely tolerate my hands on the steering wheel and found myself considering the return of the cupboard handles in favor of a pair of oven mitts. Stretch refused to scorch any part of himself on the sunny passenger seat and disappeared immediately into the shade of the rear. I couldn't blame him. I squirmed a bit myself, but had a couple of layers of fabric between myself and that frying pan of a driver's seat, so I endured until it cooled off—something I never have to do in Alaska. Northern winters are just the reverse. I start my car, turn the heater on full blast, and let the engine and interior warm up before driving anywhere. You learn so many new things when you travel—for instance, that all rental cars in desert country should come with one of those cardboard things you unfold on the dash to keep the sun from the front seats.

By the time I arrived at Chipeta Avenue, the inside of the vehicle had cooled, but, knowing the temperature outside hovered somewhere in the nineties, I parked carefully under a tree that would gradually provide more shade as the afternoon progressed. I had started across the front lawn to the Winnebago, meaning to give Stretch a drink of water and myself some iced tea, when a voice from the front porch of Sarah's house stopped me.

"Hello. Are you Maxie? Sorry. I mean Mrs. McNabb?"

A small, slender woman in her forties with short sun-streaked hair stood up from the porch swing where she had evidently been waiting in the shade, came down the steps, and walked toward me over the grass. She wore a cool-looking blue dress with a flared skirt of soft cotton material that swung gracefully around her tanned bare legs. Leather sandals confined her narrow feet, the silver links of a bracelet on one wrist gleamed in the sunshine, and matching silver swung from her ears as she moved.

"Maxie will do fine," I told her. I had never seen her before, but a hint of recognition stirred in my mind. "Can I help you with something?"

"Yes," she said, the faint suggestion of a smile lifting the corners of her full lips, "I think so."

I couldn't help asking. "Do I know you?"

"No, but I know who you are," she said, stopping in front of me. "Sarah told me you would come and that I could trust you."

My breath caught in my throat. Without hesitation I knew who she was before she spoke again, for as she came closer I could see her eyes. They were a paler, grayer shade of green than the grass on which she stood, had small—familiar—flecks of gold in the irises, and were framed with long thick lashes. They were eyes I knew as well as my own.

"I'm Jamie," she told me softly, holding out a hand. "Jamie Stover. Sarah's daughter."

When we were seated at the dinette in the Winnebago, each with a glass of iced tea, I tried to think what to say first.

I had turned up the air-conditioning in the motor home and it was running efficiently, but it took a while for the interior to become comfortably cool.

Jamie sat facing me at the table, drinking her tea with appreciative thirst, and I couldn't stop looking at her. When her glass was half empty, she noticed my attention, gave me an amused glance.

"I *am* real," she said.

"I can see that. It just takes some getting used to."

It did. How could I have anticipated Jamie? Of course I hadn't known that Sarah had a child of either sex until the evening before, when Ed had enlightened me about the reason for Sarah's absence from college that long-past fall quarter. I had assumed it was a boy because he had assumed so—and that possibly that boy was Alan— at least according to Ed. Now, suddenly before me, was Jamie—very real indeed and definitely feminine.

"Your eyes are very like your mother's," I told her.

"She thought so, too."

"You called her 'Sarah.' "

"Yes—well. It didn't work somehow to call her 'Mother.' I had a mother—a different, adopted mother.

So she said I should call her Sarah instead. When I was born she somehow arranged for me to keep the name she gave me as part of the deal, but she didn't give me a middle name, just an initial—S. When I finally met her she told me she had meant it to stand for Sarah. So I guess I'm Jamie Sarah Stover."

She hesitated for a moment, veiled her eyes with those incredible lashes as she looked down into her glass, and took another sip of tea. The gestures reminded me so strongly of Sarah that it added confirmation to their relationship. Ed had been *so* wrong in his suspicions and here was living proof. But was she *his* daughter as well? Studying her, I saw nothing of him in her appearance, not that *that* proved anything. If she was, how was he going to feel about having a *daughter* instead of a son? It was quite a switch to make.

"Did Sarah tell you who your father was?" I asked.

"No. Did she tell you?" I thought that, though it was asked rather sharply, there was a trace of wistful longing in the question.

I shook my head. "She didn't even tell me you existed, let alone who your father was. I only had a few minutes with her in the hospital before she died and she wasn't making much sense."

Was it regret in Jamie's sigh, as she glanced out the window into Doris Chapman's yard? For a second the idea that it had been relief flitted through my mind to be instantly dismissed. Of course it was regret. What child wouldn't want to know both parents?

Jamie turned back.

"So, you don't have any idea at all who he might have been? I'd really like to know."

What I had said was true—Sarah hadn't told me she had a child. I would not tell this woman lies, but saw no reason to go into Ed's suppositions, which could only add confusion to circumstances. What if he *wasn't* her father?

"Jamie, I wouldn't want to speculate," I said carefully. "I'll think about it, okay?"

She sighed again, a little frustration in it this time.

"Why would she tell you? She didn't even tell you about me, did she? And she said she was going to—as soon as you got here. That's why I waited a couple of days before coming to see you. I'd been checking with the hospital by phone, so I knew when she died."

"No, Jamie, she didn't tell me. I'm sorry. But you have to understand that she never had a chance. But she said she had written something down for me and left it in the house. I've been searching, but I can't find it. Do you have any idea what and where it might be?"

She sat up straight and her eyes opened wide in shocked response.

"Did you tear her room apart looking? That was an awful thing to do just to find some letter," she accused.

"*No!* Dear me—no. I found her room like that the night I arrived," I assured her.

"So—who did it?"

"I don't know."

If Jamie knew about the disaster of Sarah's room, then more people than I assumed had been coming and going from the house. I remembered that the room had been straightened when I saw it late the night before.

"Did you clean that bedroom, Jamie?"

She nodded. "I couldn't stand to leave it that way. So when I saw you go away with that man in his car I went up and took care of it while you were gone."

"Went up?"

"I was in the house. I had been taking care of Sarah for several days before I found her unconscious."

"*You* found her? I thought it was probably the visiting nurse."

"No, I did. I'd been out for groceries. I found her when I came back and called the ambulance. The nurse only came twice a day. But I saw you leave yesterday from the living room window."

"You have a key."

Another nod. "Sarah gave it to me."

Other pieces fell into place.

"*You* washed the mugs in the sink and left the quilt and pillow in the attic."

"Oh—yes."

"Who knew you were there?"

She shifted in her seat and shrugged her shoulders.

"Just Sarah—and the nurse who came to give her the medicine she needed."

It occurred to me that she might not know that Doris Chapman was often watching from next door who came and went from Sarah's house. Doris hadn't mentioned a woman, but I decided to ask her later.

"So you were staying—sleeping in the house."

"Yes—in the bedroom across the hall."

Not the attic, but a room I had not yet searched. Why had she hidden and not let me know she was there the night I arrived? Was it really to give Sarah time to tell me about her daughter, as she had said? After Sarah died, why hadn't Jamie revealed herself? She must have been in the attic when I was searching Sarah's room and the downstairs, for she left the pillow and quilt there.

There were so many questions for which I didn't have answers—so many things I wanted to know that might not fit. But she shifted restively and looked a little uncomfortable, so I gave up the interrogation for the moment and turned hostess instead.

"Are you hungry? Have you had anything to eat?"

A little shyly she agreed she was. I was about to find something to hold her till dinner, which I assumed we could have together, when I heard the summons of my cell phone. Opening the bag I had carried downtown earlier, I retrieved and answered it to find Westover on the line.

"I have some bad news, Maxie," he told me. "I just had a call from the hospital with the lab results."

With everything else that was going on I had all but forgotten about it. "Yes?"

"Sarah didn't die naturally of her heart condition. They believe someone tried to smother her in her bed at home and, though it didn't succeed at the time, the stress was too much for her heart. Someone made sure she'd have hours left, not weeks."

Aside from the visiting nurse, Jamie had admittedly been with Sarah in the house, I thought instantly. But she had said she found Sarah unconscious and called an ambulance for her. Would an attempted killer do that? I didn't want to think so, but it was not impossible. Would she have wrecked the house looking for something? If so, what? She said she had cleaned Sarah's room. But there had been someone else, I remembered—someone who made those larger footprints in the attic, who thoroughly went through the house hunting for something and left evidence of that search in scattered belongings.

The fact that someone had deliberately attempted to kill Sarah upended everything and left me in a state of shock and dismay. Who and why? Neither of us had mentioned Alan. He didn't know about Jamie and I couldn't tell him with her sitting right there in front of me.

"You still there?" Westover asked.

"Yes, I'm here. What should be done?"

"Nothing, for the moment. The hospital must legally

report it, and already has. I'll check and let you know if there's anything, okay?"

I agreed and he hung up.

Having heard the tone of my voice, Jamie was frowning in concern as I dropped my phone back into the open bag with shaking hands, feeling sick.

"What's wrong?"

I told her.

"I *knew it!* I *knew* there was something wrong when I found her. One of her pillows was on the floor, but I thought she had probably shoved it off the bed," she said, distressed and angry. "She said we had plenty of time to get to know each other and set things straight before—before . . . I finally found my real mother and there just had to be *something* to screw it up, didn't there?"

When I got over my surprise at her anger, I heated some of Doris's casserole, which Jamie ate hungrily. Then we talked for a while and some of my questions were answered. At least I thought they were. I may have overlooked things in my misery over the way Sarah had evidently died. That knowledge hit me harder than it seemed to hit her daughter. But I had known Sarah for most of my life and loved her like a sister. Jamie had only recently discovered she even had a mother other than the one she had grown up trusting. The time she and Sarah had spent together had barely been enough to accept each other, let alone engender closeness, hadn't it?

Jamie said she had been adopted by the Stovers, a local couple, soon after she was born in Salt Lake, Utah—where Sarah had said she spent the summer and fall of her pregnancy. This made sense, to me, looking back to the moral climate of the time, that Sarah would go away from home to avoid embarrassment for both herself and her parents. Jamie had been an only child and had never been told of the adoption. When both her parents had died in a car accident in 1998, she had found evidence of her adoption along with other family records she had inherited. But that evidence did not include the identity of her birth mother—or her father.

Working through an agency that helps people who have been adopted to find their parents, Jamie said she had finally unlocked her mother's name and tracked Sarah to her family home in Grand Junction.

"After I found Sarah, she sent me some information about her family, because I had to start searching all over again for my new—real—family records," she said with a rueful smile. "For obvious reasons, I had been completing a search of the *Stover* family lines that my mother started years ago. Then I found out it wasn't mine at all."

"You're interested in genealogy?" I asked, thinking of the family group sheets that I had found in Sarah's bookcase hiding place.

"I'm LDS and we all search our family histories. I sent Sarah some of mine."

I remembered hearing that church members did that and knew also that there was a huge amount of genealogical information that had been collected for years by the Church of Jesus Christ of Latter-day Saints in the Family History Library I had reached by phone in Salt Lake. Should I show Jamie the family group sheets I had found? Giving myself time to consider it, I moved to another related question.

"It must have taken some time to locate Sarah," I ventured, wondering how long it had taken. "When did you find her?"

"Well, at least she wasn't living somewhere clear across the country," she told me. "When I knew who she was, and figured out where, I looked up her phone number and called—about three months ago. It was an incredible phone call. We talked for almost an hour that first time and several times since. We had planned to meet this fall, when I could take time from my job. Later, when I found out she was so sick, I knew I couldn't wait, so I quit my job and drove down here to be with her. That's when she told me who you were and that you were coming from Alaska. She was looking forward to seeing you—a lot."

So was I, I thought sadly.

Behind her in Salt Lake, Jamie had left a fourteen-year-old son—with a friend, she said. She had taken back what she believed was her maiden name when she divorced, which explained the Stover.

Jamie had not gone to the hospital in the ambulance with Sarah because she assumed that, without proof of relationship, they wouldn't allow her access to Sarah, but would have called Alan, who had no more idea of her existence than I had had—still hadn't, as far as I knew.

As Jamie told me the story, I began to have an idea why Sarah might have made changes in her will and remembered that I hadn't yet read it. Whatever it contained could not be shared, though. That would have to wait till later, when Westover and I called the beneficiaries together for a formal reading in his office.

I was just going to reach for the copies of the family group sheets in my bag to ask if they were the ones Sarah and Jamie had exchanged, when I heard a call from the yard next door. Looking up I saw Doris Chapman waving from her kitchen window, which she had raised halfway. "Yoo-hoo, Maxie," she called again and, when she saw me looking, gestured for me to come around to the front porch.

"I'll be right back," I told Jamie and stood up with an amused smile to answer the summons.

"What does she want?"

"Probably to feed me again, though I still have half that casserole she gave me yesterday and part of a loaf of her home-baked bread. I can't say no. It's what she wants to do. She's missing Sarah, too."

Jamie nodded and poured herself a little more tea from the pitcher I had set on the table.

"Stay here, Stretch," I told my dachshund, who had risen to accompany me. "I'll only be a minute—I think."

I met Doris on her porch and, sure enough, she had more food—a sheet cake with chocolate frosting to offer me this time.

"This is much too much, Doris," I told her. "Give me half."

"Oh, no. You can share it with your friend," she insisted, so I had no choice if I didn't want to hurt her feelings. I had to smile to myself at the confirmation that she was very attentive to comings and goings next door.

"Did you find out when there will be a service for Sarah?" she asked, as I was about to turn away after thanking her.

"I don't know, Doris," I told her. "But it's on my list and I'll let you know as soon as I do."

"I'd appreciate that."

As I walked back to the Winnebago, I thought about that. There would have to be some kind of service—at least a gathering for the people she had known for years who would want to pay their respects. I definitely must soon examine the arrangements she had made with the funeral home to see what she wanted.

"Hope you like chocolate cake," I said as I opened the door and stepped back into the motor home. "There's enough here for an—"

The glass from which Jamie had been drinking tea sat on her side of the table, ice melting in the bottom,

but her place on the bench was vacant. For a second or
two I thought she might be in the lavatory at the rear of
my rig, but the door was open and I could see it was
empty.

I set the cake on the counter in the galley and stood
looking around as if I had simply missed seeing her
somehow. I had not. She was gone.

A glance at the bag I had left sitting open when I took
out my phone told me something else was gone, as well.
My wallet and the cash in it were untouched, so she was
no snatch thief. But the papers I had brought from Westover's office—the family group sheets and, worst of all,
my copy of Sarah's will—had vanished with her daughter—if it was her daughter.

I suddenly wondered if I had sold myself on what I
wanted to find in Jamie—who at the moment seemed
just a little too good to be true.

Chapter Twelve

I IMMEDIATELY SEARCHED SARAH'S HOUSE AGAIN, every room of it this time—even the attic and basement—but Jamie Stover was nowhere to be found and I doubted that she would be back. Disappointed and annoyed that I had been made to feel duped, I called the attorney's office to request another copy of the will and family papers, and drove down to pick them up, both Stretch and I glad that I had parked in the shade this time and the car was less than oven temperature.

Don Westover met me at the door to his office to ask what had happened.

When I related the appearance and disappearance of Jamie Stover and who she had claimed to be, he seemed at a loss.

"Sarah never mentioned a daughter," he said slowly. "She *did* make some changes to the will that seemed unnecessary, but when I asked her about them she just smiled and said it seemed a good idea. She had a book—one of those general guides to making wills and settling estates. I sort of assumed she'd been reading it and was just being meticulous. Did anything seem remarkable to you?"

I was forced to admit that I hadn't had a chance to read the will before it vanished. "You said Sarah made changes two weeks ago? That would be after Jamie said they talked on the telephone, but before she came here from Salt Lake. What changes did Sarah make, exactly?"

He spread out the original pages and went through them line by line with an index finger. "There were only a few and they were all similar to this one," he said pointing. "This originally had Alan's name as the only child beneficiary. Adopted children automatically inherit with or without a will, but she wanted him named. She changed it to read that any child of hers, natural or adopted would inherit."

"Sounds like she had Jamie in mind, doesn't it?"

"Maybe. Illegitimate natural children should inherit automatically from their mother, if not always from the father. This is getting a little complicated, isn't it?"

It was—and seemed to be becoming more so.

With the second set of copies, I went back to Chipeta Avenue, my mind awhirl with conjecture, and spent the rest of the afternoon once again minutely examining Sarah's house from top to bottom in search of whatever it was she had said she had written for me—to no avail. I found a false top on a chest of drawers in an upstairs bedroom, but nothing but dust and a small empty jewelry box occupied it. The medicine chest in the bathroom lifted out of the wall to reveal a space large enough for a diary that inspired optimism, but it was years old and told me nothing I didn't already know.

Then, in the basement, where I wound up last, a whole freestanding set of utility shelves full of old paint brushes, empty cans, wallpaper remnants, and cleaner, suddenly released on the same principle as the edge of the bookcase upstairs when I leaned against it. It swung out on hinges to reveal a door behind it—locked.

I backed away and sat down on a tall stool next to a workbench cluttered with tools and stared at that *heavy— solid—locked* door in a ferocity of frustration. After a pleasant, restful summer at home and an invigorating motor home trip, the last two days had been full of more emotional disturbance and heartache than I had experienced since the death of my husband, and it all suddenly came together in unexpected anger combined with my grief. I swore at both of them for leaving in general, then at whoever had killed Sarah, and finally, ridiculously, at her for dying before she could talk to me—for leaving me only a useless part of a letter and hiding the rest somewhere I either couldn't find, or couldn't get into. I pounded an ineffectual fist on that workbench until a pair of pliers bounded off to jangle on the cement floor below, startling Stretch away into a corner.

"Sarah—thanks a lot!" I howled. "Why couldn't you wait for me? I'm *sick* and *tired* of secret hiding games. I wish we had never started this stuff back then—not to *mention* that you kept it up. What the bloody hell were you *thinking*, Sarah? If you want me to do something about this mess, then for heaven's sake give me one damn clue that I don't have to fight for."

With that out of my system, I dried my eyes, shoved the utility shelves back to cover the door, apologized to Stretch, and carried him upstairs to the kitchen and out the back door—cobwebs in my hair, smudges on my face, filthy hands and clothes—intending to get my shower bag and spend a considerable length of time under the soothing hot water of the upstairs shower.

I turned from closing the back door to find Tomas—

the once-a-week gardener, rake in hand, still obsessed with the condition of Sarah's yard—observing me in openmouthed astonishment from the bottom of the steps. Behind him the gate into the alley was half-open. Either he had left it so—for I could see what must be his pickup parked beyond it—or someone else, Jamie perhaps, had gone through and left it open in her haste to be gone.

"You okay, Missus?" he asked.

I had suspected he would never be able to call me Maxie.

After reading the new copy of the will, which told me nothing that solved any problems or answered questions, I felt informed enough about Sarah's wishes to drive out and spend the rest of the afternoon confirming arrangements with the Callahan-Edfast Mortuary in a kind of apology and penance for my anger. I had thought to make this particular visit with Alan, but he had made no effort to contact me and I had no wish to be the target of abuse similar to what I had received in Westover's office.

"Originally, Mrs. Nunamaker said she didn't want any kind of funeral service or viewing," the manager, a Mr. Blackburn, told me. "She didn't even want it called a funeral, but a gathering of friends and family. She was very plainspoken."

"Said she didn't want people weeping and wailing over a shell in a box, didn't she?" How like her. I smiled, having heard that particular phrase from the woman herself more than once, along with the idea that we are not our bodies, they are only on loan to us.

A little uncomfortably, he agreed that that was exactly how she had worded it and told me that they had come to an agreement that a gathering of family and friends was to be held just before her cremation.

"No flowers," he said. "She didn't want flowers, either—she wanted the family wine served. It's a bit unusual, but her family winery made very good wine, you know. I'll let them know to send some in."

I did know—for she had once taken me on a tour of the winery that her father had established in Palisade, a community a few miles east of Grand Junction.

Well, Sarah, I thought, *you may have your family wine, but flowers are one thing you* can't *control.*

"I'd have a vase or two available just the same," I suggested. For I knew that I could never allow my dearest friend to depart without at least a few of her favorite blossoms, and suspected others would feel the same.

Everything else was already planned and paid for, as Attorney Westover had indicated, down to a short obituary with notice of the gathering for the local paper, lacking only the date and time. I scanned the brief obituary Sarah had left, thought about adding a few of the things I would have chosen were it up to me, but finally respected her wishes and left it as written.

I left the mortuary feeling comforted. There is something about following the established custom and ritual of the benchmarks of life—christenings, graduations, weddings, funerals—even *gatherings*—that has that effect. They are occasions for the living, and not just the person, or persons, for whom they are observed. I realized that, until I walked through it, the door of the mortuary had been another that held unanswered questions. Answering them was one of the things I had needed to do to accept the fact that Sarah was gone—one of the stages of grief—and she had helped me through it by providing some of the answers ahead of time. I hoped I would remember to be as wise when my turn came.

Thank you, Sarah.

Now—what do I do about your daughter—if she is your daughter? More than that, how can I figure out who would dare to attempt your murder? Using the word *murder* stopped me cold for a moment.

First you unlock that door in the basement, she said quietly in my mind's ear, and I suddenly remembered the key I had found in the secret compartment of the desk in the living room alcove.

It was where I had returned it to the box at the back of that one desk drawer. I plucked it out, went down the stairs from the kitchen, walked straight to the utility shelves, swung them away from the wall, and slipped the key into the lock. It turned easily and the door opened silently on well-oiled hinges into a narrow room hidden behind what had appeared to be the solid cement of the basement wall.

Well done, Sarah. Double guard: hide the key for a hiding place in a hiding place of its own.

For this one, however, she must have had help. Some unknown workman, possibly Bill, I supposed, had constructed it long ago, for all but one of the shelves that lined two walls were thick with the dust of years. That single shelf was neither dusty, nor empty. Two banker's boxes stood side by side upon it, one of them labeled *J. S. Stover* in Sarah's easily recognizable handwriting, the other unlabeled.

I took the heaviest, the *J. S. Stover* box, remembering what Jamie had said about Sarah giving her the S as middle initial. Carrying it out to the workbench, I swept a space clear of tools with one arm, and set it down.

Overhead was a shielded light bulb that turned on with a jerk of the dangling string.

The box was full of papers in file folders and a smaller box that held a collection of photographs, which I examined first. They were pictures of Jamie in reverse-chronological order, from what must have been only a year or two ago, for her hair was longer that it had been when she walked across the lawn to meet me, and going backward to the time she was born. Turning them over, I found a date on the back of each one and an indication of her age at the time the picture was taken. In order in this collection, I saw Jamie as an infant, in a sandbox at three, in a swimming suit at seven, graduating from high school at eighteen, and from college at twenty-two. I found her standing by a Christmas tree, holding a Fourth of July sparkler, and dressed as a butterfly for Halloween. There were two of her wedding to a husky young man who looked uncomfortable in a dark suit. One of these included what appeared to be the parents of the bride and groom. Later, one or two pictures showed her with a baby that must have been the son she had mentioned to me. There were more pictures of him, sitting on the front steps of a house, alone in a sandbox, but more often with her, as he grew. Oddly he never seemed to smile or turn his face to the camera. They abruptly stopped when he was nine years old, leaving five years unaccounted for. The handwriting style of the dates on the photos was consistent but unfamiliar, so someone other than Sarah had written them—whoever had sent the pictures, I surmised. Someone had known that Sarah cared about the child she had given up—someone who had been close enough to take pictures of Jamie had made sure Sarah was kept informed of her daughter's life. Who?

The adoptive mother was, at first, highest on my

speculative list of possibilities. But the handwriting on the most recent photo of Jamie matched the others and the date was May 2001. Jamie had told me her parents had been killed in 1998, so it couldn't have been the mother who had kept in touch with Sarah for over forty years. Stymied, I returned the pictures to their box and took out the first file, which was also labeled 2001. In it, and the rest, dated and going back year-by-year like the pictures, I found letters about Jamie from someone who had signed them only "Your friend." There were no envelopes, no postmarks, no return addresses—just the letters full of news about Sarah's daughter as she grew older; all details a mother would like to know.

I sat down again on that tall stool beside the workbench and wondered if Sarah had ever known the identity of her benefactor. She must have, I reasoned. Why else would she get rid of the envelopes and their postmarks to make sure that not one identifying scrap of evidence remained? What a secret to keep for all this time—even from me. It was so stultifying that I found myself on overload, without a brain cell left able to analyze the situation. I simply sat and, going through the photographs again, knew how Sarah must have treasured them.

This time I began to notice details of the various backgrounds.

The house in which Jamie had grown up remained the same—a brick residence on a pleasant tree-lined street. It had a neatly landscaped front yard and a large grassy space in back that, when she was small, held a swing set with a slide. Inside it was like most similar homes. There was comfortable furniture and the normal evidence of a family that read books, watched television, ate and lived together contentedly.

From a sign on a building in another, she had gone to

East High School, so the house she lived in must have been somewhere near where it was located. I didn't recognize it from pictures of Jamie taken there, standing proudly in her cap and gown on the occasion of her graduation.

How careful Sarah had been to keep the secret of her daughter. Why was that concealment so important to her? I could understand how it must have been at first. Girls the age we had been in college simply didn't get pregnant—it was a disgrace of major proportions. So Sarah had kept her secret, even from me, had her child adopted and moved on without a word. But was that caution necessary later, after she had married Bill and they had adopted Alan? She must have felt it was, though she might have confided in Bill. Intuition told me that Alan, conversely, had known nothing of this *sister*.

I returned to the folders, which I found all had dates that matched those on the back of the photos, and which held details of Jamie's life that a picture couldn't tell. Almost, I took them back to go through and read that evening, but changed my mind and left them in the box. Now that I had the key, they were probably safer where they were than in the Winnebago with me and I absorbed about all I was capable of for the time being.

Carefully, I put everything, except for that last, most recent photograph of Jamie, back into the box and returned it to the hidden room. Before I left, I lifted the lid of that second box and found it empty, except for a single five-by-three index card in the bottom. Carrying the card back to the light, I found an unfamiliar name recorded on it: *Mildred Scott.* Beneath the name was a Salt Lake address. Slipping it into a pocket of my skirt with the photo, I locked the door and swung the utility shelves back into position. This time the key would not go back into that hidden space in the desk drawer. I would keep it in my own hiding place in the Winnebago. Dropping it in my pocket with the picture and card, I climbed the stairs into the kitchen, thinking hard.

As I moved toward the back door, the cell phone I had dropped into the other pocket stopped me with its demanding summons and I found Ed Norris on the line with another invitation to dinner.

"I have a different rental car," he announced, when I offered to pick him up.

"Okay, but no drives to the Monument this time," I told him adamantly.

He laughed and agreed.

So I accepted his invitation with relief at the idea of leaving the confusion of the day behind me.

As I readied myself for his arrival, I wondered just how much of what the day had held I should reveal. Would he accept and adjust to the idea that what he had assumed was a son had turned out to be a daughter? Should I tell him at all? I could tell him about the plans Sarah and I had made for her gathering, however—and would. The rest I could play by ear and intuition, knowing there would be time later, if necessary.

If in doubt, leave it out is a rule I have followed most of my life and usually find advisable in the long run. You can't unsay something. It works better to keep it to yourself until you're sure, than to regret saying it later.

The other thing I would try to do that night was keep a close eye on Sarah's house, in case Jamie returned under cover of darkness. It was, I supposed, possible—depending on what else she hadn't told me.

CHAPTER THIRTEEN

"So, YOU HAVE ANOTHER CAR. WHAT ELSE HAVE YOU done with your day?" I asked Ed as we drove west out of the central section of Grand Junction in a new rental car toward a Red Lobster restaurant.

"Not much," he told me. "I spent two hours this afternoon with the rental company straightening out everything that needed to be done concerning what was left of their car. Can't say they were happy about it, but it all worked out okay and the insurance will cover it. I was glad the police report stressed that it wasn't my fault."

"Good. It certainly wasn't. Still gives me chills remembering how far I was looking down the side of that cliff for a moment or two there."

The memory made me wonder again if he had been right about Alan being at the wheel of the car that had tried to drive us off the road. It was something I hadn't thought of that day. Alan's anger in Westover's office had been enough to add to my suspicion that it could have been, so I told Ed about it.

"I'm amazed my name didn't come up in his list of

resentments as well," he commented wryly, when I had finished relating the details of the incident.

"He was focused completely on calling both Don Westover and me thieves and venting anger at not being allowed to execute his mother's estate."

"Just as well he left me out of it. You don't need more complications in taking care of the things the way Sarah wanted."

Once again, I found that enlightening him just then about the complications that—one way or another— seemed to be resulting from Sarah's wishes for some reason made me uncomfortable, though I didn't know exactly why. So I kept my own council on the appearance of Jamie that afternoon. We made casual conversation over a relaxed and welcome seafood dinner, though I had a small guilty thought or two for Doris Chapman's casserole languishing in the refrigerator of the Winnebago. Ed expressed an interest in where and how I lived in Alaska, so I told him about my pleasant summer in Homer. By the time we had reached after-dinner coffee, I was describing the arrangements for the gathering Sarah had planned.

He chuckled. "So she wanted no sepulchral sermons or spooky music—and wine instead of flowers," he said. "We could have anticipated that, I guess, couldn't we? Whatever she wanted is fine with me—all but the flowers. She'll have her usual pink roses from me."

Usual? And *pink?* I had thought Sarah hated pink. *Interesting,* but I didn't ask questions.

Instead I offered my agreement on the subject of flowers and made a mental note to double check with Callahan-Edfast on the subject.

When Ed suggested a walk by the river after dinner, I was sorry I had left Stretch at home, knowing he would have enjoyed the outing.

The confluence of the Colorado and Gunnison Rivers is located south of downtown Grand Junction and along its banks the city has wisely set aside not only space for parks, but trails for walkers and hikers that run through wetlands, cottonwood groves, across islands, and around small lakes for miles to the east and west of the rivers' intersection. Riverside Park on the north bank of the Colorado provides access to at least two of the trails, Audubon and Blue Heron, as well as playground equipment in a grassy area, shaded by beautiful trees. How could a name like Blue Heron Trail not beguile anyone into a visit, when it calls to mind one of the most graceful and dignified of birds?

Ed parked his replacement rental car and we walked across onto the lawn, where I immediately took off my shoes to go barefoot in grass damp from a late afternoon watering. He grinned and did the same, rolling up the bottoms of his pants a turn or two and wiggling his toes. The scent of the grass wafted up from under our feet and a nearby robin ignored us in favor of a tug-of-war with a reluctant worm that had surfaced as a result of the watering and was being stretched like a rubber band by the determined bird. The sun had set behind the Colorado National Monument, so the park lay in its cool shadow, though there was still a reflected red-gold glow from the top of the Book Cliffs to the north.

Like a couple of kids, we took advantage of a set of swings, coating our feet with dust from the spaces beneath them that had been worn free of grass by past swingers. It had been years since I set one in motion and it was fine to be airborne. I remembered how, as a child, I used to love making a swing go higher and higher, until I felt I could almost fly—and once sprained an ankle when I couldn't resist leaping out at the top of the arc. This was not a temptation at sixty-three, with bones that are far more brittle than those of an eight-year-old. Still, it was delicious to swing, especially with the resulting breeze cooling your bare toes. I found myself humming an old tune, some of the words echoing in my memory: *Come Josephine, in my flying machine . . .*

I wondered as I pumped myself back and forth why so many people neglect doing things that give them pleasure just because they have advanced in years. Acting old just makes you feel old, in my estimation. *Going up so high . . . touch the sky . . .*

"Sarah and I used to swing in Seattle," Ed said suddenly, and I noticed he had given up the effort and had let his swing die to a stop. "We found a park close to the university where we'd go sometimes on our bicycles and spend time talking and swinging. I'd almost forgotten that. All day I've been remembering things I thought I'd forgotten."

As I allowed my swing's momentum to die as well, I looked across and saw, in the twilight, that his cheeks were wet with tears.

"What am I going to do without her, Maxie?" he asked, turning his face away from me to stare unseeing at the riverbank in the distance. "I've always loved her, you know?"

I did know—had always known—and thought about it carefully for a moment or two before answering.

"Then I think it was good that you were able to spend time together in the last few years," I said finally. "I know it must have been comforting and a great pleasure for her to have you there after Bill died. She cared a lot for you, too, Ed."

"Not enough," he said in tight voice, and I sensed the years of dissatisfaction that had accompanied his affection for Sarah. "I would have been a better husband to her. I knew her better."

How could he think so? I was taken aback by the vehemence in his voice—had never realized how much he begrudged caring that was never returned the way he wanted it. Enough to take revenge? Surely not. What purpose could it serve now, especially so late in their relationship? He hadn't even been in Grand Junction the day Sarah went to the hospital—had he?

Why did I unexpectedly feel that he was carefully noting my reaction to his expression of pain? Was I, in the knowledge that someone had *murdered* Sarah, beginning to see everything and everyone with suspicion?

"Don't you ever cry, Maxine?" he asked suddenly.

The insinuation in his question stunned me into silence that grew into a lump of resentment, which, rather than take exception to, I swallowed. How I grieved for Sarah was my business.

I had considered telling him what the hospital had reported to Westover concerning Sarah's death—thinking he might have some clue to who had made the attempt on her life—but, again, changed my mind. It was another thing that would wait till I had examined a few ideas more carefully. Instead I gathered my thoughts, ignored his query, and defended Sarah.

"She cared enough to be your friend all her life," I told him. I get stern when people are self-indulgent, even when they may have some right to it. "That's no small thing, is it? Does love always have to be the way you want it, or measured by some personal standard to count? People only have their own kind to give. I think that every bit of what she felt for you she gave as well as she could."

We can't help loving who we love. Ed's disappointment and sense of loss reminded me how lucky I had been to have had not one, but two good marriages that were equitable and loving on both sides. Things do tend to come full circle, though not always in the way you expect.

"You're right," he admitted, turning to me a bit shamefaced. "I'm being selfish. I'm going to miss her—a lot. But then—I've always missed her, really."

"I'm going to miss her, too. But I think that as long as we remember her she's still around. I've found myself talking to her in the last couple of days."

I put my feet down to stop the swing's slight movement.

"Just think how she would have loved this—a couple of senior citizens hogging the playground equipment."

He looked around and noticed, as I had, that a couple of small boys who were standing on one foot, then the other, were clearly wishing we would abandon the swings.

Collecting our shoes, we left them to it and walked back across the grass toward the parking lot.

"Thanks, Maxie."

"You're welcome."

He drove me back to my home-on-wheels and, when he had pulled up at the curb, I turned, wanting to give him something comforting.

"Sarah left you some kind of letter," I told him. "It's sealed in an envelope, so I didn't open it."

"Where is it? Can I have it now?"

"I left it with her attorney. I'm sorry. I found it in the house with a couple of others and took them to Don Westover's office this morning. I'll ask him when you can have it—get it for you if I can."

"Please."

I hesitated a moment, deciding, then asked, "What do you know about Salt Lake, Ed?"

He gave me a blank, uncomprehending look, shook

his head and shrugged. "Nothing much. It's in Utah—
Mormon Tabernacle Choir—Winter Olympics. Why?"

"Oh, I just wondered if you'd been there and what it
was like," I hedged. "I've come through there on my
way here more than once—did this trip down—but I've
never stopped. It's not important. I was just curious."

When he had driven away, I went to the motor home to
get Stretch and give him a quick run, feeling a bit guilty
for having had my adventure in the park without him.
Glad to see me, he was even more glad to be let out and
made it clear by taking advantage of the front yard to
check out each shrub and tree, even the front steps,
where I sat down to watch him for a few minutes.

I had been considering Salt Lake as the evening progressed. It seemed to have more to do with all this than I
had originally thought, especially now that I had met
Jamie. Had she gone back there with the pages she had
taken from my bag? Could I find her if I followed?
Aside from that idea, there was now not only the name
and address on the card that had been in the otherwise
empty box in that basement room, but also *Wilson* and
the LDS Family History Library. It was a Salt Lake
number. Who were these people and how did they relate
to Sarah? Could any of them have some connection to
her death? I had a feeling Mildred Scott could be the
person who had sent the photographs and the letters
about Jamie and her son through all those years.

Her name was the best clue I had and, with Sarah's
gathering three whole days away, I was tempted to go to
Salt Lake and see if I could find some answers. Why
not? It was only a couple of hundred miles, so I could
leave early and be there around lunchtime. The idea was
appealing in another way as well.

As I said, I enjoy traveling, especially in my new

Winnebago, which I had hardly broken in. Having my house on my back, so to speak, relieves me of hunting up hotels that will accept the presence of my mini-dachshund pal, of lugging suitcases up and down stairs or elevators, of making do without my favorite coffee, traipsing up and down hallways in search of ice, eating restaurant food, sleeping in strange beds, and a whole host of similar things that weary me. The motor home allows me to stop where I want to, move around in familiar comfort when I'm parked, and see what I am passing on the way to—wherever. If I want to stay awhile and need ground transportation, I can always rent a small car for a reasonable amount and return it—and its maintenance—when I'm ready to take to the road again.

Airplane travel gives you little in the way of scenery—often just the tops of clouds or unreal scenery like the patchwork quilt of Middle America. Half the time when I fly I come home with some cold or flu that results from the recirculation of air—and germs—in the cabin, and I hate being packed in with strangers like sardines in a can. Even in first class you are always bumping elbows, or getting stuck beside someone with a restless, noisy child, or who wants to chat their way from Anchorage to—wherever. Planes are great for one thing—getting you where you want to go in a hurry. At my age there is almost nowhere I need, or want, to go in that much of a hurry. I much prefer to cruise at my own rate of speed along unfamiliar highways, explore whatever catches my interest, and make new friends in places where I can live in my own space.

So, going to Salt Lake would be no hardship—no hardship at all.

I sat on the step, one elbow on a knee, fist under my chin, rubbing Stretch's ears with the opposite hand, and considered the trip as dark crept in and the streetlights blinked on to gild the edges of the leaves on the trees by the curb and mosaic the sidewalk with their shadows. Across the street the television was entertaining its watcher again and once more I heard another cricket chirp somewhere under the hydrangeas beside the steps.

A car turned off Seventh and did a slow, almost silent cruise along Chipeta. I watched it pull over to park in front of where I sat and realized it was a police car.

Two men got out—a tall one in uniform and a shorter, wider one in slacks and a rather baggy sports jacket—and came up the walk. I recognized the uniformed one from his unexpected appearance in Sarah's doorway the night I had arrived to find her bedroom in such a state of chaos.

"Ms. McNabb?" he questioned, when they were halfway up the walk.

"Yes."

"Officer Bellamy. I was here the other night."

"I remember you." I got up and held out a hand, which he shook.

"Detective Soames," he said, introducing his companion, who nodded in my direction. "I had a call from Don Westover and told him we'd check to make sure everything was okay here. Understand you had another break-in. You should have called us."

"Probably, but there was no one in the house by the time I discovered it and no evidence I could see that would have helped you." .

He gave me a half-indulgent smile and shook his head at my seeming lack of common sense.

"You couldn't know that. We have methods . . ."

"I'll call you if there's another," I interrupted firmly, "but I'm sure there won't be. It turned out to be a relative and everything's fine now. By the way, who was it that called about the break-in that first night?"

"We don't know. It was made from a stolen cell phone and hasn't been used again."

Interesting.

Detective Soames had taken out a notebook and was clearly waiting for an end to our exchange.

"Was there something else?"

"Yes," he stepped forward and raised a pen over paper. "I'm investigating the suspicious circumstances of Mrs. Nunamaker's death and I need answers to a few questions. When did you arrive in Grand Junction, Ms. McNabb?"

I related my day of travel and arrival on the day of the thunderstorm.

"Is there anyone who can assure us that you were on the road between here and Pocatello, Idaho, that day?"

"You're investigating *me*?" I asked in disbelief.

"We have to follow up on everyone who was here that day," he told me smoothly. "You were inside the house when the call came in about the break-in, so you're on that list."

Biting my tongue against my first response, I thought back to that day of approximately three hundred and fifty miles of driving.

"The restaurant was crowded where I stopped for lunch on the way down, so I doubt they'd remember me. I hesitated at service stations a couple of times, but didn't talk to anyone, even an attendant," I told him. "I put my gas on a credit card."

"Do you have the receipts?"

When I had retrieved them from the Winnebago, he checked the time and dates, and nodded. "These will do."

"I want them back."

Another nod. "I'll make copies and be sure you get

them. Is there anyone that you know was with her in the house the day she was hospitalized?"

Jamie, I thought, but didn't say so. How could I explain a tangle of relationship I didn't completely understand or even know was legitimate, for that matter? I could give them her name later, if appropriate.

I shook my head in answer to his question. His eyes narrowed in response to my denial, but he shrugged and put away his notebook.

"Oh," I said, remembering. "I almost forgot. There was a nurse who was coming twice a day to give Sarah her medicine."

He took out his notebook again. "You know her name?"

"Never met her."

He wrote something and put it away again.

"You're sure everything's okay here?" Officer Bellamy asked. "Want us to check the house again?"

"No, it's fine. I've already gone through it and cleared up the mess."

His slightly pained expression insinuated that in the process I had carelessly destroyed any possible evidence. Under the calm exterior I had determined to maintain, I was feeling a certain amount of derisive amusement at the officiousness the two of them displayed. It must have showed when I glanced up at him, because he suddenly grinned and shrugged his shoulders in a more friendly, I'm-not-really-such-a-bad-guy sort of way. He was younger than he looked.

"We're really on the side of the righteous, Ms. McNabb," he told me. The grin was so infectious and almost adolescent that I couldn't help returning it.

"Does your mother know you harass old ladies?" I teased.

"Yeah, she does—and would want me to apologize."

Detective Soames watched this bit of friendly nonsense with evident cynicism and did not smile, but turned with Bellamy and walked toward the car without another word.

I waited for him to get into the passenger seat and close the door before I called out to Officer Bellamy, who was on his way around to the driver's side.

He came trotting back up the walk with a questioning look.

"You said to let you know if I was leaving town," I told him. "Tomorrow I'm going to run up to Salt Lake for a couple of days, then I'll be back. Is that all right?"

"Sure," he said, still smiling. "You're not under arrest. Here's my card—give me a call when you get back. I want to be sure no one *else* harasses you, okay?"

I agreed and watched them both pull away before I took Stretch home to bed.

Once inside the Winnebago, with the shades drawn and everything closed up for the night, I decided to take a break from all speculation and picked up a book I had been meaning to read on the Northern Rockies and the Colorado Plateau. Settling at the dinette with a cup of tea and a piece of Doris Chapman's chocolate cake, I leafed through page after page of beautiful pictures of places I would like to see, until I found a section of text that told me how natural stone arches are formed. It was a fascinating book and the cake—with homemade frosting, not that sticky stuff from a can—was great. In no time at all, I had eaten a second piece and was falling asleep over the pages somewhere between Canyonlands National Park and Monument Valley.

I stuck a marker in the book and, setting it aside for another night, headed for bed, yawning and totally forgetting that I had intended to keep an eye on Sarah's house in case Jamie Stover returned.

CHAPTER FOURTEEN

WHEN THE SUN ROSE THE NEXT MORNING BEFORE SIX, I was already up and cheerfully anticipating a day on the road. After a quick breakfast for Stretch and myself—scrambled eggs and toast for me from Doris's loaf of bread—I cleaned up the galley and stashed away everything that could roll, rattle, or fall before I set the rig in motion. I turned off the gas and made sure the refrigerator was switched from AC power it ran on when parked to the DC the automotive system would provide as we traveled.

I made phone calls—one to Westover's office, to make sure there was nothing I needed to do before leaving—and one to Ed Norris, to let him know I would be gone for two or three days. Ed wanted to know why I needed to go to Salt Lake, but I put him off with a comment or two about the need to get away by myself for a space. I was a little anxious that he would offer to come along, as he had made it clear he was inclined to count on me for company, but to my relief he didn't. He was a grown man, after all, and could take care of himself. I had other things I needed to do—questions to answer that I didn't want to share.

Stretch, who always knows when I'm about to go somewhere, padded around eagerly, getting under my feet at every turn. Finally, I picked him up and deposited him in his basket over the passenger seat, where he could watch without tripping me.

"Take a gander from there," I told him. "No worries, mate—I'm not going without you this time."

When everything inside was shipshape, I let him outside for a bit while I unhooked the lines for water and electricity from Sarah's house, filled the water tank, coiled and packed the lines away neatly in an outside compartment, and was ready to go.

Before leaving, I took the clean casserole dish and cake pan that had held Doris's food offerings, the leftover contents of which I had transferred to plastic containers, and walked across to knock on her front door. She answered almost immediately with a smile.

"Going somewhere?" she asked as I handed her the dishes, along with additional thanks.

Did nothing get past this woman?

"Just a quick trip to Salt Lake," I told her. "I'll be back day after tomorrow."

To forestall questions, I gave her the details of Sarah's gathering. She immediately offered to provide food, of course, and looked disappointed when I told her we would keep it simple and serve only the family wine Sarah had requested.

"Well, I guess if that's what you think best. But it seems a little . . ." she let her comment drift off, rather than sound critical.

"That's it," I told her. "We'll do it just as she wanted."

"Would you like me to pick up the newspapers from the front porch?" she offered. "So the house won't look empty—considering that burglar the other night, I mean."

News does travel fast, doesn't it? Well, the police *had* been rather obvious with their shouts and flashing lights, and neighbors *will* talk.

"If you wouldn't mind," I told her, and, as I went back to Sarah's to check the front porch before leaving, thought about daily mail delivery which, coming and going through the back door, I hadn't remembered, either.

There were two newspapers on the porch, which I collected and took inside, using the same key that fit the back door. In the vestibule, I, for the first time, noticed a box on the wall into which mail fell as it was pushed through a slot from outside. In it were several envelopes that I flipped through and found were nothing but an electric bill and some advertisements. Along with two accompanying catalogs, I laid them on the desk in the alcove and went out again, locking the door behind me.

As I pulled the Winnebago out of the driveway onto Chipeta Avenue, Doris waved from her porch. I waved back and was on my way.

In just under half an hour I had found a service station along Horizon Drive with facilities where I could empty my holding tanks and fill the gas tank, and had driven up the entrance ramp onto Interstate Highway 70, headed northwest. Having passed Fruita and the turnoff to the Colorado National Monument, I went over the Colorado River, up a long rise and was crossing the state line into Utah at eight o'clock—the sweeping curve of the Book Cliffs visible on my right.

Highway 70 is a comfortable two lanes each direction with a wide median, easy to drive and to allow other drivers to pass a motor home—as many of them think they must, even if one is traveling as fast as they want to go. From past experience, I can understand their wish to be able to see the road and possible obstacles ahead, but often they cut back in too close for safety, and do not consider how much farther it takes a much heavier motor home to slow down or stop.

The road rose and fell over low clay hills scattered with sagebrush, an arid introduction to the northeast edge of the Colorado Plateau that takes up huge parts of Four Corners Country—Utah, Colorado, Arizona, and New Mexico. It tempted me to turn south and explore an area I had always wanted to see that is even more spectacular than the Colorado National Monument.

Southeast Utah near Highway 70 is peppered with wonderful names—Mule Shoe, Yellow Cat Flat, Winter Camp Wash, Professor Creek, Hotel Mesa. Passing the town of Cisco, I knew that Arches National Park was not far away, with the town of Moab just below. With a mission established, I resisted. The canyon-filled country could wait for another day, when I had no commitments. Rather than travel two sides of a triangle and in order to save myself sixty-five miles, just past Green River I turned north on Route 6, which is a narrower two-lane road that runs about one hundred thirty miles to join north–south Interstate Highway 15 just below Provo, Utah.

The Book Cliffs swung north with me and I soon crossed the Price River where for the first time I noticed a few pinion pines and cedar on a low mesa not far from the highway. The land slowly spread itself out into farmland. I passed through Price and when I came to the small town of Helper, I couldn't resist turning off the highway to find out about the town's interesting name— and lunch, if possible.

As I drove into Helper I had the feeling that this was

a town that rolled up the sidewalks when the tourist season ended, for there was no one on the street and only a few cars and pickups at the curbs. In the center of the main five-block street, which was lined with small shops, a couple of banks and hotels, a theater, a grocery, a hardware store—and the Western Mining and Railroad Museum that was unfortunately closed—I found a café that was open.

A small bell tinkled as I pushed open the door and walked into a soda fountain straight out of *American Graffiti*. Except for a clerk who popped out of the kitchen in the rear, the place was empty of people, but full of old-time wire-back chairs and tables to match. At the long counter that took up most of one wall I perched on the kind of revolving stool I had loved as a child and was cheerfully handed a menu in a plastic cover that folded open like a book—more nostalgia. It took me a minute to get to it, however, for my eye was caught by an ice cream aficionado's fantasy list on the wall behind the counter. No low-fat supermarket frozen yogurt, this. I was informed that it was homemade ice cream with whole milk and cream, *real* strawberries, blackberries, and other taste sensations long forgotten, or ignored, by the current commercial world of artificial flavors. I found lemon custard, a childhood favorite, on the list and knew I would have terrible trouble choosing between it and a huckleberry swirl. But a peanut-butter milk shake was definitely the selection to accompany the rest of my lunch order. Remembering that I had a freezer in the motor home, I ordered quarts of the other two to go, feeling smug. As I waited, listening to encouraging sounds from the kitchen, I examined the other walls that were covered with antique tools, kitchen utensils, and such. One front corner of the place was filled with displays of candles and colorful gift items.

Spotting a jukebox across the room, I dropped in a quarter and was soon finding my thrill on Blueberry Hill along with Fats Domino.

The hamburger that arrived in record time, on a home-baked bun with a scoop of old-fashioned potato salad on a lettuce leaf beside it, was a scrumptious reminder that burgers used to be made one at a time to the customer's specifications and have slices of dill pickle and tomato that you couldn't see through. As I consumed every crumb between slurps of the peanut-butter shake, the nice lady behind the counter told me about the town's name.

This had been coal-mining country, I learned. The grade through the hills to the north had proved too steep for a single railroad engine to be able to pull a train of loaded cars, so the company provided *helper* engines to assist. Thus the name of the town—Helper.

What a treat. I love place names. I traded her one of my favorites: Damfino Creek, somewhere in Wyoming. Can't you just imagine one old prospector saying to another, "What's the name of that there crick?"

It has always amused me that Nome, Alaska, was the result of the misinterpretation of some cartographer's scrawled question on the border of a map: "Name?"

They are everywhere, if you look. The country's history and humor is recorded in its names, and some of the best in the West are to be found in its small towns, abandoned mining claims, and the imagination-inspired titles for natural features.

Evidence of coal mining was just around the edge of the bluff that rose to the north of Helper, as I took the Winnebago slowly up the steep grade between the walls of a narrow canyon and was reminded of those helper engines. In a large pull-off, I also found evidence of the Old West on a bronze plaque: "Near this site stood the

Pleasant Valley Coal Company office and store. On April 21, 1897, in one of the most daring daylight robberies, Butch Cassidy, Elsa Lay, and Bob Meeks robbed paymaster E. L. Carpenter and made off with over $8000.00 in gold and silver of which only approximately $1000.00 was ever recovered."

Besides old mining buildings, there were signs that told about Utah's coal industry and a commemorative plaque with a long list of the names of miners lost in a tragic accident. With one hundred miles to go before I reached Salt Lake, I drove on and soon crossed Soldier Summit in a rainstorm that blew in and out in less than half an hour, washing the dust from the windshield and, hopefully, the rest of the rig.

I filled up with gas and picked up a map of Salt Lake at a service station outside Provo. It was almost two in the afternoon when I turned off Highway 15 into downtown Salt Lake and, somehow, found my way to the VIP Campground at 1400 West North Temple. Actually, I think I just got lucky and drove past it by accident.

The streets in the main part of Salt Lake City are very well organized and easy to understand—*if you can crack the code!* For anyone unfamiliar with the arrangement, they can be totally, leave-you-scratching-your-head bewildering, for they seem to be nothing but letters, numbers and compass directions at first.

Eventually, one gets used to what appears to be a maze of confusion and it begins to make perfect sense. It conspired to make sense to me on the second morning and, thereafter, I had little trouble finding my way wherever I wanted to go. Upon arrival, I simply searched until I located North Temple, then drove up and down it, watching like a hawk, until I finally spotted the VIP Campground and turned in with a sigh of relief.

To give Salt Lake its due, however, from another

point of view it is an unusually stress-free place in which to drive. Usually, guiding a thirty-foot Winnebago through the center of an unfamiliar city requires careful attention and skillful navigating, but downtown Salt Lake is a motor homer's dream. In 1847, within a few days of its Mormon founding, the city plan was laid out in a grid pattern of ten-acre square blocks. These blocks were separated by streets that were an unbelievable one hundred and thirty-two feet wide, because, at that time, it made sense to make them "wide enough for a team of four oxen and a covered wagon to turn around." This early planning was so generous that the width makes the streets feel half-empty of traffic and there is plenty of room to make turns and shift lanes—even for a thirty-foot motor home—with, or without oxen.

At the VIP Campground I registered in their A-frame office and, finding a number of spaces from which to choose, parked the Winnebago in a lovely, isolated spot under a large shade tree. In response to a quick phone call, a local car rental agency soon delivered a compact car for my use. So, leaving the Winnebago where I had hooked it up to water, electricity, and sewer, I made a short trip east on North Temple to a shopping center with an Albertsons grocery, where I picked up some fresh fruit, milk, on which I was running low and like in my coffee and tea, and a new red ball for Stretch, who, we discovered, had forgotten his yellow one in the yard at Sarah's.

Upon our return, we took a walk around the campground. Then, while Stretch took a nap I borrowed a telephone book from the office to do a little sleuthing. Settling on the sofa with the unopened phone book in my lap, I did nothing for a few minutes. It was quiet, except for the hum of traffic on North Temple beyond the registration office and, far away, the faint sound of a

siren of some kind—police or ambulance, going somewhere I didn't need to know. It felt—satisfying.

I had not anticipated what a relief it was to distance
myself from complications, though those very complications had inspired my trip north to Salt Lake City.
There is something liberating about being on your
own—alone in a new and unfamiliar place with no one
to make demands or judgments about what you should
or should not be or do. I know that kind of freedom is
part of why I like to travel and have taken to the road so
easily after years of living in the same place with the
same people. I have friends at home that I can't do without forever, which is part of why I return frequently to
my house in Homer on Kachemak Bay in search of
reassurance that my roots are still firmly planted in
Alaskan soil. But I do enjoy wandering to places I have
never been, seeing things I've never seen, and meeting
all kinds of interesting people in the process. I like
doing it alone, accommodating no one but Stretch, who
demands little and is great company.

When my husband Daniel died, it seemed for a while
that half my life had gone with him. At first I kept
myself busy doing things at home and refusing to allow
grief to take up residence in the empty space. But in a
couple of months I found I had run out of projects—the
house was immaculately clean, closets and cupboards
all in order, lawn mowed and manicured, garden planted
and weed-free. I realized that you could read only so
many books, rent so many movies, repeat the same
walks so many times. When a friend asked me to join
her on a trip to Denali National Park, I was enthusiastic
in accepting, just to get out of town for a bit, though the
closest I had been to a motor home was swearing at them
on the highway between Homer and Anchorage during
the summer months of the year, when they travel the

Kenai Peninsula in migrating herds of pale behemoths. I was astonished that one trip to Denali was all it took for me to develop a yearning for a rig of my own. Within six months I had it parked in my driveway and was getting ready to attempt my first trip down the Alaska Highway. It was a most welcome surprise to find how very well a new singular lifestyle on wheels suited me.

Running away from home was no problem. My two children had both grown and flown to follow their own stars.

Carol, my daughter, is married to an attorney with political ambitions and lives in Boston in a whirl of social life that would make me dizzy, but seems to suit her. Neither she, nor her husband, Philip—never *Phil*—approve of my gypsy lifestyle and let me know—frequently—that it isn't *socially acceptable*. The past summer, for instance, upon learning that I was driving north to spend the summer in Homer against their advice, they had refused to allow my grandson, Brandon, to visit me, pleading summer sports as an excuse, but really as a sort of punishment, I suspected.

I see my son, Joe, on a more regular basis. He is a criminalist for the Seattle Police Department and is able to visit me fairly often, bringing with him the casual Alaskan attitude he has retained and, sometimes, his cheerful, realistic, live-in girlfriend, Sharon, who runs her own travel agency and has no uppity airs about her. I imagine they will eventually marry—when it suits them—which is fine with me. When they learned of my new acquisition and travel plans, they expressed nothing but approval and once or twice have even come along for short parts of the ride.

As I sat there in the middle of Salt Lake City, I thought about calling Joe to check in, but decided to let it wait until later, when he would be at home and not in the middle of something forensic. Instead I looked through the phone book for the names on my mental list.

First I checked for Stover, any Stover. There were seven, none of them J. or Jamie. I considered that possibly the phone might still be listed under her ex-husband's name, though that seemed unlikely, as she had said they'd been several-years divorced. I didn't know what his name was anyway.

Strike one!

I gave Stover up for the time being and tried Scott. There was a whole page of Scotts, but no Mildred. There was an M. Scott, so I called it, but that turned out to be a Michael Scott who didn't know anyone named Mildred.

Strike two!

I did have the address that had accompanied Mildred Scott's name and could try finding it tomorrow. No! I decided. I would try it later that day. More people are at home in the evening and, if I couldn't find her, I might find someone related, or who could help me find her.

Not strike three—not yet!

I considered calling the Family History Library and asking for Wilson again, as this was the day they had said he would be back. Explaining what I wanted—when I was confused about who, what, and why—would be difficult at best, however, and *best* might be to go there in person to talk with him.

Tomorrow, then.

Giving up until after dinner, after which I intended to brave the bewildering checkerboard of Salt Lake City and try for Mildred Scott's address, I succumbed to my former impulse and joined Stretch in a nap.

CHAPTER FIFTEEN

IN MY DREAM SARAH HAD COME TO VISIT ME IN HOMER, as she did one long-ago summer. We were young again and walking side by side along the beach on the long spit that extends out into Kachemak Bay. It was late afternoon and there was no one else on that smooth crescent. Except for the screams of the gulls, the soft gurgle of waves on sand and gravel, and the wind that tossed my hair, it was quiet. A gust plastered her green slacks to her legs and she laughed as it snatched off an old fishing hat she was wearing and sent it rolling away. I chased and caught it but, when I turned around, she had climbed into a boat that hadn't been there before and was steadily rowing out into the bay without me. When I called to her, she didn't answer, but smiled and kept on rowing. So, helpless, I could only watch her grow smaller and smaller in the distance until she disappeared and left me standing with the brim of the hat in my hand.

My hand was full of an edge of the comforter when I woke to find my pillow soaked with the tears Ed had asked of me in the park the day before. I seldom cry. When I'm alone, I don't fight it and didn't then. There are good results from tears and one of them is the release of tension. In a few minutes they stopped, so I dabbed at my eyes with that edge of the comforter, got up feeling better and went to open the door to let the warm breeze dry my face.

Stretch came to stand with me and look out through the screen door, as we often do. We watched a woman with a basket under her arm and a small girl in tow walk across to the office building and disappear into the laundry room.

A glance at my watch told me it was after five o'clock. I had slept for well over an hour. Time to think about dinner, after which I would see what I could do to find Mildred Scott's address.

I took Stretch.

There's something about a mini-dachshund—especially with a sixty-three-year-old woman at the end of his leash—that is nonthreatening. People are attracted to Stretch for obvious reasons—he's cute, he's friendly, he's too small to be a menace. They talk *about,* then *to* the dog—and then *to* the woman-with-the-dog. With the ice broken, they usually extend more communication to the woman. It almost always works. Stretch doesn't mind. He expects to be adored.

Having scrutinized the map with the assistance of the sympathetic manager in the office, I drove my rental car east on North Temple until I arrived at Temple Square, with its six unmistakable towers rising from a cluster of other buildings associated with the LDS church. Turning right on West Temple, I drove by the Family History Library, where I intended to go the next day in search of Mr. Wilson, then made a left onto South Temple. The ten or twelve blocks of this wide street to the east of the square are the most historic in the city, including Beehive House, residence of LDS Church President Brigham Young who founded Salt Lake City; the Utah Governor's Mansion; and many other impressive mansions, churches, and buildings. Tree lined, it was a pleasant drive with those ten-acre square blocks on the right and smaller blocks on the left between the alphabet streets of the northeast quarter.

Two-thirds of the way along it, according to the map, I located South 1100 East and, making another right turn, followed it along until I reached the 700 block. There, in the area I had anticipated, close to both East High School—and the University of Utah, I had located on the map—was the address I had found linked to Mildred Scott's name. I pulled up in front and sat looking at an ordinary sort of house with a walk that led up the center of the yard to a short flight of steps and a front door under a small roof that protected a narrow porch. There was a light behind thin curtains in a front window. Someone was at home.

I got out, took Stretch on his leash, and went up the steps to ring the doorbell. Waiting for an answer, I could faintly hear some kind of classical music from inside. I didn't hear anyone approach, but the door opened suddenly and a man about my age stood looking out at me. He reached to one side and turned on a porch light.

"Yes?"

"Excuse me, please, but does a Mildred Scott live here?"

He stared without answering for a long moment and a hint of a frown lowered his brows.

"Who wants to know?" he asked.

"My name is Maxie McNabb," I told him and hastened on, as he raised a hand to the doorknob as if he meant to close it. "It's a bit hard to explain, but I found her name and this address on a card and she may know and have corresponded with a friend of mine in Grand Junction."

"Damn," he half-spit at me. "She's *dead*, for God's sake! Go away."

He stepped back and began to swing the door shut.

"Please," I said, reaching one hand to restrain it. "I'm sorry. I don't mean to upset you. My friend in Grand Junction has just died and I need some information. Please."

He hesitated, still scowling at me.

"And who the hell *are* you?"

Then Stretch worked his magic, stepping forward with tail wagging in such a friendly fashion he was impossible to ignore.

"Hello, pup," the man said, looking down, and smiled before he could help himself.

As I said—irresistible.

Still reluctant, he let me into the hallway—probably to avoid the curiosity of a neighbor, who had stepped onto her porch at hearing what must have sounded like an argument, reminding me of Doris, back in Grand Junction. Inside, with the door shut, he kept me standing in the hall and waited to hear what I wanted, still glancing down at Stretch, who exhibited his best behavior by sitting at his feet and not attempting to check out the living room.

I explained, as best I could, about Sarah's death and finding out she had a daughter; about finding the picture, letters, and the card with Mildred's name and address; and that I was trying to find out something that would tell me who had tried to kill Sarah and why—starting with Mildred Scott, who was my only real lead.

"So she did live here?" I asked.

"Until she died in June of 2001," he said. "It was our home."

Just after the date on that last picture of Jamie that I had found in the basement room.

"And you were . . ."

"Her husband."

"Did she know a Jamie Stover?"

"Oh, yes. We *both* knew Jamie. She grew up right next door—lived with her parents until she got married and moved away. They died a few years ago. Still, she used to drop in to see Milly now and then."

He sighed and waved a hand toward the living room.

"Might as well sit down, I guess. They're both dead now, so I guess it can't matter to talk about it finally. What else do you want to know?"

I perched on the edge of the sofa. After he had given Stretch a pat or two, he sat down in a recliner so worn it retained the impression of his body.

"Did she know Sarah Nunamaker?"

"Only met her that one time, years ago. Milly was a nurse at the hospital where her babies were born."

"Babies?" He *had* said "babies"—plural—hadn't he?

"The twins she put up for adoption. But Milly was only able to keep track of Jamie, because the Stovers next door adopted *her*. The boy got adopted by some other people."

I sat back and stared at him, taken aback to the point of speechlessness. It had never occurred to me that Sarah might have had more than one child. Why should it? All the information I had found was related to Jamie, with no mention of anyone else. Could Ed have been right and Alan *was* really Sarah's son? Had she adopted him after she married?

"You didn't know about the boy?" he asked.

"No. I didn't. Sarah was my best friend, but she

didn't even tell me about Jamie. I don't know why. Was the boy adopted immediately, or later? Did Mildred know who adopted him?"

"He was adopted almost as soon as he was born, but Milly didn't know who the adoptive parents were. She tried every way she could think of to find out, because she had promised Sarah. But he just disappeared and the court sealed all the papers."

So, I thought as he continued, it couldn't have been Sarah who adopted Alan.

"Not knowing upset both of them. Milly always blamed herself—but Sarah never did," he finished.

"Did you know Sarah?"

"Nope. Just knew about the pictures that Milly sent with the letters. A letter from Sarah would come once a year—about the time of Jamie's birthday always—usually with a present that we gave her like it was from Milly. I never pried. It was Milly's secret when we got married. She told me about it, but she wasn't going to let it go, so we just kept it like that."

"Did you know that Jamie had found out that she was adopted and that she had located Sarah?"

"Yes, I knew that. She was pretty upset when she found out—after her folks died in that accident. She kept insisting that Milly must know something about it, because Alice Stover and Milly were pretty good friends, but Milly never told her that she knew Sarah, or anything about having a brother. I think she was still keeping loyal to Sarah. Jamie may still not know about her twin. I don't know. She found out about Sarah through some agency that helps adopted people find their real mothers. She should have left it alone, I think. She's got enough on her plate with raising that boy of hers by herself."

I didn't know what to say to that. So I asked him if he knew where Jamie lived. He didn't—just somewhere in, or near, Salt Lake. Did he know the name of her ex-husband?

Harris, maybe Harrison—or something similar.

"We went to the wedding. I didn't like him much."

My head full of new information, there wasn't anything else I could think of to ask, so I thanked David Scott and got up to take myself back to the VIP Campground for the night. Before I left, he said he was sorry to hear that Sarah was dead, but I thought I recognized relief in his voice and could understand why. The burden of the secret relationship between his wife and Sarah must have been a thing he felt she could have done without—and *knew* he could.

As I drove back through the wide streets, I wondered if Jamie had been able to find out anything about her twin brother—if she even knew she had one. Where was he? What had his life been like? If his family had lived in Salt Lake, being the same age as Jamie, they could have been in the same place any number of times without knowing. It was improbable, but not impossible, that they had gone to the same schools. If not, they might have attended the same football, or basketball games, or gone to church together. They might even have researched their family history at the library near Temple Square, if he was also LDS, and the majority of people in Salt Lake are. How ironic—each of them researching families that were really not their own. But he might have been told he was adopted, as she had not. Had he looked for her—or Sarah? Now *there* was an interesting thought.

Speculation—all speculation, with a tangle of possibilities. I was glad my children knew who they were and that their lives would hold no such surprises. They might have lost their father, Joe Flanagan, but they knew who he was, know who their mother is and, most important of all, who they are. There is stability in continuity. I had trouble imagining how being adopted would feel.

The next morning I left Stretch in the Winnebago, not wanting to leave him in a hot car and having no idea how long it would take me at the Family History Library to find Mr. Wilsón. When I parked in a lot just around the corner from Temple Square I was glad I had, for the cement paving was already reflecting heat like an oven and there wasn't a single tree anywhere under which to park.

Finding a walkway that led to West Temple Street at one corner of the lot, I took it and was startled when I came out next to a rough log cabin between two multi-story modern buildings—a display to illustrate what early settlers had originally built and lived in. Around it were flowers similar to those pioneer women had cherished enough to carry seeds all the way across the plains from their eastern gardens—hollyhocks and sunflowers, among others.

Next door to this educational display was the Family History Library, a large attractive building with a tall modern entrance that provided shade for low walls retaining attractive beds of pink, red, and white flowers. Several people were sitting on the walls, taking breaks from their research of the records contained in the library. A sign on the wall of the building identified the Genealogical Society of Utah, Established 1894. No wonder they were reputed to have the most extensive collection of family history in the world. They had certainly been at it long enough.

For the first time I wondered if I could find the names of any of my ancestors in their voluminous collection of information. *Not today you can't,* I told myself. Today I was on the track of Mr. Wilson and whatever, if anything, he could tell me about the family group sheets, or the names on them, that I had found in Sarah's house.

Inside the front door on the northeast corner of the building, I found myself in a large atrium that held a reception desk with several people behind it who were answering questions and giving directions. As I waited my turn, I picked up a floor plan from the counter and found that the library was much larger than it appeared. The main and second floors held records in books and on film for the United States and Canada. There were, also, two basement floors; one that held records for Europe, Scandinavia, Latin America, and International; and one below it that did the same for the British Isles. A brochure next to the floor plan told me that the library had been gathering records for over a hundred years and that every year it preserves and catalogs an astonishing hundred million new pages of historical documents. Somewhere in the library were over 12,000 books, 50,000 microfilms, and 25,000 microfiche, all carefully organized and cataloged.

I was still absorbing this information when one of the women behind the desk sent a researcher downstairs to the Scandinavian collection and turned to me. "May I help you?"

Given Mr. Wilson's name, she directed me upstairs.

"He should be at the reference desk," she told me. "If not, someone there will know where to find him."

There was an elevator, but I climbed the stairs. Exercise at my age is never a bad idea. The reference desk, a large square counter with space for workers in the middle, was the first thing I came to in a huge room of bookshelves and lots of microfilm and microfiche readers, most with people searching records in front of them.

I asked a woman at the counter for Mr. Wilson.

"Michael," she called, and at the other end of the square a short gray-haired man in a business suit turned to look back over his shoulder. His face was wider than it was long, which made his smile look even broader beneath the bushiest pair of eyebrows I have ever seen. He came bustling across to where I stood and looked up at me from behind his side of the counter.

"Yes? May I help you?"

They must train all their volunteers—and, I learned that most are volunteers—with the same phrase, but it works for me. Everyone I met in that library was friendly and helpful—some overly so. The IRS and a few other government agencies—Medicare for instance— could—no, *should*—make their employees go through training at the Family History Library before they are allowed to meet the public.

I laid my copies of the family group sheets on the counter in front of Mr. Wilson and showed him the note with his name and the phone number, explaining that I had found it in the belongings of a now-deceased friend. "She may have called and talked to you sometime in the last month or so. I thought perhaps you might remember a Mrs. Sarah Nunamaker, or recognize some of the names on these pages. I'm the executor of her estate and am trying to figure out what she was looking for and if it is important for me to know."

The brows went up and down, and he gave me a help-less glance over the granny-glasses he had balanced on the bulb of his nose.

"I am the only Wilson here, so it must have been me," he said. "But we assist hundreds of people, in person and on the telephone, with questions. I'm sorry, but I couldn't remember most of the names I helped yester-day, let alone a month ago."

Until I walked in the door, I realized that I had had the picture of a regular library in mind. Having found something so different, I had feared this kind of failure would be the answer to my questions. In the few minutes I had been in the library I had seen dozens of people in motion, books and papers in their hands, and many more working at film readers, copy machines, and filing cabinets. The place was like a hive of busy worker bees, with pleasant helpers around for guidance.

"I'm really sorry," Michael Wilson said again. "Was there anything else I could help you with?"

I was already there and interested, so why not?

"You could tell me a little about how this all works," I said. "Is there anything in print for novices who might like to do a little family research here?"

"Oh, *yes,*" he said. Eager to make up for not being able to provide an answer to my initial question, he reached behind the counter and pulled out several brochures and sheets of information, including another floor plan. On top of these he laid a two-page form titled *Where Do I Start?* and a *Family History Materials List.* Before I could even consider a protest, I was carrying a pile of Mr. Wilson's introductory gifts and he had come from behind the desk to give me a tour of the second floor of the library.

He was explaining the variety of census records that were on file, and we had come to a large area full of filing cabinets with a row of carrels for film readers off to one side, when someone else caught my attention and I abruptly quit listening to his nonstop explanation of what was available to researchers. I stopped moving as well when a man stood up from one of the carrels, pushed back a chair that had a jacket draped over its back, and turned to walk toward us with a roll of microfilm in one hand.

His appearance before he turned gave me a start because for a moment I had thought it was Ed Norris. This man's hair was as dark as Ed's had once been and he was as tall and thin but, as he came toward us and gave me a disinterested passing glance, I could see there was no other resemblance—or only what my imagination had provided. Still, it made me suddenly aware that, consciously or not, I was now on the lookout for Jamie's brother—Sarah's other twin.

CHAPTER SIXTEEN

I STOOD LOOKING AFTER THE MAN WHO HAD JUST passed me in the Family History Library.

He had glanced at me with no reaction and walked on to stop in front of a bank of drawers where he opened one and replaced the microfilm he had been reading.

"Someone you know?"

Mr. Wilson, who had noticed I wasn't tagging along, followed my gaze to the man with the microfilm.

"I don't think so. Do you?"

"No." He turned to continue the tour.

But I couldn't stop watching while the man at the drawer ran a finger down the top of a row of films, selected a new one, and took it out. Closing the drawer, he started back toward his carrel and, as he passed me for the second time, glanced my way again.

Something in my expression must have registered, or he was uncomfortable being stared at, because there was a hesitation in his step and his glance turned into a look with a question in it. When I didn't respond or look away, he gave me a self-conscious almost-smile and moved on.

I went on with Mr. Wilson, who led me out of sight of the carrel between two bookshelves, but I wasn't hearing a thing he said.

How could I, the evening before, have found out about a person the existence of whom I had never suspected and, the very next morning, have seen someone I thought might *be* that person cross the room in front of me—twice?

Get a grip, I told myself. If you hadn't met Jamie, then learned that she had a brother, you wouldn't have noticed this man at all.

Politely I listened for another few minutes as Mr. Wilson did his best to give me an informative tour, but I didn't understand or retain much. When we came back through the microfilm area on our way to the reference desk I glanced over again, looking for the man I had seen. Pausing in front of the carrel, I saw that there was film in the reading machine, but the paper upon which he had been taking notes was gone. The chair was empty, the jacket missing from its back, and the man who had been working there was nowhere to be seen.

Mr. Wilson assured me that researchers are honor bound to return materials when they finish using them. Since the microfilm was still in the reader, he thought the man was probably still in the library and had merely stepped away for some reason.

Honor bound or not, I thought otherwise. I thanked him for his time and assistance and went back down the stairs and out the front door with my armful of informative brochures. There, I sat down on the wall with people taking breaks from their studies and turned so I could watch the doors. I couldn't help it, though I knew

I was being silly, I wanted another look at the man if he hadn't already come out and gone.

It was a bright sunny day, but pleasant in the shade. Scores of people were coming and going from the library and a variety of buildings that occupied Temple Square across the tree-lined street. At least half the researchers who were chatting together along the wall were senior citizens, probably freed by retirement to be able to spend the majority of their time searching their family histories for lost ancestors. The two women closest to me were discussing the merits of working at the library rather than online. It was something I hadn't thought of, but evidently there were numerous sources that could be studied with a computer. Maybe I should get out my laptop from the cupboard where it lived in the Winnebago and take a look. It was about time for my weekly e-mail check anyway and I might have something from Joe and Sharon in Seattle. I filed away a reminder to do so and returned my attention to who was coming and going through the library doors.

As I waited, I did not try to unscramble the potential piece of the puzzle I had just stumbled upon, but tried to figure out how I could find Jamie—if she had returned to Salt Lake, as I suspected. It was very possible that she had not—that I had left her behind in Grand Junction. From what she had said she must have been there for at least a week. How long would she leave her son with a friend? Was there any way I could locate that friend? Had she purposely left me with no names, no addresses, nothing of help in finding her? I could search unsuccessfully for weeks in a city this large.

An hour later I gave up. Mr. Wilson had been mistaken. The man I had seen was long gone and had simply forgotten to return the microfilm before he left for some other, completely innocent reason. I was being seduced by my overactive imagination. Collecting my bag and brochures, I headed for the car that I knew would once again be too hot to drive.

Strike three!

The car was once again a furnace. As I had in Grand Junction, I started the engine, turned the air conditioner on full blast, and stood around waiting for it to cool to endurance level. This was September? Not the kind I was used to in Alaska.

As I waited, my cell phone suddenly came to life in my bag and I had to dig hurriedly through the contents to find it. Finally at the bottom I recognized it by feel and fished it out before it stopped ringing.

"Hello."

I could hear the line was open, but there was no response.

"Hello. Who's calling please?"

Still nothing, though I had the definite feeling that someone was listening.

"Do you have the wrong number? I'm going to hang up, if you don't answer."

"Wait," said a voice I didn't recognize. "You'd better listen."

"Who *is* this, please?"

"You don't need to know that. But if you're smart, you'll get out of Salt Lake."

The voice was higher than normal and oddly muffled, as if this person—male, I thought—was talking with something in his mouth to disguise his voice.

"Why? *Who is this?* What do you mean?"

A pause, then, "You remember how close you came to the edge that day on the Monument? Next time you might not be so lucky. Get out of Salt Lake. Then get out of Grand Junction."

"What . . . ?" But before I could ask, or say, anything else, there was a click on the line as the connection was broken.

Hot as it was in that parking lot, there were goose bumps on my arms that had nothing to do with the air-conditioning as I got into my rental car. Who was this person, and how did he know my phone number? Was the caller somewhere close? I looked around nervously and saw only two women talking together as they headed for their car. I had no idea what it meant, but it had been a definite threat—of something that could be very nasty and I hadn't any kind of idea what that could be. I had been willing to accept that Ed had been the target in the incident on the Rim Rock Drive of the Monument—because he thought so. Now I had a very unpleasant feeling that, for whatever reason, someone had now turned the focus in my direction.

The day before I had felt relief at being alone and distancing myself from complications—liberated to be on my own in a new place. As I drove back to the VIP Campground, I was not feeling the same satisfaction. Instead, I was aware that someone had *killed* Sarah and could have tried to kill *me*—with Ed along for the ride; that I was in the middle of an unfamiliar city where I knew no one and there was no one to turn to if I needed help.

Whatever was going on had suddenly become less of a puzzle and taken a more deadly turn. I had some sense of safety when I was in the Winnebago, but am not stupid enough to think that a sixty-three-year-old woman with a shotgun is a total deterrent. I know that people my age are more vulnerable than those who are younger. We are not as strong as we once were, or as quick to respond. Far from falling off the perch—as my Daniel would have put it—I am aware that my age makes me more susceptible to accident or misadventure and I compensate to the best of my ability.

I am not inclined to take unnecessary chances, but I will not let my life be ruled by fear—fear of what *might* happen or be out there. On the other hand, if I know of something specific that I *should* be afraid of, you won't find me hesitant to yell for help if I need it—or to take off and leave it behind if that's the best option.

By the time I had reached my Winnebago, climbed in with Stretch, and locked the door behind me, I had made up my mind that leaving this potential threat behind was exactly what I was going to do. What could staying do for me? With a lot of effort I might be able to find Jamie, but I was more likely to come up empty and waste that effort with no positive result. What would finding her tell me? If it turned out anything like our first interview—very little or nothing at all.

It was time to be gone.

In less than an hour I had checked out, gassed up, found Highway 15, and was headed south. I decided I would drive until I grew tired. If that happened before Grand Junction, I would find an RV park, spend the night, and complete the journey the next morning.

Stretch, good traveler that he is, was happy enough to watch the passing scenery from his basket. I slid a Singers & Songwriters CD into the player and shifted my mood with some of the good old stuff: "Brown Eyed Girl" by Van Morrison, Carole King's "I Feel the Earth Move," and Dave Loggins wandering through "Please Come to Boston." I remembered how fine it had been, on our Alaskan deck, to slow-dance with my first husband, Joe, to Dan Fogelberg's "Longer."

But under the memories and surface of my appreciation of the music was an awareness of everything around me that reminded me of my snake-watch on the Monument. There was also a thread of anger that it had seemed necessary to run. Oldie or not, I hate running.

I watched other cars that passed me, and, in the rearview mirrors, those that followed. There was no sign of anyone I thought might be following me, but I hadn't seen it when I was going the other direction, either, and I now believed that I had been followed from Colorado. How else could this person have known where to find me? And why was it so important to do so?

It stuck in my mind that the caller had said not "the Colorado National Monument," but *"the Monument,"* as the locals usually do.

I tuned back in to "Sunshine Superman" and refused to speculate.

By the time I had crossed Soldier Summit, gone by Helper without stopping for ice cream, passed Price, and reached Green River, I was tired enough to hunt up the KOA Kampground and park us for the night. I hooked up to water and electricity, then went inside and retrieved the shotgun from its hiding space, leaning it against the sofa while I fed Stretch and got something— I don't remember what—for my dinner.

That shotgun is a Remington 1100 LT-20 that holds and will fire three shells before it has to be reloaded— which should be enough in any circumstance I care to imagine needing it. I am not of National Rifle Association mentality, but not opposed to guns, either. The shotgun is protection and I view it as such. I would not hesitate to use it defensively if necessary, and wouldn't have bought and learned to use it, otherwise. I had never before felt it necessary to take the shotgun out of its hiding place, but that night, having it within reach gave me confidence.

Opening the ceiling vents, I locked the coach screen door, but, in what I felt was half bravado under the circumstances, left the door itself open, unwilling to shut out the soft blues of the twilight and the cool breeze that wandered in from the river a short mile away.

When it was almost dark, I shut and locked all the doors, made sure all the windows were securely fastened, and all the blinds closed tight. With the air conditioner running on low it was bearable—just. I detest sealed spaces, as I have mentioned, but that night I needed security more than fresh air. I tried to read, but found myself repeating pages I had just completed. I jumped at every sound and listened attentively until I could identify it as ordinary. There were a lot of ordinary crickets, ordinary crunching of gravel as a rig or two drove in to park for the night or under the feet of people going back and forth to the showers or laundry, and the ordinary periodic hum of a vehicle passing on the nearby highway.

When I gave up and decided to try to sleep, I laid the shotgun beside me on the bed, just in case. I intended to make an early start the next morning, expecting I would be wakeful and up before daylight, if not more often during the night.

The reclining figure on a grassy space at the rear of a large Class A motor home next door to the Winnebago waited in the dark a long time after the lights had been turned out in both rigs. Silent and watchful, face turned to take pleasure in the slow progress of stars across the sky, it rested, serenely patient, until there had been no detectable movement or sound from inside either for the better part of an hour.

Then, with care to remain in the shadows, it rose and, one step at a time, moved stealthily across to the side of the Winnebago. Bracing a cautious hand on the side of the motor home, the figure rested and listened, hearing nothing from within.

Two more guarded steps brought it to the coach door, but the last step sent a single pebble skittering against another with a small click. The figure froze, all attention focused on the slight movement inside just before the fretful barking of a small-sounding dog began from behind the door.

The Winnebago moved again, with the weight of a person in motion, though no lights came on. As the motion continued to the forward part of the coach and the dog hushed its yapping, the figure reached out and lightly tried the handle of the screen door, which it found locked.

"Look," a voice called out from inside. "Whoever you are, you should know that I have a loaded shotgun aimed in your direction and will not hesitate to use it if you don't get the hell away from my door. I also have a cell phone and am calling nine-one-one."

Taking something from a pocket, the figure reached out again to slip it between the screen and its handle. Trying for as much quiet as possible on the gravel surface, it walked quickly away, climbed into a car left nearby, and drove off into the dark without turning on the headlights.

CHAPTER SEVENTEEN

WITHOUT TURNING ON A LIGHT, I SWUNG MY FEET OUT of bed and took the shotgun as I stood up and crept barefoot into a position close to the coach door, but far enough away to level the barrel at it as I thumbed off the safety.

Not intending to stay more than one night, I hadn't bothered to use stabilizers. Without them you can hardly go from one end of a motor home to the other without it moving slightly, so Stretch was aware of my presence and stopped barking. In the ensuing silence, I heard something gently rattle the handle of the screen door I had locked earlier.

I waited, listening—with the distinct impression someone outside was waiting and listening as well.

"Look," I said loudly and with more confidence than I felt. "Whoever you are, you should know that I have a loaded shotgun aimed in your direction and will not hesitate to use it if you don't get the hell away from my door. I also have a cell phone and am calling nine-one-one."

There was no answer but a soft, crackly, zippery sound as something brushed against the screen outside the door, then the cautious crunch of someone attempting the impossible—to go silently away on gravel.

I listened without moving as the footsteps faded. A car door closed, its engine started, and, as I heard it start to move, stepped to a window, pulled open the blind a crack, and caught a glimpse of a shadow vehicle without lights disappearing behind another motor home.

Stretch whined at my feet.

With hands that shook a little, I put the safety back on and carefully laid the shotgun on the dinette table. Then I dropped onto the sofa and lifted him into my lap for a cuddle—more for me than for him.

"Thanks for the warning, lovie," I told him. "You have the heart of a lion."

I gave us both a little warm milk before heading back to bed, leaving the shotgun on the table, for some reason feeling certain there would be no more disturbance that night.

There was not. I slept soundly until I woke at six to the grumble of a large Class A diesel rig pulling out of the space next door. Putting the coffee on to brew, I put the shotgun away in its hiding place and felt better without it in view. The sun had come up and I could already feel a hint of the heat to come, so I collected my kit and clean clothes, intending to take a quick shower in the campground facility.

I unlocked and opened the coach door, and was reaching for the handle of the screen when the sight of a foreign object stopped me. A crumpled sheet of paper had been slipped between the handle and the screen wire. I recalled that crackly, zippery sound I had heard just before my night visitor walked away from my door.

Laying down the things I was carrying, I unlocked the screen, and retrieved the paper.

It was very simple and specific in threat: a rough circle had been drawn with a felt-tipped pen. Inside it was a line that curved down for a mouth and two Xs for eyes. The meaning was clear—it was supposed to represent a dead person. Underneath, written in block letters, were the words STOP DIGGING INTO SARAH'S AFFAIRS. GO AWAY BEFORE YOU GET HURT—OR WORSE.

I stood staring down at it in shock, the apprehension I had felt the day before, back—with a vengeance.

So much for a shower.

There was no way I was going to leave Stretch, or the Winnebago, so I splashed water at myself and dressed in a hurry. In ten minutes I had unhooked and stowed my water and electricity lines, cleared the galley and was ready to go. Then a sense of reason settled in and I sat down at the table to drink my first cup of coffee with a piece of toast and jam and think the situation over while allowing Stretch to finish his breakfast.

Perhaps I should have made the 911 call I had threatened in the middle of the night. But aside from the fact that someone had tried to open my door, what could I have told the police when they arrived to find a tourist— a senior citizen, nonresident, granny with a dog? I'd have made sure, of course, that they would not have seen the shotgun. I have found that some law enforcement officers are inclined to assume that senior women are either senile or timid—often both. What they would think of a senior like myself traveling alone in a motor home was anyone's guess. But I would probably have had to try to explain at least some of the background I suspected for this incident, which would have sounded not only incredible, but confusing enough to sustain their suspicions that I was round the twist—thank you

Daniel. Better, I decided, to go on to Colorado, where the police—and Ed, and Don Westover—at least knew part of what had already transpired and would be inclined to take me seriously.

Getting up to rinse and stow my coffee cup and Stretch's dish, I felt more positive about my course of action.

First of all, I had to fill the tank with gas or I'd never make Grand Junction. And though I felt like taking the advice I had been given and heading down the road to just about anywhere else, I knew I was going back to Grand Junction. Once there, I decided that my first goal should be a call to Officer Bellamy—or Detective Soames, if necessary. The kind of threat I had just found in my screen door was beyond handling alone. It was time to share everything—what I had held back the last time I saw them and what I had learned in Salt Lake. Though I was sure it all fit together somehow, I had few answers to the question of how.

The more I considered the threat and my lack of answers, the more disgruntled I became. Why was this menace directed at me? What have you pulled me into by keeping secrets, Sarah?

In preparation for leaving I had opened all the blinds, so the sun was now shining directly into the interior of the Winnebago and heating it up along with my ill temper. Pouring another cup of coffee into a travel mug, I took it forward to the holder I could reach from the driver's seat. Reminded of the heat I would be driving into on my way east, I retrieved a tricky little item I picked up somewhere on a past trip, a battery-operated fan with a spray bottle attached that can be filled with ice water. When you pump the spray handle with the fan running the result is a fine mist that you can direct at yourself, dampening and cooling whatever you're wearing along with your face. This is, of course, best used after removing your sunglasses or you're suddenly blind to the road ahead. It fit neatly into a holder next to the mug that held my coffee and I was ready to hit the road.

Gas tank full, we were shortly on the broad expanse of Highway 70, with less than a hundred miles to travel before we reached Grand Junction. Once again, as I passed the turnoff to Moab I was tempted to take it and lose myself in the fantasy lands of southern Utah, leaving behind the sinister coils of menace I had evidently roused, like the snake on the Monument, with my curiosity and persistence. Concern that I might be followed there as well—and my own stubborn refusal to allow myself to be intimidated—negated the consideration of that option. I bypassed the exit for Highway 191 and continued east into the glare of the morning sun.

As I backed the Winnebago in next to Sarah's house at just after ten o'clock, Doris Chapman came flying across her yard to meet me.

"Thank God you're back!" she called, eyes wide with relief and excitement as she began to spill out details as fast as she could speak. "Someone was in Sarah's house again last night. I called the police, but they didn't find anyone when they got here. They went through the whole place though—every bit—from top to bottom. Somebody must have a key because they didn't break in—but they were already gone before the police got here. I think that . . ."

"Whoa, Doris," I told her as I climbed down from the driver's seat with Stretch under one arm for a run in the yard. Putting him down, I took off my sunglasses and turned to walk around and hook up the water and electricity. "Slow down. Let me take care of the hookups and come inside before you tell me."

Necessaries taken care of, I switched the power back to AC and got us both a glass of iced tea from the refrigerator.

"Now, sit down and start again—slowly—okay?"

She sat, gingerly, on the edge of the sofa, glass in hand, and took a breath and a sip of tea before speaking.

"I woke up just after midnight and got up to get a drink of water. From the window I saw that there were lights in Sarah's kitchen and in the basement. I thought it was you for a minute, but then I remembered you weren't there. If you'd been there I couldn't have seen the kitchen window, because your motor home would have been in the way, you know? So I watched for a minute or two and saw someone moving in the basement."

"Who?" I asked.

"I couldn't tell who." She took another sip of tea and sighed in apology for criticism. "Those windows haven't been washed in years."

What basement windows in old houses are? I thought, but didn't say, just nodded encouragement. "And?"

"And—so I called the police."

"How long did it take them to get here?"

"Not long. But the lights went out downstairs before that and someone went out through the backyard to the alley and a car drove away. They left the kitchen light on though."

"What kind of a car? Could you see it?"

"No, I just saw the lights come on through the lilac bushes back there—then the glow of the lights as it went away down the alley to Seventh."

"Was it a man or a woman?"

"I don't know. It was too dark to tell, but he was carrying something."

Perhaps this time it had been a thief. "What kind of something?" I asked.

She shrugged. "I don't know. About this big." She held her hands, one still holding the glass, about eighteen inches apart. "A box, maybe?"

"And the police went through the house?"

"Yes, they found the back door unlocked and went through every room of it. That nice young man that was here before came across to talk to me—the tall one in uniform. Officer . . . ah . . ."

"Bellamy?"

"Bellamy. Yes, that's right. He seemed to know you weren't here. He gave me his card."

"I saw him the night before I left," I told her, thinking that the police were probably tired of making unsuccessful runs to burglaries at Sarah's address. "Did they lock the back door before they left?"

She nodded assurance. "I know they did, because I loaned them my key."

"You have a key?"

Why did that startle me? Neighbors often have each other's keys. The woman who cares for my house in Alaska while I'm on the road has one.

"Sarah and I traded keys years ago," Doris confided. "It makes it easier to water the plants and things like that when either one of us is gone." She stopped and put a hand over her mouth, eyes wide as she remembered that Sarah was dead. "When one of us was out of town, I mean. Sorry."

Who else, I wondered, had a key to the house? Alan? Westover? Why should I have assumed I had the *only* key?

Stretch, who had been padding around outside where I could keep an eye on him through the open coach door, scratched on the screen to be let in. I got up and opened it for him. Ignoring me, he headed straight for Doris, who gave a chirp of delight and leaned to pet him.

"Oh, what a sweetie you are."

Accepting her accolade as nothing less than his due, he gave her wrist a lick of appreciation and encouragement.

He can be such a ningnong.

"Well," I said, setting down my empty tea glass. "I guess I'd better take a look and see if I can tell what this person took away with him—if it was a him."

Doris rose as I did and we went out the door, leaving Stretch inside. She hesitated. "Would you want me to come with you?"

Clearly, she had no desire to do so and was offering because she thought it was the thing to do.

"No thanks. I'll be fine. There won't be anyone there now."

Relieved to be let off the hook, she went home and I went to unlock the back door with the key that I had retrieved from my bag.

Sarah's kitchen looked the same as it had when I left for Salt Lake. The only difference I could see was that the basement door had been left open, perhaps by the police. I left the basement till last and made a tour of the first and second floors, but found nothing out of place or missing. A quick trip up the stairs to the attic had the same result.

I could feel the temperature drop as I descended into the cellar. Like many old basements, it smelled damp and dusty. A few cobwebs festooned the joists of the floor overhead and the windows that, as Doris had observed, had years of grime obscuring them. By the time I reached the cement floor at the bottom of the stairs I knew that, however dirty those windows, I had evidently been observed through them more closely than I suspected. How else could anyone but Sarah have known that the utility shelves hid her secret room?

They held no secret now, for they had been swung away from the wall and the door had been kicked in. It stood splintered and wide open.

What the thief had carried out was obvious. The box of letters and photographs was missing and only a dim square in the thin film of recent dust lingered to show it had ever occupied the shelf next to the empty one that remained, its lid askew.

I stared at the space with a sinking feeling that I had seriously let my friend down. If Sarah had treasured those letters and pictures, then I should have, too. Now I might never be able to read those letters that I had put off until later.

Who could have taken them? Jamie was the first name that came to mind. Would she have been able to kick open that solid door? It could not have been the person who left the threat on my screen door the night just past. A person can't be in two places at once and there was too much distance between Green River and Grand Junction to reach either one from the other fast enough to kick in the door *and* leave the warning note.

I closed the door as best I could and swung back the shelves in front of it. But the horse, so to speak, was already gone.

I'm sorry, Sarah. But you didn't leave me much to go on.

Back upstairs, I wandered through the living room, checking things again to be sure nothing else had been taken. In the vestibule I remembered the mail that had probably come while I was away and retrieved several items from the box under the mail slot. Walking back toward the desk, I shuffled through them—a magazine, one of those *You Are Pre-qualified* envelopes from some credit card company that must gobble up trees by the square mile at least once a week at the rate they harass the public by mail, and a large manila envelope the sender had wasted tape to seal, rather than moisten the flap. About to lay them all down on the desk with the mail I had retrieved before I left for Salt Lake, I flipped them over and found that the manila envelope had been sent to Sarah's address, but the name printed on it in ink was *mine*!

Something from Don Westover's office, I thought at first. Then I noticed that in the upper left corner the sender's address was the same as the address under my name and above it were two initials: S. N.

Sarah Nunamaker—without a doubt.

If anyone should know, I should, for I had seen those initials in the same familiar handwriting—on every piece of mail that I had received from Sarah in over forty years.

At the house, Maxine . . . I wrote it all down. You can read it, she had said. And here it was—I knew—in the best hiding place she could think of—the U.S. mail.

CHAPTER EIGHTEEN

WITHOUT BOTHERING TO FIND A LETTER OPENER IN THE desk, I ripped open the flap of the manila envelope. What I pulled out was a similar envelope, folded once to fit. It was even more carefully sealed with tape, this time all around the edges, so it was impossible to open without irrevocably tearing the brown manila paper, and was addressed to Sarah Nunamaker at her Chipeta Avenue address.

TO BE OPENED ONLY IN THE PRESENCE OF MAXIE MCNABB AND DONALD WESTOVER had been written in block letters across the face of the envelope. Under that: MAXINE: READ THIS BEFORE OPENING had been underlined with an arrow that pointed to a sheet of paper folded in quarters and paper-clipped to the envelope. I pulled it from under the clip and opened it to find a half page written in Sarah's familiar hand:

> *Dear Maxine,*
> *I may be able to do this myself, but just in case*

I can't: Please DO NOT OPEN THE ENVELOPE TO WHICH THIS IS ATTACHED.

It is very important that you take it directly and as soon as possible to Don Westover.

I have mailed this first to myself, then, in the envelope you have already opened, to you. Without opening it, you must take it straight to Don so he will be able to prove from the way it is sealed and the date on the postmark that it was mailed and, therefore written, after the copy of my will that he helped amend several days ago and assumes is final. The changes in this will postdate and invalidate parts of that document.

Inside with these changes is a letter to you explaining why this course of action is necessary so far as I know and understand it.

If this is necessary, I'm sorry to land you in the middle of this without prior knowledge, but you and Don Westover are the only people I can trust and all this is crucially important to me and will be to others.

Thank you, my dear friend.

All my love,

Sarah

I stood staring at what I held in my hands for a long minute, then read it again as I reached for the phone and called Don Westover's office.

June answered.

He was in court, she told me, but would be back by lunchtime.

I told her if he came in before I arrived that it was critical to keep him there, which she promised to do and didn't ask why.

Taking both envelopes and the note back to the Winnebago with me, I grabbed up the kit and clean clothes I had expected to use in Green River and headed to Sarah's upstairs bathroom for a quick shower. I locked the door and put the envelope on the toilet seat, where I could keep an eye on it, determined that this time nothing that had been trusted to my keeping and was so important was going to disappear.

Leaving Stretch behind, I took the rental car I had left parked while I was in Salt Lake and headed into downtown Grand Junction, where I took care to park in the shade of a tree on Main Street, though I had to hike a block and a half to Westover's office as a result.

Don Westover was in the outer office by June's desk when I walked in, examining some papers he evidently had brought back from his trip to court. She looked up and smiled as he left what he was doing and came to meet me anxiously, gesturing that we should go into his office.

"Are you all right?"

I assured him I was.

Once again sitting in a chair in front of his desk, I took the manila envelope and accompanying note from my bag and handed them over without a word.

He raised a questioning eyebrow.

"It came in the mail," I told him. "Maybe yesterday, or the day before. I found it less than an hour ago, when I got back from Salt Lake."

He read both the note and what was written across the envelope, then went back and read them again.

"Smart woman, Sarah," he commented. "Mailing this to herself *will* legally establish the date from the postmark. As she says, it is perfect proof that any changes in this sealed envelope were written after and will invalidate the last one I drew up for her. It'll hold up in any court of law."

Laying the envelope on the desk in front of him, he frowned and pursed his lips for a moment of thought before speaking.

"Well," he said finally. "We'll open this and find out what Sarah has to say. But I think it would be wise, under the circumstances, to have witnesses. If this is a final change to Sarah's will, as she indicates, there is a lot at stake that could be contested—by Alan, for one. And I think we could count on that, if it doesn't go his way."

I agreed—thinking also of Jamie and how the will Westover and I had reviewed when I was last in his office had seemed designed to include her.

"There was another break-in at Sarah's house last night," I told him, "and a theft this time. There are also some things I found out in Salt Lake that you should know. There may be another child besides Jamie Stover."

"Who?"

"I'm not sure yet, but . . ." I started, but he interrupted.

"One thing at a time. Let's open this envelope and find out what's in it first," he said, laying a hand on the envelope in question as he got up from his chair. "Then you can tell me the rest. Stay here while I scare up a couple of witnesses and we'll open it."

In five minutes he was back with June and a woman attorney in tow. He introduced his colleague, Karen Keller, and we all sat. He handed the envelope across to Karen Keller and June, who looked it over thoroughly, then signed their names with the date on a lower corner, attesting that it had been sealed when they examined it. We all watched, as Westover took a pair of scissors from his desk drawer and carefully slit the envelope and tape at the top, preserving evidence of the way it had been sealed. Just as carefully, he removed a few pages that were paper clipped together and a sealed white business-sized envelope with my name across the front that was exactly like the three I had found for Alan, Ed, and Jamie.

"Better sign this, too," he said, handing the white envelope to the two witnesses, who complied and handed it on to me.

"Read the will first," I suggested, laying Sarah's letter in my lap, not sure if I was ready to read and make public what she had written to me just yet. "It's the most important thing, after all."

Before reading it, Don had his witnesses sign and date each page that had been in the envelope and asked June to make copies, so we could all see what he was about to read. In a quick first glance I could see that it was composed in Sarah's unmistakable penmanship, though her writing looked a little shaky here and there.

Westover cleared his throat and began.

"In sound mind, I, Sarah Anne Nunamaker, affirm that these are the final changes and additions to my last will and testament, written in my own hand and witnessed by Doris Chapman, my longtime friend and next-door neighbor, and by Tomas Navarro, my trusted gardener, whose signatures appear with the date on each page and formally on the last."

I flipped through the three pages of the document and found that she had been cautious enough to make sure each of them was witnessed, as she said.

Well done, Sarah. But you never did do things by halves.

That established, I listened and followed along with the other two as Don Westover read the rest aloud. It was completely lucid and to the point.

She mentioned that before Westover had gone to her

house to amend her will, the one she had on file had left everything to Alan, and that the amendments Westover had made at her request had changed it to include *any child of hers, natural or adopted.*

"That re-establishes a reliable chain of events within the document," Westover stopped to comment.

He turned back to Sarah's instructions.

Though this new document delineated items that should remain the same as the amended version—the life insurance and investments that listed Alan as beneficiary. Two changes were startling.

The first concerned the family businesses—namely the orchards and the vineyard and winery. Sarah indicated that their worth and future profit or loss, or their worth should they be sold, should be *"divided equally between any and all my children, natural, adopted by me, or adopted by others, and who are not convicted of a felony by any court of law."*

Upon reading that line, Don Westover paused again to comment.

"Interesting instruction, considering the question of how Sarah died. She didn't say who *have been convicted.* She carefully said who *are not convicted.* There's a very significant difference between the two. She must have known she was in danger."

I was thinking the same thing. Though she hadn't said so specifically, it seemed to indicate that she had been aware and afraid of the possibility of an unnatural death. Or was it someone else's death she had feared?

The second change addressed the disposition of the property and house on Chipeta Avenue. She had unconditionally left them to *"Jamie S. Stover of Salt Lake City, Utah, to occupy or dispose of as she wishes."*

Evidently Sarah had been convinced beyond doubt that Jamie was her real daughter. She had also left Jamie her jewelry. I thought of the box I had found in the upstairs closet and remembered the pin I had slipped into the pocket of my sweatpants. I told myself I must remember to take it out and put it away, but I did not regret taking it.

One other bequest was new—as if she were adding something she had forgotten in the past. She left a thousand dollars *"with thanks to my faithful gardener, Tomas Navarro."* I had to smile at the rightness of it.

By the time he finished reading, Don Westover was shaking his head in perplexity, but he waited until June and Karen Keller left his office before he turned to me with his questions.

"You went to Salt Lake?" he asked.

"I did—and found out some interesting things."

"What did you mean that there might be another child?"

He picked up a pencil to take notes and waited.

"It's a long and complex story," I told him, hesitating. "First, about the break-in at her house last night. Doris Chapman called the police, but whoever she saw was already gone. I was about to call them again this morning on another issue, but I found the envelope in the mail and came here instead. If I'm going to tell everything I know about this situation, I can't see any reason to tell it twice. Could we get Officer Bellamy or Detective Soames to come here?"

We could, and did. Bellamy showed up almost at once—Soames, twenty minutes later. Bellamy and Westover chatted about another case while we waited and I took the opportunity to open the letter Sarah had enclosed for me.

There were several pages in the white business-sized envelope, more than there had been in the document

Westover had just read. I unfolded them to find to my dismay that the top two were threats similar to the one I had found in the screen door of my Winnebago that morning. The first had the same circle face with turned down mouth and Xs for eyes. The warning beneath it read, "DO WHAT IS RIGHT AND FAIR OR YOU WILL REGRET IT." The second had two smaller faces, side by side, and read, "SHE IS A FRAUD. BELIEVE HER AND SHE DIES WITH YOU."

"Dear Maxine," Sarah's letter to me began on the third page.

> *Along with several phone calls from someone whose voice I do not recognize, I have received these threats in the mail, both within the last week, and since my daughter Jamie came here from Salt Lake to stay with me I will not run away. I am almost as stubborn as you are, you know?*

I did know and had to smile.

> *So, if you are reading this I probably am dead, as both threats imply I could be.*

Oh, Sarah.

> *If that is true, Jamie will have seen you, told you who she is and all about searching and finding me after so many years. I have kept track of her since she was born through a woman in Salt Lake who was my nurse at the hospital and who has regularly sent me letters and photographs of my girl and her poor little boy. In a secret hiding place in the back of a drawer of my desk you will find a key*

that unlocks a room hidden behind a set of shelves in the basement. There you will find those letters and pictures of Jamie's life.

Ahead of you, Sarah, but where are they now?

Give them to her, please, and tell her again how happy it has made me to have her with me at last. I would like her to know that I always knew who and how she was and loved her.

She went on to tell me what I already knew; that she had, as Mildred Scott's husband, David, had confirmed, given twins up for adoption during the fall of her junior year of college—a girl and a boy. She apologized for not telling me at the time and for keeping such a secret through the years.

There never seemed to be a right time to tell you back then and as time went on I let it be. Back then, I was afraid to tell anyone but Ed, who was the father, of course, so he was the only one in Seattle who knew I was pregnant. He wanted to marry me, but I didn't love him and knew it would never have worked. So I went home and then to Salt Lake instead. No one but my folks knew where I was and, though he demanded to know, they refused to tell him. He has always been convinced that Alan was that child and Bill and I found and adopted him later, which is not true, but I have let him think so rather than complicate the issue with the truth and thinking he might go hunting for his real children. Perhaps I made a mistake in that. He has been determined in this belief and persistent in demanding assurance, particularly in the last few months.

My only grief is that my friend in Salt Lake lost track of my son and I have never known where he is, or who adopted him. I named the boy James G.—for my maiden name, Grayson—and the girl, Jamie S.—for Sarah, which I have already told her. I gave them no last name, nor did I reveal Ed's name as the father, but was able to stipulate that after adoption they would be allowed to keep the names I had given them. I have not told Jamie that she has a brother and I hesitate to tell her now—or to tell Alan about her or her twin, for that matter. Poor Alan. Perhaps it was another mistake to tell him from the start that he was adopted, for he has always had a resentful streak and that may be part of it. But hindsight makes everything easier to see, doesn't it dear?

Oh, yes, it does. But I couldn't help wondering if not knowing would have made Alan much different.

I honestly have no idea who is making these threats, but trying to scare an already dying woman with death is a bit redundant, don't you think? I <u>will</u> <u>not</u> allow them to make wrong what I feel is right.

If you are reading this, you will have taken the pages that came with it to Don Westover, as directed. I know you too well to even consider that your personal ethics would allow you to open it otherwise against my wishes—and isn't it a joy that we have always been able to love and trust each other so? So you will have seen the final changes I want made to my will and understand that it is the only way I know of being fair in what I have to leave to <u>all</u> my children. If it should turn out that one of the three of them actually is the author of these threats, or of my death—I can't

*imagine it could, but should it—the line I have
included, after much thought, about a felony conviction will take care of the inheritance part of it.*

*One last thing: in a secret space between the
shelves of the bookcase near my desk you will find
letters I have written to Ed and my children. They
are personal and not part of this thing with the
changes to my will. Would you see that they are
delivered? Perhaps at the gathering I have
arranged with the Callahan-Edfast Mortuary.*

*There isn't much more to say, really, and I will
soon be rambling on unnecessarily. Please, always
remember how much I have loved you, my dearest
of all friends. You must be the keeper of all the
memories now. Go walk in the rain for me some
warm September day, will you? Splash in the pud-
dles and laugh for us both.*

It's been a great adventure.
Sarah

A great adventure? Oh yes! Life had always been full
of adventure for Sarah, as for me. I think that in that
regard we inspired each other. Her laughter had been
giggles and my much lower one a hearty bray of appreciation, but how I would miss that harmony. And how I
resented being deprived of it before I could share it to
the last. I looked again at the two threatening pages she
had received and realized again, through tears, how
angry I was.

I was still staring at them and considering possible
perpetrators when June came to the door to announce
Detective Soames.

Chapter Nineteen

When all four of us were seated around Don Westover's desk and June called in with her shorthand notebook, they turned to me and waited.

It took over an hour—with a few interruptions—to tell them everything I knew, or speculated, and to answer their questions.

First I had Don Westover read the letter Sarah had sent me.

"You have to know how everything began and continued before you can understand how the people I'm going to talk about fit into all this," I started. "The letter will give you some of the history."

When he had read and handed it back to me, I started with my arrival in Grand Junction and told them everything that had happened since, including my experiences in Salt Lake. When I came to the Green River part, I took out the threat I had received there in the campground and laid it on Westover's desk along with the two that had come to Sarah. It was plain that the same hand had drawn and written all three of the threatening messages.

Officer Bellamy stood up and leaned over to examine them without touching. "Better get these to the lab to check for fingerprints," he said. "Probably wasted effort, but we might get lucky."

For a long minute he just looked, then sat down again and gave us his thoughts.

"The note you got in Green River is pretty straightforward—directed at you and no one else, with specific intent. Whoever sent this may have something to do with Mrs. Nunamaker's death and feels you're getting too close for comfort. The two that came to Mrs. Nunamaker leave questions. What does *right* and *fair* mean? It refers to something specific, but doesn't say what. It assumes that Sarah would know, and she probably did."

"It must be related to the amendments she had me make in the legal dispersal of her property, or these last changes," Westover suggested.

"Possibly. But who is the `she` the second threat includes—this woman, Jamie Stover, who claims to be her daughter?"

"It has to be," I told him. "There isn't any other woman involved that I know of and Jamie was there with Sarah before she died."

"That concerns me, too." He leaned back in his chair, frowning, and chewed on his lower lip.

"Tell me about the car you say was used in an attempt to force you off the road on the Monument," Soames said. "You've seen it three times?"

I hesitated, thinking back and counting. "Yes—three. Once the night I arrived here—as the intruder drove it away from in front of the house. Once when the driver tried to force us over the cliff between Cold Shivers Point and the Serpents Trail. But I think we saw it before that, though I can't be positive, because I didn't see the taillights that time. We had stopped to look at the Book Cliffs and were pulling back onto Rim Rock Drive when it almost hit us, but went on past, headed east."

"Same person driving?"

"I don't know. I didn't ever see the driver. Ed Norris thought it might have been Sarah's son, Alan."

"Why?"

"He thought he recognized Alan during the cliff thing on the Monument."

"And he's the one who thinks Alan is his son?"

"Yes."

"Where is he now?"

"Ed?"

"Yes."

"As far as I know he's still staying at the Holiday Inn on Horizon Drive, where he checked in the morning Sarah died."

"And where are Alan Nunamaker and Jamie Stover? We'll need to talk to all these people."

I couldn't tell him where to locate Jamie now that she had vanished. "Maybe Salt Lake. She said she lives there with her son, but didn't say where, and she's not listed in the phone book. I checked."

"She may be unlisted. I can find out."

Don Westover had been writing on a yellow sticky, which he handed to Soames across the desk.

"Here's Alan's home address and phone number. He runs the family businesses, so he may be either at the orchard or the winery. I've listed them."

Still frowning, Officer Bellamy sat up with a question for me.

"You're the only one of us who's met her. Do you believe this Stover woman actually *is* the daughter?"

How should I answer that? Sarah had obviously been

convinced. I thought back to how much Jamie had looked like Sarah the first time I saw her as she walked across the lawn to me. It made me also remember the man I had seen in the Family History Library. It was such a tenuous and seemingly unrelated incident that I let it go for the moment and concentrated on sharing my mixed perceptions of Jamie rather than confusing the issue.

I had to confess that I couldn't be absolutely sure. "She fits," I told them. "She looks and at times even moves so much like Sarah that I find it hard to believe she's not. But she stole the copy of Sarah's will from my bag and disappeared. Why would she do that if she wanted to convince me she was for real? And she was angry—or frustrated—that Sarah hadn't told her who her father was. I could have, but I wanted to make sure first."

"Did you?"

"Tell her? No. I haven't seen her since she disappeared that afternoon. Make sure? Yes. This letter from Sarah confirms that Ed Norris was the father of her twins."

"But he still thinks Alan is his child?"

"As far as I know—yes. I haven't told him otherwise."

There were a few more questions, some of which I could answer, some I could not.

"If we step away from the details, all this seems to come down to a conflict over inheritance," Westover suggested toward the last of our conversation. "I'm wondering now just where the other child is—the twin, Jamie Stover's brother. Any way you can help us find that out? From the nature of these last changes, Sarah meant him to share in the inheritance—and it's considerable."

"It would take some time and opening sealed adoption records to find out who adopted him," Soames said. "I'll look into it and let you know."

"What are you going to do now, Ms. McNabb?" Officer Bellamy asked me, a note of concern in his voice. "I'm not sure you should stay by yourself on Chipeta Avenue."

Don Westover chimed in with harmonious agreement.

I hadn't really considered staying anywhere other than my usual parking place beside Sarah's house.

"You really think I'd be better off in some RV park?"

"Less vulnerable, at least. You could leave town, you know."

"No, I couldn't—or wouldn't. Sarah's gathering is tomorrow. Besides, I hate running."

"Sometimes the better part of valor is to run like hell," he suggested, flashing me a grin that immediately faded. "I was there last night when that woman next door called about another break-in. I saw that broken basement door and it took someone with a fair amount of strength to kick it in. You should consider that the same person may have left you the threat in Green River and could show up again."

"I'll think about it, but I rather think I'll stay put," I told him. "I'll be careful, keep my cell phone handy, and Stretch is a good watchdog."

He shrugged and an uneasy grimace flitted across his face and was gone.

"I'm off duty, but I'll make sure a patrol drives by regularly to check on you tonight."

I considered telling him about my shotgun, but unless I ever have to use it I see no reason to inform law enforcement officers that I have it, however nice and well meaning they may be. Law enforcement officers look askance at regular people with defensive weapons.

I think they may be right about handguns. It's harder to hit anything with a handgun anyway and easier for one to be taken away. You have to be serious to pull out a shotgun and if, or when, mine comes out, I *am*. It would definitely be within reach tonight. Meanwhile, I kept my mouth shut and smiled my thanks for his offer of surveillance.

"You know," Westover said to us, leaning forward on his desk, "some of these people will be at the gathering for Sarah tomorrow afternoon. Alan and Ed Norris will be there for sure, right, Maxie? Maybe Jamie Stover, as well."

Detective Soames nodded. "Then so will I," he said, closing his notebook and depositing it in his shirt pocket.

They left together, taking the written threats to me and to Sarah with them.

Don Westover and I sat back in our chairs and looked at each other for a long moment in silence.

"Well," he said with a resigned sigh. "This certainly changes things, doesn't it? I'd better get these last changes of Sarah's into some kind of understandable format, as I'm sure as hell going to be asked to explain them. We'll also have to amend the paperwork that has already been filed, or submit again. I'll get that done soon so you can sign it."

"What about those letters she left for Alan, Jamie, and Ed?" I asked. "Should you bring those to the gathering?"

"I'm reluctant to hand them out until we've settled everything legally," he said, frowning. "Let's wait, shall we, until later. You could deliver them when we disclose the amended contents of the will. I don't see how we can notify beneficiaries or transfer allocations of inheritance until we see if Jamie Stover's twin can be found.

Knowing he exists makes a difference. Of course both of them will have to prove they *are* related to Sarah. If that proves out, Alan will probably contest it, you know. Legally this could take months—years. Who knows?"

I sympathized and agreed, hoping it wouldn't take that long, and left him to it, thanking June on my way out for keeping her boss in the office as I had requested on the phone.

What a tangle of complications, I thought as I drove toward home, stopping once to replenish the groceries my trip had depleted—vegetables for a salad and pork chops for my dinner. Finding myself unexpectedly in the frozen food aisle, I almost fell off the wagon and picked up some lime sherbet for dessert, but remembered the ice cream I had bought in Helper.

I had a suspicion that I would hear from Ed with a suggestion that we meet again for dinner, but this time I intended to refuse and stay put in my own comfortable space for the rest of the day. I had had enough of discussing Sarah's children, the threats, the will, the police, and all the rest of it for the time being. I intended to either put some amusing movie from my collection in the DVD player, or escape into a good book I hadn't yet read—possibly both. Settling down for a quiet evening with only Stretch for company was what I wanted.

As I traveled the few blocks back to Chipeta Avenue, I couldn't help wondering about Alan and how little I had seen of him. I had left a message for him at home and at his business office with the information about his mother's gathering the next day, but no response had been forthcoming. He had successfully avoided me since I arrived, but angry, upset, or not, he surely wouldn't absent himself from this occasion out of spite. He was not going to be happy about the rearrangement of what he clearly considered *his* inheritance and he could, I supposed from Don Westover's remarks, make things legally difficult, though ultimately he would probably be forced to face failure and conform to his mother's wishes. She had seemed to anticipate that from the way she so carefully delineated her wishes.

Why was everything so hard for him to accept? He and Sarah had made a happy pair when he was a cheerful, adventurous child. He had loved to be read to, I remembered. There had been a golden retriever puppy with enormous feet. It had grown almost as big as Alan and, inseparable, they had gone everywhere together. He had even wanted to take to it to school. Denied, Gully—for Gulliver—had faithfully waited for him on the front porch every afternoon, met him with wags of total joy in reunion, and had often slept in his bed if undetected by Sarah and Bill. What had happened to that happy little boy? Had he ever gone searching for his birth parents, like Jamie?

I hadn't meant to spend the rest of the day thinking about Alan, or any of the other people involved, but had allowed myself to fall back into it. I gave myself a mental shake as I turned the corner onto Chipeta, looking forward to a walk with Stretch before finding some lunch for us both. Before we went to the park, I needed to call Mr. Blackburn at the Callahan-Edfast Mortuary to be sure all would be ready for tomorrow's gathering for Sarah.

A blue pickup truck occupied the space at the curb where I had been parking the rental car, so I pulled in behind it where there would be enough shade to keep my car cool, though I didn't intend to go anywhere else that day. Carrying my single sack of groceries, I started across the lawn toward the Winnebago, but hesitated at sight of the figure I saw sitting on the low extendable doorstep of the coach.

Is it sometimes possible to materialize people just by thinking about them? At that moment, I felt it must be. For in the shade of the house, leaning back against the screen door, legs stretched out in front of him, fingers laced across his waist, Alan Nunamaker appeared to have been waiting long enough to now be taking a nap.

CHAPTER TWENTY

ALAN HAD EVIDENTLY BEEN THERE LONG ENOUGH FOR Stretch to decide he was no immediate threat and quit barking. I stood looking down as he slept like an angel, or the child I had recalled, total innocence on his face, peaceful and trusting that nothing unpleasant would disturb his rest. Always slim and muscular, I knew he moved with an easy natural grace that had allowed him to excel at sports. At forty-three there was not yet a hint of gray in his dark hair. A little damp with perspiration, it had a tendency to form waves around his ears, and I remembered that at kindergarten age his head had been a mop of curls. Sarah and I had more than once looked down at him asleep in his bed and marveled at the miracle of such a beautiful child.

Remembering that as I looked down at him on my step, I thought I saw more of his mother in his face than many natural children. Was it possible that he really was . . . ? No, I knew it was not and that I simply wished it were. But she had loved him more than many natural parents love their children, for he had been a choice—

fulfillment, perhaps even atonement. What could have made him so angry and determined to prove his worth, especially with her gone? Or could it be *because* she was gone?

I didn't move or make a sound. Neither did he, but I was suddenly aware that he was no longer asleep. Without moving any other part of himself he opened his eyes and looked up at me.

"Hello," he said, then smiled a friendly smile that caught me off balance because it was not at all what I had anticipated. "I figured you'd have to come home sooner or later."

"I surely did," I replied. "But I was not expecting to find an angel napping on my doorstep."

"An *angel*?" A curl of the lip turned the smile a bit crooked. "More like a devil, maybe."

"Oh, I think not. Will you come in? Finding you here was a kind of déjà vu. It made me recall how Gully would lie on the front porch and wait for you to come home after school. Remember?"

"Old Gully," he said, getting up and reaching to take the sack of groceries so I could unlock the coach door. "He was a good old boy. Who's the guardian of the hearth inside this rig? Attila the Hun?"

"That's my dachshund. Barked at you, did he?"

"Ferociously—for ten or fifteen minutes."

"He's a little territorial."

I opened the door to find the subject of our exchange waiting just inside, impatient as usual.

"Meet Stretch."

Stretch has one trick that Daniel taught him. He will not perform it on request, but only when *he* decides it's appropriate, whatever that means to him. He startled me by performing it then—holding up one front paw for Alan to shake, charming him instantly and completely.

This is no dumb dog.

Inside, I put away the groceries while they made each other's acquaintance.

"Iced tea?" I asked Alan.

"Please. Even in the shade it was warming up out there. It's good for the fruit—we've got a good crop this year. We'll be harvesting the apples and pears soon."

I handed him a glass, took my own and sat at the dinette. He dropped onto the sofa across the aisle, loose limbed, one arm stretched casually along the back.

"Look," he said, with the most sincere of repentant expressions. "I must apologize for my behavior in Westover's office the other day. I know it was uncalled for and unfair—that you're doing what she wanted and that's okay. It was just so unexpected, because she always said she wanted me to take care of things, you know?"

His contrition was the last thing I had anticipated. I accepted his apology, but I couldn't suppress a suspicion that there might be a smidgen of manipulation in it. Having failed at anger and insults, was he now attempting to charm me onto his side? I knew that Alan had discovered at a fairly young age that temper tantrums were not effective in getting his way, especially with Sarah. I could almost hear her saying that *You catch more flies with honey than with vinegar*. There had always been a knowing gleam in his eyes when his charm succeeded, and behind it a more serious satisfaction had lurked in confirming his accomplishment.

Obligation taken care of, he asked about the arrangements for Sarah's gathering and approved of what I described.

"It's what she wanted and I know that she had it all taken care of," he said. "I have to admit that I didn't pay very careful attention. Planning the whole thing for herself seemed pointlessly gruesome to me."

He shifted on the sofa, leaning forward with elbows on knees, and shuddered.

"I *hate* the idea of dying—even being sick. Can't stand hospitals and all that. I didn't want to think about her dying."

She! He kept saying *she* or *her.* Not once had he said *mother.*

But when he glanced up at me there were tears in his eyes.

Looking back down at my dachshund, who was lying between us on the floor, Alan reached to rub his back. Stretch immediately rolled over and presented his belly.

Opportunistic, gullible dog.

Alan stood up abruptly, drained his glass in a long swallow, and took it across to the sink in the galley.

"Work to do. Gotta run," he told me and headed for the door, filling the void with words. "Thanks for the tea. See you tomorrow."

The screen door closed and I could hear Alan whistling as he crossed the lawn to his pickup. *No tears now,* I thought, and wondered if and how much they had been calculated for my benefit—wondered, too, if that gleam of satisfaction was back in his eye. I am not prone to take the world and its inhabitants at face value.

It was too early for dinner and Stretch needed some time out of the Winnebago, so I thought again about a walk, but decided I didn't want to go blocks in the heat and took him instead to the backyard, where I unexpectedly found Tomas, the once-a-week gardener on his knees, trimming the edge of the grass around a flower bed. He got to his feet, tugged off his cap, and gave me a smile as I walked across to where he stood.

"*Buenas tardes,* Tomas."

His smile widened at my attempt to speak his language, but he stuck with English in reply. "And to you, Missus McNabb."

"Will you come to the gathering tomorrow to say good-bye to Mrs. Nunamaker?" I asked him.

His eyes widened in surprise. *"I should come?"*

Perhaps he would rather not, I realized. Still, I wanted him to know he would be welcome.

"Yes, but only if you like. Would you like to come?"

"Oh, *yes*. I like very much to come—if it is . . ." He searched for an English word, found only Spanish, *"propio,"* and settled for "okay."

"It would be very *okay*," I assured him. "All her friends will come. You were her friend and she would be sad if you didn't come."

"Then I must come. *Gracias*."

I started to turn away, but remembered the changes to Sarah's will that he had witnessed and turned back.

"Thank you, Tomas, for helping Mrs. Nunamaker—for writing your name on her papers. It was very important."

From where he had returned to his knees on the grass, he looked up a little warily, but saw that I meant my thanks sincerely. "You have the papers?"

"Yes. They are—okay. I have taken care of them. *Gracias*."

The twinkle returned to his eyes and I recognized his reply for the unspoken compliment he intended, *"De nada,* Senora—*Maxie."*

I called Mr. Blackburn at the Callahan-Edfast Mortuary and found that all was on track for the next day and there was nothing he needed from me.

In the middle of leafing through the yellow pages to

find a florist, I suddenly realized that I didn't want a commercial offering. In the yard, thanks to Tomas, were all the flowers Sarah had loved best. Early in the morning, while it was still cool, I would take time to make an arrangement of them that would be perfect for her.

Not contented to stay in the Winnebago for the rest of the afternoon, I took water, a book, a blanket, a pillow, and Stretch, and drove back to the park by the river, where Ed and I had commandeered the swings. For an hour I enjoyed the shade in an almost empty park, all the children confined to their first weeks of school. Though I left the swings alone, I came close to falling asleep where I had spread the blanket, plumped the pillow, and leaned against a tree to read. But a dragonfly buzzed around my head and woke my attention to the blur of its gauzy blue wings before it zoomed off to find a landing place on some reed near the water.

Stretch came to life from his nap when an elderly man came walking through the park with his mini-schnauzer. They stopped to say hello, as dog owners often do, then moved on down one of the trails along the riverbank, headed west. As I watched them disappear out of sight, a shadow suddenly swept across the park and I looked up to see a dark bank of clouds billowing out across the sky, obscuring the sun and threatening to shower on us. I collected our gear, we made a dash for the car, and reached it just in time to toss everything at the backseat and climb in as the first fat drops splattered on the roof and hood.

Back at Chipeta Avenue, I put the pork chops in to bake with a favorite recipe for rice, and opened all the windows to let the cool air blow through the screens. Pouring myself a Jameson and a glass of ice water, I settled on the sofa with the book, to read and listen to the grumble of rain on the roof of the motor home, reminded of the storm that had welcomed us to town a few short days earlier. This was a softer rain. Without the percussion of thunder and lightning, it tapped gentle rhythms on the leaves outside and splashed harmoniously from the gutters and downspouts of the house.

It was still raining when the predictable call from Ed came about an hour later, and I turned down his invitation to dinner, as planned.

"Well, if you're sure," he said. "Shall I pick you up for Sarah's gathering tomorrow afternoon?"

"I have to go a little early, so I'll just see you there, but thanks," I told him.

"You trying to avoid me, or something?" he teased.

"Not in the least. I just need some time by myself tonight. It's been rather busy the last three days."

"What's up?"

"Oh, nothing I really want to get into now. I'll tell you about it when I see you. When are you leaving for Oregon?"

"Depends. I haven't decided yet. Did you get me that letter Sarah left?"

I had forgotten that I had mentioned it to him.

"I'll bring it tomorrow, okay?"

"Can't I come by and pick it up?"

Forced to admit it was still at Westover's office I told him he could have it the next day. "I'll bring it, or have him bring it. I promise."

As soon as he hung up I called Don Westover and caught him just as he was about to leave the office. When I told him I thought we should give the letters to their intended recipients, he half-reluctantly agreed to bring them along.

"I guess it can't do any harm," he said. "It's just that I wish we knew what Sarah had told them all, so we could anticipate the reaction. Someone killed her, Maxie. It could be one of them."

"Do we have the right to keep them to ourselves? Sarah did suggest that they be given at the gathering. I'd rather find out now what's in them than wonder, wouldn't you?"

"They may not share the contents."

"Maybe not. But they also may. If Jamie shows up they'll all be together tomorrow. Let's give them the opportunity."

"All right, then. Tomorrow."

Chapter Twenty-one

The rain continued through the evening and I went to sleep hearing the gentle beat of it on the roof over my bed. When I got up for a drink of water at almost three it must have just stopped, for when I opened the door to look out there was still the sound of water dripping from the shrubbery around Sarah's house and trickling musically from the nearest downspout onto the pebbles below.

Everything smelled fresh and clean and a star or two winked from dark gaps between the retreating clouds. A three-quarter moon slid out between them as well, with enough pale light to cast long shadows from the trees at the curb onto the grass of the lawn. Startled, for a moment I thought I saw a light moving in the attic, but it was only the reflection of the moon on the glass of that diamond-shaped window that faced the street. Enough of a breeze had sprung up to set the porch swing moving slightly and, though I couldn't see it behind a curtain of ivy that grew up a concealing trellis, I could hear the small rhythmic creak of it over the water sounds.

It had been an evening to remember Sarah, knowing that the next day would bring closure of a sort, with her as its focus. I wondered who would attend of the people she and three generations of her family had known for the better part of a century—four generations if you counted Alan, and Alan must be counted, of course. I wondered again about his appearance earlier and what he had been hoping for in a peacemaking effort with me. Did he think it would be that easy to pacify me, or was he actually sincere? Fear had to be a basis for at least some of his anger. What could have made him so afraid? With no answers handy, or inclination to hunt for them, I returned to considering Sarah.

Her house stood solidly there beside me, dark and dignified in its Victorian emptiness, still full of her possessions and presence. How long before someone else's spirit would replace hers and whose would it be—Jamie's, as Sarah evidently wanted? It was not difficult to imagine her in the house, perhaps because I had seen her first coming from the porch swing, as if it belonged to her, or because she reminded me strongly of Sarah. Would Jamie be willing to move to Grand Junction and live in the house, or would she let it go to someone else, breaking the chain of family ownership and tradition? Would whatever had Sarah written to Jamie in the letter we would give her the next day make a difference?

Maybe it was the rain, for out of nowhere came memory of walking across the University of Washington campus with Sarah, arm in arm to keep both of us under the same umbrella, on our way to play bridge in the Student Union cafeteria and drink its terrible coffee. How adult we had thought we were. How long ago it had been. How—I would miss her.

Stretch came padding out from his bed to stand beside me at the door of the Winnebago. I bent to pick him up and he didn't struggle to be put down again as usual, but leaned against me and laid his chin on my shoulder.

"What a bonzer boy you are," I told him.

I stood there for a few minutes more, looking out into the silent dark that followed the moon's disappearance behind a cloud. Then I closed the door, took him to spend the rest of the night beside me on the bed, climbed in myself, and we both slept.

The figure in the swing on the porch of Sarah's house watched closely until the woman closed the door and when no lights came on in the Winnebago, assumed that she had returned to her bed. Cautious and silent, it rose and crept the length of the porch to the side opposite the motor home and circled the house to the back door, which stood open a crack to allow access. Shadow within shadows, it slipped through the dark house and quickly up the two flights of stairs to the attic.

A whisper, "She's gone back to bed. Have you found anything?"

"Not yet."

Ribbons of light from a flashlight held between fingers swept across the floor over which papers had been cast from the boxes piled in one end of the four spaces that formed a cross under the peaks of the roof.

"There's nothing here but old bills and financial records."

"They have to be somewhere."

"I know, but we've looked everywhere I can think of."

A sigh of discouragement. "What now?"

"Nothing more tonight."

"And tomorrow?"

"Tomorrow we'll go as planned."

"I'm still not sure that's wise."

"What else?"

Carefully shielding the light, the two figures moved to the stairs and went down them quietly. Walking the length of the hallway, they descended the second stairway and made their way through the silent house to the back door, which the taller of the two locked with a key before they took hands to dart together across the backyard and disappear through the gate into the alley.

It was bright as a new penny the next morning, all the colors washed clean by the rain—green grass and trees, blue sky with a few fluffy white clouds, an assortment of pinks, yellows, reds, and whites in the flowers of the yard. Residual damp was quickly evaporating, but everything looked fresh and more vivid from the gift of water in a dry country.

I threw open the door and all the windows to let in the sweetness of the air and, while it was still cooler than it would be in an hour, stepped out with Stretch to gather a huge armful of Sarah's own flowers, which I took to plunge into water and leave in the coolness of her kitchen until time to take them to the mortuary.

Stretch and I were just finishing breakfast when there was a rap at my door and I answered it to find Detective Soames peering in through the screen.

"Good morning," he said with such a winning smile it made me wonder if I was addressing the same person—or if, like Alan, he had decided I needed skillful handling—as I invited him in and offered him coffee, which he accepted with thanks. I removed my breakfast plate from the table and we sat across from each other at the dinette.

He took a sip or two without comment and looked around the interior of the motor home with interest.

"I've never been inside one of these things," he said. "It looks comfortable but I bet it drives like an Zamboni."

The comparison was original, but I couldn't let him get away with it.

"That might be helpful in Alaska," I told him. "Actually, it's very easy driving, or I wouldn't go all the places in it that I do—as well as back and forth to the far north every so often. It handles well and it's helpful to sit high enough to see over cars on the highway. Like any heavy vehicle it takes a bit farther to stop than a car and because of its length you need to calculate turnoffs ahead of time if you need to change lanes. But the benefit of having your house with you outweighs a lot of other considerations. I love traveling in it."

"You mind if I look around?"

"Be my guest."

I watched from where I sat while he, like others in the past, wandered through the Winnebago, examining its compact storage, neat galley, lavatory and shower facilities, pausing to scrutinize the control board next to the kitchen with its indicators for the levels of black, gray, fresh water and propane tanks, battery charge, and switches for the water heater, pump, and generator.

"What's this for?" he asked, pointing to the Slideout Control.

I joined him to demonstrate the retraction and extension of the stove and sofa section.

"The bed in the rear slides out the same way."

"Wow. How do you keep your refrigerator cold when you're not connected to electricity?" was his next question.

"When I'm driving, I switch it to DC power and the cab engine takes over. Parked without a hookup, it can run on gas."

He took a quick look at the bedroom and the cab, nodding approval. "Pretty slick. They seem to have thought of just about everything. I can see how you could get addicted to going places in one of these. And you travel all by *yourself*?"

How many times have I been confronted with that question? Somehow people, even some RVers, seem to think that a woman—especially a woman my age—can't possibly be capable of motor homing alone. Any woman who has hauled a vacuum cleaner up and down stairs, sorted supplies into a small kitchen, or dragged hoses around a garden can easily understand that there isn't much about the everyday care of a motor home that is more difficult. Like many Alaskans, I've chopped my own wood for winter fires all my life. My father wouldn't let me learn to drive until I knew how to change a tire and prime a carburetor if necessary. I know how to adjust the setting on a generator for different elevations. Several feet of snow seldom impedes my driving ability, but if it does I'm smart enough to wait for the plow. I'd much rather drive the wide, well-paved stretches of the Alaska Highway than the congestion of most American cities, but I'm capable of either.

I told him so.

"What if you have mechanical problems?" Soames asked.

"That," I told him, "is what other people are for—and tow trucks and repair shops. Though I could gap spark plugs, or change my own oil and filters, I don't. I have the rig serviced regularly, including all the systems, but I understand how they work and carry extra fuses, fluids, and belts."

"It's kind of like a boat," he observed.

"Did I mention that my first husband was a commercial fisherman and that I helped run his boat?"

"I give up." He grinned, sliding back onto the dinette bench as I refilled his coffee.

"So what can I do for you, besides be a saleswoman for motor homes?" I asked as I sat down again.

I watched him mentally shift gears and the law enforcement officer reappear.

"Thought I should have some idea just what this—ah—gathering . . . *Gathering!* What *is* that? Why can't you just call it a *funeral*?"

My accommodating mood dissolved in a hot spark of irritation. I liked his alter ego better.

"Because it's *not* a funeral," I told him a little sharply. "Gathering is what Sarah wanted it called. She didn't like the baggage the word funeral suggests to most people."

Chastised, he accepted responsibility for my annoyance. "Okay—okay. I apologize. Makes sense the way you put it, I guess."

"It will be more of a recognition of Sarah's life—a sort of celebration in a way."

"And I understand there'll be wine."

"Yes—another thing she wanted. She always said she didn't want spooky music or preaching and wanted the family wine instead of flowers—though she's going to have to put up with both."

He gave my use of the present tense a half-dubious glance.

"Okay, here's the thing. The lab did find fingerprints on those threats with the faces—three sets that belonged to you, Mrs. Nunamaker, and Don Westover. But there was one partial they couldn't identify. There's about half a thumbprint on one edge of one of them that doesn't match up. I'm thinking that we might be able to get some prints for comparison off the wineglasses at this *gathering* this afternoon. Glass takes good prints and the other people I have on my list as possible suspects will be there, won't they?"

"I'd guess that would depend on who you have on your list," I said, wondering about the word other, in terms of possible suspects. Was I still on his list—was Don?

He nodded and took out his seemingly ever-present notebook. Flipping pages, he found the one he wanted.

"Mrs. Nunamaker's son, Alan, the woman that claims to be her daughter, Jamie Stover, and this old friend, Ed Norris. Those three, but I'll be on the lookout for anyone questionable. Any other you can think of?"

There was not, but I couldn't know who would be coming, could I?

What he wanted was to have two of his people assist at Callahan-Edfast as waitstaff. They would circulate through the assembly, offering wine in glasses and collecting empties, carefully segregating for testing those from the people Soames had designated as suspect.

"As long as they aren't obvious, I have no problem with it. But you'll have to clear it with the director."

After Soames agreed and left with the intention of doing so, I sat thinking how sad it was that the police found it necessary to use Sarah's gathering as an opportunity to collect clues to the identity of her murderer. On the other hand, had it been my death, I knew she would have been relentless in helping to track down the person responsible for such an offense and would expect no less of me.

I hoped that Soames would keep his people strictly in the background. So far there had been no mention by the local press that her death had been anything but natural and I wanted it kept that way. The disclosure of law enforcement in attendance with such a purpose could inspire all kinds of unpleasant rumors. It could also interfere with Soames's hope to find an identity to go with that single partial print.

His plans, however, were not my first priority. I wanted Sarah to have the kind of gathering she had planned, without speculation from the people who had cared about her and would be present to give her a good send-off.

The event as I—and Sarah—had imagined it, however, would not take place precisely as planned.

CHAPTER TWENTY-TWO

THE CALLAHAN-EDFAST MORTUARY WAS AN ATTRACtive building on Patterson Road with a sweeping drive and a waterfall in the entryway.

Mr. Blackburn met me near the front door shortly before three and called an aide to take and arrange the armful of colorful flowers I had brought from Sarah's yard.

We had walked through the facility on my initial visit and agreed that rather than set up a table in the central area, waitstaff would bring wine on trays from the kitchen to serve to those attending, leaving more space for people to mingle casually as Sarah had wanted. There was a chapel that could seat close to two hundred, but with no formal service planned it would be used only for those who would like a place to sit, or to add the flowers some were sure to bring to those already around her closed coffin at the front of the large room.

"You know," Mr. Blackburn asked hesitantly, "she didn't want a service, but someone should say something, don't you think? People will expect it. Would a toast be in order—because of the wine, you know—perhaps by her son? That would provide an informal kind of recognition without the speechmaking she didn't want."

I thought about it for a minute and agreed.

"I'll ask Alan when he gets here."

It wasn't long until people began to arrive and Mr. Blackburn went off to the kitchen to send out the waitstaff with wine in glasses while I greeted the early birds, offering them each one of the cards Sarah had prepared, had printed, and sent to Mr. Blackburn before she died.

Under her smiling picture were a few of her own words of explanation and expectation for the rather unusual gathering she had planned.

> *Because I don't believe that*
> *goodbyes are forever, or that*
> *they should be sad affairs, I*
> *invite you to raise a glass*
> *with me and remember only*
> *happy things today.*
> *No speeches, no tears, no*
> *solemn farewells.*
> *Please know that I've had a*
> *fine life, filled with more*
> *than my share of warm memories*
> *of the things and people that*
> *count the most—friends and*
> *family.*
> *It's been a great adventure.*
>
> *Sarah*

It was so like her that I had to smile, but somewhere inside still lay that hot coal of anger that someone had deprived me of the last pleasure and comfort of her company and sent her off ahead of schedule, against her plans and wishes.

Alan came then, striding across the room to where I stood and smiled down at me a little cautiously. I had not remembered that he was so tall until we stood next to each other.

"Will you give a toast for your mother?" I asked him. "Mr. Blackburn thinks something should be said and it would be appropriate for you to do it, wouldn't it?"

He nodded. "Yes, I can do that, I guess. Do you think . . . ?"

He stopped, his focus shifted, eyes narrowing in dislike as he looked past me toward the door. I swung around to see what had caused such an intense reaction and saw Ed Norris on his way in with what looked like a dozen pink roses.

"Damn," Alan muttered, scowling. "Does *he* have to . . . ?"

"Stop it!" I interrupted him, turning my back on Ed and laying a hand on Alan's arm. "This is your mother's day. Whatever you may think of him, she and Ed were friends. Leave it alone, Alan."

Glancing back I saw that Ed had obviously seen Alan's furious expression, for he was veering away from a confrontation and heading in the direction of the chapel with his flowers.

A little of the tension seemed to leave Alan as Ed disappeared. He was still not happy, but at least he was paying *some* attention.

"All right," he snapped, "but keep him away. He has nothing to do with me."

"I know."

"You know *what*?" he demanded, giving me his full and sudden attention.

"I know that he's not your father, however much he may think he is. Will that do for now?"

"How could you—?"

"Never mind how. We'll discuss it later, if you want. For now, *behave yourself* as your mother would expect."

"You sound just like her." Though it was reluctant, he managed a crooked grin. "I'll thank these people for coming and give her a toast, okay?"

I smiled back.

"Good boy."

Though he was far from a boy.

It took a while for me to work my way around the room and warn Ed to stay away from Alan, for many people began to arrive and the flood continued until the central area was congested and at least a third had spilled out into the sheltered reception area in front of the building.

"Where did they all come from?" Ed asked, looking around the crowded space. "Who are they?"

"They're people who knew and loved Sarah," I told him, amazed he seemed to have no concept of how much a part of the community she and her family had been. "Her father was once *mayor* of Grand Junction. You can't have imagined people didn't know and respect her."

He shook his head, bewildered. "I guess I knew, but I had no idea . . . I put her roses in the chapel and thought they'd stand out, but there're dozens of others."

Men simply focus on one thing at a time. He had imagined what he wanted and nothing more. It was his way, but good for him to have a fresh and more realistic perspective. I left him to new discoveries and went to meet and thank a few more people for their presence as a tribute to my friend.

Mr. Blackburn had provided a string quartet that

included a harp and, in a small room off to one side, was playing classical background music—but none of the *spooky stuff* Sarah had refused to consider. There was no formal reception line, which, along with the wine, encouraged people to form small social groups and talk to each other. They all appeared to at least know who Alan was and sought him out to express their condolences. At one point he brought the current mayor over to meet—and, perhaps impress—me. Several others stopped to introduce themselves, including an attractive blond woman with a pleasant smile.

"I'm Cathy White," she told me and leaned closer to avoid being overheard. "I'm the pathologist who helped do Sarah's post, but I knew her before from a reading group we both belonged to. She was a fine person with a great sense of humor and life. I liked her a lot and was sorry to find that her death wasn't natural, as we had expected it would be. I hope you don't mind that I'm here."

How thoughtful of her to ask.

"Of course not," I told her. "You've done her a great service and I'm very glad you came. I don't need to know the details, but you were completely sure about what you found?"

She nodded. "Yes, and I'm sorry that we were. Of course the first opinion was from the coroner—I assisted. I hope they find out who was responsible soon."

So did I.

Seeing a woman go into the chapel with a bouquet of blue delphinium, I followed her to the door and found, as Ed had indicated, that Sarah's closed coffin was rapidly being covered with an almost dizzying assortment of bright flowers of all kinds and more stood on the floor around it in the vases I had requested. Most had not come from florists, but from people who had brought the best of their gardens, as I had Sarah's. It was lovely and bright and I knew that, no matter what she had said she wanted or didn't want, she would have been pleased. In the center of it all, someone had lit a tall candle that glowed softly in the restrained lighting Mr. Blackburn had wisely chosen.

"Beautiful, isn't it?" a voice spoke beside me and I turned to a heavyset woman I didn't recognize.

She held out a hand. "Beth Gleason—her nurse. I went by twice a day to make sure she was comfortable. You must be Maxine. She talked about you often and was looking forward to your visit."

"If only I had arrived sooner," I said, and thanked her for taking care of Sarah. She moved away to speak to Doris Chapman, who smiled and nodded to me.

There were so many people it was almost impossible to see across the room, but in a momentary space between the mayor and Don Westover, who I hadn't seen until that moment, I glimpsed Tomas hesitating at the door, a slender woman beside him.

Threading my way slowly through the crowd, I finally reached and greeted him. "*Buenas tardes,* Tomas. Thank you for coming."

"My wife, Jovana," he said, proudly presenting her.

With a warm smile, she extended a hand and spoke with only the hint of the accent that gave his words so much character. "Hello, Mrs. McNabb. I'm pleased to meet you. Tomas says you were a good friend to Mrs. Nunamaker."

This was no shy or retiring, stereotypical wife, but a self-assured and lovely woman, who I soon learned was a teacher of Spanish at a local high school. What a handsome older couple they made—he in a dress shirt so

white it almost glowed against his dark skin, so different
from the casual clothes of the man I knew from Sarah's
garden—she in soft, flowing, butter yellow, her dark
hair a heavy curve that fell to just above her shoulders
without a hint of gray. She was as erect in stature as a
Flamenco dancer, and as graceful.

As we spoke, just beyond Jovana's shoulder, I saw
one of the waitstaff go up to Ed and offer him a fresh
glass of wine, which he accepted, draining the last of
the one he held and handing the glass over in exchange.
Rather than take it, the waiter indicated that Ed should
set it on the tray he held in one hand and gave him the
full one with the other. As he turned away, Ed gave him
a quick questioning glance and frowned slightly before
turning back to the conversation in which he was
involved. I wondered if he had recognized the man as
part of the local police department.

The waiter walked straight across the room and into
the kitchen, where I could see Soames waiting among
the crew. With fingers spread to apply pressure inside
of the mouth of the glass, the detective deftly lifted and
slipped it into an evidence bag, which disappeared into
his jacket pocket, all out of Ed's line of sight. Success-
ful, he glanced up to find me watching and—to my utter
astonishment and amusement—winked.

"What was that about?" asked a quiet voice in my ear
and I whirled to find that Alan, standing beside me, had
followed my close attention to the sleight-of-hand
going on in the kitchen. "The waiters stealing the glass-
ware now?"

"I've no idea," I lied.

He shrugged and seemed to forget it in favor of what
he had come to ask.

"Whatever. Shall I do the toast now?"

"Oh yes, I think so."

As he walked away to do his duty, Soames appeared at my elbow.

"That son of hers keeps refilling his glass," he said with a frown. "So far my man hasn't been able to get it away from him. Any ideas?"

I looked over to see that Alan *was* carrying a glass half full of wine.

"Maybe," I told Soames. "Let me give it a try."

From the tray of a passing waiter, I took a fresh glass of wine, followed Alan across the room and stopped next to him while he waited for someone to bring him a chair to stand on.

"Here," I told him, holding out the fresh glass. "You can't raise a toast with a half-empty glass." As he took it, I reached out and lifted his old glass out of his other hand by its stem, turned and walked away toward the kitchen, where Soames emptied it and repeated his sleight-of-hand.

"Well done," he grinned. "You ever need a job, come see me."

I left him to his evidence collecting and went back to hear what Alan would have to say.

High enough to be seen by everyone but a few who had stepped outside, he smiled and nodded to the crowd now quiet and listening.

"I'd like to thank you all for coming today to honor with your presence a grand lady who will be greatly missed," he said. "As you know, she didn't want a fuss or a funeral, so she planned this friendly gathering herself, as she wanted it—with no speeches. So instead of a eulogy I offer a toast that was Sarah's favorite." He raised his glass and said simply, *"Love and friendship, life and laughter,"* then, as I remembered Sarah adding whenever she used it, "lots *of laughter.*"

Everyone ceremonially sipped the wine amid a mild ripple of appreciative and understanding amusement.

Nicely done, Alan, I thought.

But once again he had avoided saying *mother*.

It was then, as the laughter died away and he had stepped down from the chair he had used as a platform, that I turned and caught my breath at the sight of Jamie Stover coming through the door. In her hands were several slender stems of yellow freesia and fern caught together with a white ribbon.

Moving beside her was the tall, dark man I had seen in the Family History Library in Salt Lake.

A person in the crowd stepped in front of me before I could be sure, but neither of them noticed me as they disappeared into the chapel. I was about to follow when the crowd closed in completely between us and Soames spoke suddenly beside me.

"Someone you recognized, Mrs. McNabb?"

"Maxie," I corrected him absently, still looking in the direction of the chapel. "*Mrs. McNabb* makes me think of my mother-in-law and I never liked her very much."

"Who did you see?"

Persistent, wasn't he? I swung around to give him a frown.

"I'm not sure. It might have been someone I saw in Salt Lake."

"Who?"

Not being sure, I refused to be drawn.

"You got the prints you wanted?"

"Yes. Thanks to your quick thinking with her son's, I have all but the Stover woman's. Is she here? Have you seen her?"

I bit my lip before nodding. "She just came in and went into the chapel with some flowers."

Taking my elbow, he pulled me after him through the

crowd, which parted like the Red Sea at his "'Scuse me, please—pardon me—'scuse me."

We arrived at the doorway to the chapel, moved around several people conversing in the opening, and stopped in the long aisle that ran down the center of the room. From where we stood I could plainly see that the spray of yellow freesia Jamie had carried now lay among the flowers that covered Sarah's coffin.

But neither she, nor the dark-haired man who had accompanied her, were anywhere in the room.

"Well—*hell*," Soames said in disgust. "You're sure you saw her come in here?"

I was, but didn't bother to inform him that someone had accompanied her.

Like wraiths, the two had slipped in and, somehow, out again. Probably they had gone through some back door, avoiding all contact with anyone they knew, or didn't want to acknowledge—myself included.

CHAPTER TWENTY-THREE

BY FIVE O'CLOCK THE CALLAHAN-EDFAST MORTUARY was empty of guests. Even Soames and his pair of pseudo-waiters had gone from the kitchen.

"I'll let you know what I find," he had assured me.

Except for the staff engaged in cleanup, the only people left were Don Westover, Ed, myself, and, reluctantly, Alan, who had agreed—when I all but shook my finger under his nose in admonition—to once again *behave*. He stood as far as possible from Ed, however, and glowered at him as Westover handed over the envelopes he had, as promised, brought and removed from an inside pocket of his jacket.

"Sarah left letters for several people," he told them. "These were for you. Mrs. McNabb and I thought this would be an appropriate time for you to have them."

Ed gave me a nod as thank you, took the envelope he was handed and tucked it away in his own inside jacket pocket. "I'll read it later," he announced and walked off toward the front door.

Alan, as I suppose I should have expected, once again couldn't leave it without contention. His amenable disposition of the day before was now evidently a thing of the past.

"How long have you had this?" he demanded. "Why wasn't I told?"

"Your mother suggested it should be given to you today," Westover said calmly, avoiding his first question. "We could have waited until time to notify her beneficiaries and transfer the allocations of the inheritance as designated in her will. But we decided not to do that—to give these to you now."

"*We?*"

"Mrs. McNabb is the executor—with my assistance."

"So the two of you get to make all the decisions?"

Alan's voice was loud enough to cause Mr. Blackburn to appear in the door to his office and give me a questioning look.

I shook my head at him and he disappeared, relieved, I'm sure, not to be involved.

"Yes, Alan. Legally, we do," Westover answered.

Without another word, Sarah's son whirled and strode angrily out the front door, ignoring Ed, who had paused there, and swearing under his breath for as long as we could hear him, which wasn't long.

I was grateful that we had waited until *after* Sarah's gathering to present the letters. We would not, however, have any satisfaction in finding out what Sarah had written in either one of them.

"And this one?" Don Westover asked, turning to me and holding out the third letter with Jamie's name on it.

"Give it to me," I suggested. "She came to me once and, who knows, might again. She doesn't know you."

"True." He handed it over and I tucked it into my bag. Another chore to add to my list, I set my bag on a chair near the chapel door and went to Mr. Blackburn's office to thank him.

"It was lovely," I told him. "Just what Sarah had in mind. You and your people have done a great job."

"You're welcome and I'm glad it went well," he said. "Are you sure you want all the flowers sent to St. Mary's Hospital?" he asked.

I assured him I was, but went back to the chapel, where I sat down for a minute to look again and feel pleased with the colorful display covering Sarah's coffin. No matter that she had said she didn't want them. I knew that she had been cringing at the thought of wreaths and baskets from florists, not this bright remembrance from gardens all over Grand Junction.

You would have loved this, Sarah, I told her and remembered her smile.

Before I left I took one sprig of the honeysuckle I had put with the flowers I brought from her yard. It would press nicely in a favorite book and be an unexpected reminder whenever I ran across it that, sweet as honey, it had been a favorite of hers.

Retrieving my bag, I slipped the honeysuckle inside and headed for the front door, where I was not surprised to find Ed waiting.

"Ready for dinner?" he asked, as if we had made plans ahead of time.

Well, why not? I had a hunch he didn't want to go back to an empty hotel room by himself and wanted company, which was fine with me as I had planned nothing beyond the gathering.

"Sure, Ed. Thanks."

"Gladstone's?"

"Why not?" It was a pleasant place with good food and it was nice to have someone else make a decision for a change.

"I need to stop and give Stretch a break first, so I'll take my car back there and you can pick me up, if you don't mind."

Stretch, as usual, was happy to see me and, I think, even happier to be allowed out. I do not usually leave him to spend as much time alone as he had in the last few days. I made sure he had plenty of water and a rawhide bone to chew on after our quick trip to the backyard, where I waited with a plastic bag to collect his deposit from the grass and trash it in a can by the alley.

Ed waited patiently and we were soon ensconced once again in a booth at Gladstone's, waiter hovering to take our drink order and provide us with menus.

"It was a fine gathering," I said, when I had settled comfortably and had my first sip of Jameson.

"It was," Ed agreed, then shook his head, a bemused expression on his face. "I just can't get over how many people came. There must have been well over a hundred."

"A hundred and sixty-seven all together, according to Mr. Blackburn and counting Soa—" I stopped, realizing I had been about to reveal that we had had the police among us.

"Counting who?"

"Ah—counting some people from the hospital and the nurse who came to the house twice a day," I managed—I hoped—to cover my almost-slip.

"Alan certainly made it plain he was anything but pleased to have *me* there."

"Well, let's give that a rest, shall we? I'm just glad everything went as Sarah wanted. Let's talk about something besides Alan. I'm tired of his childishness. When are you going home?"

"Trying again to get rid of me?" he grinned. "I'll

have to make a reservation for tomorrow—maybe the next day. We'll see how it goes—how booked they are, for instance. I haven't seen you since you came back from Salt Lake. How was your trip?"

"Oh, it was fine—an interesting drive."

I was thinking of my lunch in the café in Helper, but *interesting* would also have had to include the threat I had found in Green River, though I didn't mention it.

"Maxie," Ed said, after moment of thoughtful silence. "You didn't go just to get away from here for a day or two, did you? It had something to do with Sarah's death, didn't it?"

I guess I shouldn't have been surprised at his suspicions. The trip had been abrupt and unplanned under the circumstances and Ed was no mental slouch.

"What makes you think so?" I asked, stalling for time and not knowing what to tell him.

"I just do," he said flatly "Tell me I'm wrong."

"What did Sarah tell you in the letter she left?" I asked.

"That's really my business, isn't it? But I haven't read it yet."

This statement startled me into silence. When he had leaned forward to help me with the seat belt in his car, I had seen the ragged edge of that white envelope in the inside pocket where he had placed it after saying he would read it later. If he hadn't torn it open hastily, it wouldn't have been tattered. Was there any other reason to rip it open than to read while he waited for me outside the mortuary door? I couldn't think of one.

"Oh," I said and picked up my glass for a swallow of ice water, which went down wrong and resulted in a fit of coughing. Jameson expected is great stuff. Mistaken for a gulp of ice water it can take your breath, as it took mine. I could feel its burn in the top of my nose between my watering eyes.

"Sorry," I said, when I could speak to apologize and had made a quick trip to the restroom to splash water on my face and blow my nose. "That certainly cleared out the cobwebs."

As a distraction, however, it worked well enough in avoiding the answers to unwelcome questions.

Salt Lake as a topic was not resumed. As we ordered and ate dinner, Ed did not talk about Sarah, which surprised me, for I had expected him to once again expound upon his feelings for her and how much he missed her. Instead, he asked innocuous questions about Alaska and my trips back and forth in the motor home, told me about his work and travels, and was a generally pleasant dinner companion.

Tired from the day's activities and concerns, I would have turned down the offer of another walk in the park, but Ed didn't offer, seeming a little distracted and anxious to go home himself. We said little during the drive to Chipeta Avenue.

"I'll let you know when I'm leaving," he told me, when he had swung into a space at the curb and left the engine running. "Where are you going from here—and when?"

"I don't know *when*. It will depend on what Don Westover still has for me to do in taking care of Sarah's estate—there've been a few complications. But when that's finished I'm going to New Mexico for a warm and quiet winter—Taos, perhaps."

"Good plan. Have a good rest tonight—you've earned it. It was a great day for Sarah. Talk to you soon."

I got out and watched him pull quickly away, bands of light and shadow from the streetlights and trees alternately playing across the roof of his rental car. Walking slowly to the Winnebago, I could hear Stretch barking an *It's about time*.

* * *

Having tucked the sprig of honeysuckle from Sarah's bouquet between the pages of my journal and changed from my dress clothes into comfortable casuals, I let Stretch out and went to sit in the porch swing while he poked about in another circuit of the yard. The last of that wonderful blue of twilight that makes artificial light seem so bright in contrast was gradually growing deeper and I could see that once again the across-the-street neighbor was watching television. This time his wife had joined him in a nearby chair and, between glances at the television, was knitting something green that covered most of her lap and may have been an afghan.

It reminded me that I hadn't even thought of getting out my yarn and needles since I left Alaska. I like to knit. Because my mother had rheumatoid arthritis, she had been forced to give up many things, including any kind of needlework. Assuming it was probably an inherited trait; I checked on it years ago and found, thankfully, that it did not seem listed on my menu of possible future aches and pains. By that time, however, knitting had become such an integral part of my life that I've kept it up anyway. It keeps my hands busy and supple and, according to a friend's humor, "It's a bit like what they say about sex—a *use it or lose it* sort of thing, I think. But knitting is less likely to get you into trouble."

Part of going to New Mexico was the idea of a visit to a group of weavers and dyers in Taos from whom I had ordered yarn in wonderful textures and colors from time to time and looked forward to meeting. With that in mind, I thought perhaps I would get back to my knitting in the next day or two.

Stretch suddenly barked, but only once, so it was someone he recognized, and hearing footsteps on the front walk, I stood up to see who had attracted his attention.

Doris Chapman was coming up the shallow steps with Stretch right behind her. She was carrying two tall glasses, one of which she handed to me.

"Thought you might welcome some iced mint tea," she said smiling. "I heard the porch swing, so I knew you were out here. Someone really should oil that thing."

"Sit down," I invited, scooting over to make room. "I'll ask Tomas the next time he shows up if he can do something. It was complaining a little in the breeze last night."

"Really? There wasn't much last night. It usually takes a pretty big wind to move this heavy old thing enough to make it whine."

She went on to what she *really* wanted to talk about—the gathering.

"Wasn't it a lovely afternoon for Sarah? And weren't the flowers wonderful? I wasn't at all sure about not having a regular funeral, you know. But it turned out just fine, didn't it?"

It had, indeed, and I could understand her need to share her observations with someone. Many women have a predisposition to make things more real for themselves by talking them over in detail. Living alone can be frustrating at times in that regard.

It made me remember Ed that afternoon and how singularly focused he had been on what he had assumed, or wanted things to be concerning Sarah. Men do tend to focus on one idea or thing at a time. Women, on the other hand, seem more capable of dealing with several at once, like jugglers. Multitasking comes easily to most of us, at home or at work—balancing chores, professions, and family.

"I hardly recognized Tomas all dressed up like that," Doris said. "And wasn't his wife a surprise. I'd never met her."

Thinking back to my own pleasure at meeting Jovana Navarro, I agreed, amused that Doris seemed to have been every bit as watchful of who came and went as she was at home.

"And who was that couple that came in late?" she asked. "The woman had some yellow freesia? I think I've seen him before somewhere."

It was a comment that caught my complete and serious attention.

"Where?"

I held my breath while she leaned back in the swing, closed her eyes, and thought aloud.

"I can't quite remember, but it'll come to me. It was back before Sarah died. Or was it? Maybe right after you got here. I don't know, maybe I just imagined I'd seen him. No, I've definitely seen him, and more than once.

"I *know!*" she said, sitting up so suddenly it set us both rocking hard enough to slosh some of the tea over the rim of my glass.

"It was that first day you were here—you know, the day I gave you the tamale pie—the day Sarah died," she remembered, hesitating sadly. "There was a man went in the back door of her house that morning while you were gone to the hospital. Do you remember? I asked you if he had come with you, but you said he hadn't."

I thought back and did remember. "You said he had dark hair and wore sunglasses."

"That's right, he did. Well, I *think* it was the same man. If it was, I may have seen him the day—or maybe two—before that. Didn't think of it until just now. He came in the same way, through the back."

"A day or *two*? Which, Doris?"

Considering when Sarah had been found unconscious, it could be extremely significant.

She frowned and made an attempt, but shook her head. "I'm sorry. I can't recall for sure. Is it important?"

I had no way of telling, but wished I knew if it *had* been the man I thought I had recognized with Jamie at Callahan-Edfast that afternoon—the man I had seen in Salt Lake who resembled Ed Norris. It raised all kinds of possibilities, none of which I cared to discuss with Doris.

"Not so you should worry about it. There were so many people this afternoon I'm not sure who they were." Then hoping to distract her, if possible, "What did you think of Alan's toast for Sarah?"

"Oh, he did very well, didn't he? And the music was just lovely."

Doris settled back into a replay of other details, including a critique of the wine's quality, allowing me to nod and put a word or two in here and there, while considering the ramifications of what I might have just learned.

In ten minutes we had finished our tea and she had gone happily home, having relived the afternoon to her satisfaction.

I took Stretch and went back to the Winnebago, still attempting to sort out just how this man could fit into the rest of what I knew, or thought I knew, about everyone else involved.

Where was Jamie and, by extension, this unknown man who just might actually be her twin? I remembered the letter for her that Westover had given me and started to get it out of my bag when another thought struck me.

If the man Doris had seen had gone into Sarah's house while she was alive, she must have known who he was. If he was her son, why hadn't she left him a letter similar to those she had left for Ed, Alan, Jamie, and me? Or had she? Could I have missed one in that secret space in the bookcase where I found the others?

It was possible and I decided it shouldn't wait. I wanted to know—right then.

Taking the key and a flashlight, I went in the front door and directly across the room to the bookcase, where I pressed the release to the hidden space between the shelves. Far back in one corner I felt paper and drew out exactly what I had hoped to find—a fourth envelope. Written across the front of it in Sarah's hand was his name, *James G. Curtis*.

I stood staring down at it for a long minute, wishing I hadn't missed finding it sooner. Recognition and understanding began to settle in. Sarah had evidently, before her death, been able to meet her natural son. How did I know for sure? I knew because she had given both children clues to their natural identification in the names she had been careful they would continue to keep. Jamie had S as a middle initial, which she had been told stood for *Sarah*. I knew, without a doubt that the G as the middle initial of this man's name stood for Sarah's maiden name Grayson. Jamie *Sarah* Stover. James *Grayson* Curtis.

If I had only had the name *Curtis* during my search in Salt Lake I might have found him.

Closing the secret space in the bookcase again, I took the envelope back to the motor home, laid it on the table, and reached for my bag to set Jamie's letter beside it.

Not finding it immediately by feel, I opened it wide under the overhead light to see where it was. Nothing. In frustration, I dumped the contents of the bag onto the table and pawed through them.

*   *   *

The letter for Jamie was missing. It had vanished as completely as if Don Westover had never handed it to me at the mortuary hours earlier.

And who had been there when I choked and left my bag at the table in Gladstone's to go to the restroom?

My cell phone lay in the middle of the contents of my bag that now cluttered the table. I snatched it up and dialed the number of the Holiday Inn. When the desk answered, I asked to be connected to Ed's room and waited, seething with anger, as it rang—and rang— and rang.

Would I like to leave a message?

"No, thank you."

He had said he was going back to the hotel. Where the hell was he?

But, as I had listened to the empty ringing, I had realized that Ed was not the only possible thief.

I had left my bag on a chair in the entry to the mortuary when I went to thank Mr. Blackburn, then when I went into the chapel to see Sarah's flowers just before leaving.

Both Ed and Don Westover had been there, along with several staff members busily clearing up after the gathering.

As Ed and I left to go to dinner, I had also seen that Alan's pickup was still in the lot. Could he have gone back inside while I was in the chapel?

I did not understand *why* any of them would have taken the envelope from my bag, but, obviously, some-one had.

All of them had known I had it and *where* I had put it.

CHAPTER TWENTY-FOUR

I SLEPT BADLY THAT NIGHT, WAKING SEVERAL TIMES and getting up twice. The whole confusion of what I knew— or thought I knew—was a jumble in my mind, with many questions and few answers. Worries always seem worse in the middle of the night. Solutions are harder to come by when you feel weighed down with problems that grow huge in the dark.

Finally, I gave up trying for reason and hunted up something to read, but was unable to concentrate and, tossing the book aside, went back to bed for an hour or two.

Tired to bed and tired to rise, when the sun came up I heard the birds start their cheerful chorus of welcome to another day from where I sat at the dinette, transfusing myself with a first cup of strong coffee.

Somehow it seemed that the gathering for Sarah the day before had been some kind of line that I had crossed and now everything felt different and more confusing. I felt drained by untrustworthy people—wanted new ones and new places—wanted to unhook my rig and be gone to—somewhere else. The motor home walls seemed to close in around me and I felt unpleasantly crowded in space that I usually found warmly enclosing and comfortable.

Getting up, I took my coffee to the door where I could look out into the yard and feel fresh air on my face. It helped, but there was an odd disagreeable awareness of Sarah's Victorian house, dark and silent, that seemed for the first time to loom ominously above me.

I thought about the letter to James G. Curtis that I had retrieved from the bookcase hidey-hole the night before and put away for safekeeping in the concealed space with my shotgun. Something would have to be done with it—*and* to get back the one for Jamie from whoever had taken it if I could. The idea depressed me. Why couldn't people just tell the truth, keep their hands off things that didn't belong to them, and let all work out fairly, the way it was supposed to?

It made me annoyed with everyone involved. Once again, the desire to be somewhere else swept over me in a wave of dissatisfaction. I couldn't give in to it. I still had responsibilities. But I could go somewhere else for the time being—get into the car I had rented and drive away for a few hours until I could find myself a more positive mood.

"Come on, buddy. How'd you like to go for a nice long walk?" I asked Stretch. Having finished his light breakfast, he came wagging his anticipation at the word *walk*.

It was enough to decide me.

A good wash made me feel better still and I dressed in jeans, a light blouse, and my walking shoes, before making a substantial bacon and egg breakfast of my own. Leaving the dishes soaking in the galley sink to clean up later, I was out the door by eight, headed for the Monument, alone this time.

* * *

The most beautiful times to visit the Colorado National Monument are early morning or late afternoon, when the angle of the rising or setting sun allows it to draw the richest of hues from the red and gold of the stone and blue-purple of the shadows. Even the dusty gray-green of the sage and yellow-green of the juniper seem deeper.

It was still cool enough to leave the car windows open and traffic was picking up with people heading to work as I drove through downtown Grand Junction and on toward the east entrance to the Monument. By the time I reached the kiosk the road was empty and the attendant greeted me with enthusiasm, warmly pleased to see someone so early.

"Please be sure to keep your dog on a leash," she cautioned me, and I thought of the encounter with the rattlesnake the day Ed and I had visited.

Assuring her I would, I told her I wanted to hike the Serpents Trail and asked what was the best way to go about it, considering that I would have to leave my car either above or below it.

"You can leave your car below and hike both directions," she told me. "But there is no transportation between the top and bottom of the trail. Most people who hike one way or the other have someone drop them off and pick them up when they finish."

"Drat," I said, feeling foiled and a bit foolish for not thinking of that earlier. "Well, I guess I'd better give it up, then, and just go for a walk somewhere else, but I was really hoping for that particular hike."

She nodded sympathetically and glanced at a truck that had just pulled up behind me, waiting to go through.

"Wait," she said with a conspiratorial smile. "Here's my replacement—late as usual, and I have to drive up to the visitor center before leaving. We don't usually do this, but since I'm off duty now, if you like, you can park in the lot at the bottom of the trail and I'll give you a lift to the top on my way up."

We did exactly that. In the small parking lot at the bottom of the Serpents Trail near the Devil's Kitchen picnic area, I parked. Collecting Stretch *and* his leash, my daypack with water, snacks, and small first-aid kit, I clapped my wide-brimmed hat on my head and climbed into the bright yellow Jeep Wrangler in which she was waiting for me.

Sometimes people renew your faith and are unexpectedly generous. I thanked her and we went winding up and up the curves of the twisted road, through a short tunnel, and she dropped us off in the small parking lot at the top of the Serpents Trail. When she had gone, with a wave and a smile, I realized I had neglected to ask her name.

Putting Stretch on his leash, I walked across the lot to the northernmost edge and stood for a minute or two looking out across the Grand Valley far below to the wall of the Book Cliffs. They swung away to the west, much in shadow now with the morning sun mostly behind them and just gilding the edges. On either side of the trailhead rose buttes of red and gray sandstone, not towering, as some places in the Monument, but wide apart and tall enough to make a sort of gateway for the start of this hike. Below my feet a narrow canyon fell away steeply. It was a long way down, but far out on the flat below I could see the ribbon of road that I had traveled to reach the Monument entrance rolling away toward Grand Junction in the distance.

The sound of the Jeep had died quickly away as it vanished over the hill above us and it was very still. As I listened, I could hear the descending notes of a canyon wren's *tee-tee-tec*. When it stopped, there was a silence, then a meadowlark's distinctive call came rising from somewhere out of sight in a sweet gift of music. There was not enough of a breeze to move the nearby sagebrush, but enough so that the soft sun-warmed scent of it drifted pungently into my nose. My spirits lifted in being outdoors, alone and with a new adventure ahead.

In Alaska, I am so used to having the incredible vistas of Kachemak Bay and the Kenai Mountains that frame it spread out in front of me that for days at a time I almost forget to notice them. But when I leave Homer I am often made aware of its lack, which makes me notice and appreciate the other kinds of natural wonders I find in my travels. For the last few days so many people and details had taken my attention that I had forgotten how much I, consciously or subconsciously, need the restoration of time spent in the outdoors. This hike was exactly what would recharge my personal batteries.

As I stood there, I suddenly noticed a sign that indicated dogs were not permitted on this trail and for a minute my disappointment rose. But the park ranger had brought me here—with my dog—and had said nothing about this prohibition—only to be sure to keep him on a leash. Adding to that the fact that the only way back to my car was to go down to it, I decided to ignore the sign and proceed with my hike. Still, I felt a slight bit of guilt as we started off and hoped that no one would admonish me for this mental justification of rule bending.

The Serpents Trail was once a part of an original twenty-three-mile main road into the high country of the Colorado Plateau from the valley. Members of the Civilian Conservation Corps, or CCC, with shovels, picks, and sledgehammers, dynamite and dump trucks, built the road in the 1930s. In some places the roadbed had to be built up in order to make the hairpin turns that were required, so rock fill was laid and retaining walls built to hold it. When it was used as a road it was sixteen feet wide and had fifty-two hairpin turns.

The lower part, which now formed the trail that I was about to hike, still zigzagged back and forth in turns that were mostly sharper than curving switchbacks on a regular road. They formed acute Zs over the surface of a giant outcrop of solid sandstone that lay at an angle from the top of the trail to the parking lot at the bottom, about a mile away. The open spaces between the Zs were scattered with sagebrush, and a variety of grasses and flowering plants, many of which, in September, were long past blossoming and were ripening dry seed. The juniper, however, was heavy with berries that were beginning to turn a reddish brown and the jays were busy collecting them. A popular short hike, the trail's bed, a combination of bare rock and sandstone fill, had worn to grit and powder from the passing of many feet over the years and my shoes were soon covered with reddish dust.

The trail started with a curve to the right and we headed down its wandering course, taking our time to enjoy the walk and the view. Stretch, of course, was much more interested in everything off the trail than on it and when he heard the rustling of some small animal in the brush it was a hard sell to convince him to come along and ignore it.

At the first corner, we came close to the edge of the huge sandstone outcrop and I was startled to find that it fell away in a cliff that I decided must be close to a hundred feet from where I stood to a talus slope at the bottom. Picking up a smallish stone, I dropped it over the edge and counted, "One-hippopotamus—two-hippopotamus—three . . ." and I heard it strike a rock below. Well over a hundred feet. The talus was a jumble of jagged rocks, large and small, that had fallen away from the cliff face.

It was a beautiful lookout point, but would have been a nasty and probably lethal place to take a fall.

Taking a careful step back from the edge, I looked across into the canyon to see that the new road we had traveled not long before looped back and forth on its way up, resembling nothing so much as the coils of a giant snake writhing gradually to my level where it disappeared into the tunnel. High above that tunnel was a low rock retaining wall behind which the unseen road ran along the top, and I was startled to realize that it was the same wall I had looked over from the car window in panic the day Ed and I had almost been forced over it.

Turning back to continue the hike, as I had the day with Ed, I couldn't resist crushing one of the dusty-blue berries of a juniper that grew beside the trail, its slow-growing trunk twisted into gnarls. The scent clung to my fingers long after I finally completed my walk that day.

We had rounded several more corners and the trail had taken us away from the edge of the cliff, when a flash of scarlet caught my attention and I investigated to find a favorite Indian paintbrush blooming between two large chunks of sandstone a few feet from the track. Paintbrush will grow almost anywhere, from desert sagebrush country to high in the mountains, as long as its feet are dry. It comes in a variety of reds, oranges, even yellows. I love it for its color and tenacity.

One of the rocks by the paintbrush was flat, so I sat down on it for a rest and some water, knowing that, as it was growing warmer, Stretch, too, would be ready for a drink. Pouring some in the plastic bowl I carry for him when we go on long walks, I drank from the bottle, recapped it, and put it back in my daypack. While I waited for him to finish his, I took off my wide-brimmed hat, closed my eyes, and raised my face to the sun. How fine it was to be off on my own.

As it was a weekday, I had expected the trail to have few hikers, especially this early in the day, and had seen none at all, for which I was grateful. Something went skittering in the rocks a little ways away from us, the leash pulled taut in my hand, and I opened my eyes without moving to see what Stretch was up to. A mottled rock squirrel ran out onto the trail, took one look at the dachshund quivering in eagerness at the end of its tether, and dashed frantically for cover. It vanished so quickly Stretch barely had time for a single yip before it was gone. I reined him in and went back to my half-nap.

I was considering that it was about time to go on when I heard footsteps and a voice on the trail above me and a man of about my age with a camera and a cell phone came into view around the last corner I had turned. Unbelievably he was talking into the phone as he walked.

"No, I haven't seen any ravens," he said. "But there's an eagle over the canyon. Yes, a golden eagle, I think. The trail goes away from the edge and around a large raised part of the rock. I'll call you back when I come to the next part—at the edge—the one where the wall is, okay? Bye."

I have begun to believe that the world is infested with cell phones. This man's use of one on a hiking trail was bizarre. He must have seen the incredulous and disapproving look on my face as he approached, for he stopped with a grin.

"I can see," he said, "that some kind of explanation is in order."

Taking off his sunglasses, he dropped the phone into a pocket and sat down on the rock on the other side of the paintbrush. "Nice," he said, and took a picture of it with his digital camera.

Stretch, who had given up on the squirrel with the approach of more interesting company, came trotting back to be admired.

"Hey, there," the man said, reaching to give him a pat. I waited, dubiously, already resenting the interruption.

"I don't usually make phone calls when I'm hiking—honest. But you see I have this sister," he said. "She's been to the Monument, but has never been able to hike the Serpents Trail. My wife's parents live in Grand Junction, so we visit fairly often. This time I offered to hike the trail, take lots of pictures, and call her on the cell phone in the process, so she can follow me on a map and ask questions."

I had to chuckle, forced to alter my perception of his use of the phone in this unusual location. What a concept. I had brought my own along in the daypack, but only for emergencies.

"I exonerate you," I told him. "It's probably a first in the annals of cell phone history—a kind of virtual hike."

"Hadn't thought of that," he said standing up again. "My wife's hiking up from below to meet me, so I gotta go. Have a good one."

You just never know, do you? But it alerted me to expect other people on the trail.

Stretch and I went more slowly down behind him and he was soon out of sight.

We reached another outside point of a Z, where the trail came back to the edge of the cliff again and, as the man with the phone had told his sister, it did have a low retaining wall between it and the sheer drop into the canyon. I sat on it for a minute in order to look down without feeling the dizzying pull heights tend to inspire. As I sat there, looking out into the canyon, a small side-blotched lizard darted out from under one rock onto the top of the wall near me, but too high for Stretch to see. Realizing it had company it stopped, watching me, and lay so still it seemed unreal. It was gray-brown with small spots or blotches that covered its back and sides, giving it its name. Part of its long tail was missing, as if it had had a narrow escape from some predator— another larger lizard, perhaps. I moved one finger and it darted away and was gone, as fast at it had appeared.

As I stood up from my place on the wall I heard the click of small stones falling on rocks somewhere on the slope above me and looked back up, expecting to see someone coming down, but saw no one. Another squirrel, I imagined, or a rabbit, maybe. Something large enough to have sent a small cascade of pebbles rattling in any case. For some reason it gave me an uneasy sense that someone was following and watching me. Then I noticed that three hawks were cruising overhead in slow graceful curves as they rode the thermals of rising air, on the lookout for lunch below. I was obviously not under consideration, but I thought they might have spotted Stretch, who isn't that much larger than a rabbit, and kept him a little closer.

We hiked on along the lower side of the Z, where I soon found that this time it went farther away from the dangerous drop at the edge of the cliff to swing out around a low sandstone butte. The stone, higher than my head by several feet, was a kind of boat shape, longer than it was wide. When the trail turned back and headed once again for the cliff's drop, I could see that its length was lined with huge stones too tall to see over to the upper parts of the trail.

Once again I heard a scrambling somewhere uphill, closer now as if something larger than a squirrel were making its way over the field of large rocks and boulders that ended beside the trail where I walked. I stopped and listened, but the sound, once again, had stopped.

We walked on and in a few minutes reached another sharp turn in the Z. This time it had no retaining wall and the outside edge of the trail went right out to where the cliff fell away into the canyon. A little nervous of the height and long drop to the talus below, I was about to make the turn without stopping to look down and take the lower section of trail safely away from the edge.

But someone not far behind me spoke my name.

CHAPTER TWENTY-FIVE

HEARING YOUR NAME WHERE YOU LEAST EXPECT IT
and think you are alone is startling. To whirl toward the
sound and find that someone you know, but certainly
didn't anticipate, creates a combination of relief and
uncertainty. There is relief, because it *is* someone you
know—but how and why they came upon you without
your knowledge creates uncertainty.

Mixed with this, for me, were identifiable amounts
of resentment for the interruption, confusion about the
reason behind such a sudden appearance, and a growing suspicion that I had been followed down the Serpents Trail and that Ed had carefully picked this spot
to confront me for some definite reason. He had evidently cut across over the rocks I had walked around
and hidden until I went past, then stepped out of a
space between two large rocks that I could now identify from where I stood. Otherwise, I would have heard
him coming behind me on the rough surface of the
trail.

First things first.

"How did you know I was here?" I asked.

"I followed you. I watched your place all night, so you couldn't slip away from me again, and I've been following since you left this morning."

Slip away again? What was he talking about? But I now knew why he hadn't answered his phone the night before.

"Whatever for?"

"Because it's a perfect place for you to explain to me why you and Westover are conspiring to cut Alan out of Sarah's will—and why you keep insisting that he is not my son, when you know he is."

This pronouncement stunned me, almost to silence.

"You aren't serious."

"I am deadly serious and ready to expose your conniving, whatever that takes."

Ed stepped closer, almost hissing at me, and I could see he was more than just angry. There was a fury about him that suggested a man as close to his emotional edge as I was close to a vertical one.

I took a step backward and glanced back to see how much space there was between the cliff and my feet.

"This is no place to discuss anything. Let's go down to my car, where we can sit down and talk it over rationally."

He took another step toward me—clearly uninterested in that suggestion.

"Not a chance. You're going to tell me now how you've got it all fixed up—so I can put a stop to it. You can't get away with it. I have evidence, you know."

The rocks on the uphill side formed a complete barrier. Over the downhill side of the trail was a rubble of fallen stones that made it an impossible escape route.

"What evidence?"

But I knew what it was before he reached into a

pocket to retrieve the letter he had stolen from my bag.

"This, for starts," he shook it at me. "What are you paying this *Jamie* for her cooperation? And how did you fake Sarah's writing? She was supposed to be your *friend*, but you've always hated her, haven't you? It's because I loved *her*—not *you*, isn't it? That's the basis for all of this. Admit it."

I realized that there had always been something obsessive about Ed's singular focus on Sarah. Maybe she had known it, too. If so, it was probably why she had never told him the truth about the twins; her real children—and his. She had been protecting them. Probably his obsession had ruined his marriage—set his wife running from him.

"You stole that from my bag. It doesn't belong to you."

"It does now. It's proof." He moved another step toward me.

I cautiously took one away from him and closer to the edge of the cliff that was making me extremely nervous. Stretch was staying very close, all but huddled, tail between his legs. He's courageous, but not stupidly so. This was more than he could handle and he knew it, but I could hear his low growl just the same.

As I stepped back, Ed suddenly lunged forward, grabbing my arm, wrenched me around to face the drop-off at the cliff's edge.

"Tell me!" he demanded through clenched teeth. "Tell me, or I'll make sure you never tell anyone anything again."

I could feel an unyielding pressure and tension as he used his furious strength to force me toward a sickening fall.

"All right," I said, trying not to struggle and accidentally pull us both over. "Whatever you want. Just let me go."

It would be better to try for another chance by telling him lies than to insist on what I saw waiting for me in the debris of the talus and the curve of the new road far below.

"Not until you tell me."

Then, as I was frantically trying to think of what to say, his grip on my arm and shoulder suddenly eased slightly and his snarl of words turned to a howl of pain.

I looked down and back to see that Stretch had sunk his teeth deep into Ed's leg just above the ankle.

We all three struggled on the edge of that precipice, as Ed danced and tried to kick Stretch loose without letting go of me. We almost went over. I was looking straight down in panic and clutching at air when, unexpectedly, someone was yelling and I was yanked back from the edge as Ed's grip fell away.

A scuffle was going on behind me and I whirled to find the man I had seen with Jamie the day before forcing Ed to his knees and holding him there, Stretch still determined to remain attached to his ankle.

Behind them, Jamie watched, ready to help if necessary. When she could see her assistance wasn't needed, she came quickly around the two men to me.

"Are you okay?" she asked anxiously.

I assured her I was—or thought I would be—and went to make Stretch let go, which he did, reluctantly, before Jim—as I later found he was called—took his belt and wrapped it tight around Ed's forearms.

"Who the hell are you?" Ed yelled at him furiously. "And what do you think you're doing?"

Jim looked down at him with a look of distaste and regret.

"*I*—God help me," he said quietly, "am your son. And this," maintaining a grip on Ed, he laid his other arm around Jamie's shoulders to pull her forward, "is your daughter."

I blame myself for not having put it all together much sooner, for all the hints were there had I only looked more closely at them—asked more questions. With what I knew, an outsider probably would have attached much more significance to the narrow focus of Ed's obsession with Sarah and the doggedness of his assertion that Alan was his son. But one often tends to be blind to the faults of old friends, accepting them as you remember them, not necessarily as they have become. My face-value acceptance of Ed *was* based on lingering assumptions from those long-ago college days. One phone call to the Holiday Inn would have told me that he had not arrived in Grand Junction when he said he did, but several days earlier. The discovery of that single lie might have set alarm bells ringing in my mind. I suppose that old saying about spilled milk should be some part of the equation now, but my inattentiveness still bothers me some.

Had it not been for Jamie and her newly found brother, Jim, my lack of awareness might well have proved fatal, to me and, possibly, to Ed as well. As I found later, the two of them had come to the house on Chipeta Avenue the night before to set everything straight with me. But, as they were walking from where they had parked, they had come up behind and noticed Ed watching the Winnebago from his car and didn't like the look of it. So they had spent the night watching him in turns from inside Sarah's house, then followed him following me and, thankfully, wound up on the Serpents Trail in time to save my life.

With Jim keeping a close hold on Ed, we walked the rest of the way down the trail to the parking lot where I had left my car. Before we started down I used my *emergency* cell phone to call the police, bringing both Soames and Bellamy so fast they were almost there to meet us. As we waited the few minutes before they pulled in to take charge of Ed, I noticed a descriptive signboard in the lot—the kind you find in many national parks—with the story of the Serpents Trail. It was titled "The Crookedest Road in the World," which seemed appropriate for more than historical reasons.

Soames came with the news that the partial print on the threatening page belonged to Ed. They took him off to jail, where he later broke down and confessed that he had not only followed me to Salt Lake, but also sent all three of the threats. The day before I arrived in Grand Junction, while Jamie was away from the house, he had also made the attempt on Sarah's life so she couldn't change her will and leave Alan less than everything she owned, not knowing she had already done so.

Alan, who hated Ed enough to have tried to drive him off the road on the Monument, and me with him, had always known he was not the son Ed wanted so badly for him to be. Alan had been the intruder I surprised on the night I arrived. He had torn Sarah's room apart hunting for her will. I wondered if Ed would ever really believe that, for, though he admitted smothering Sarah, when I left Grand Junction two days later he was still adhering to his twisted vision of plot and conspiracy between myself and Westover.

When Soames and Bellamy had driven away with Ed, I took Jamie and Jim to the parking lot at the top of the

Serpents Trail to retrieve their car and we all went back to
Chipeta Avenue, where I found us something for dinner.
We talked late into the evening, getting to know each
other, asking questions and getting answers, and I
learned enough to fill in all the blanks and more.

Jamie had found her brother shortly after she located
her mother and brought him to Grand Junction with her
when she came to care for Sarah. Sadly, it was the only
time he and Sarah were able to meet each other, but he
had come back for her gathering.

"She was so happy to have us here," Jamie said. "She
had lost track of Jim when he was adopted, so it pleased
her more than you can imagine to be able to see us both,
alive and well, before she died. I will always be thankful
for that. I stayed, but Jim had to go back to work in Salt
Lake. Besides, his wife was taking care of Billy for me
and needed his help."

"Tell me about your boy," I asked her, thinking of the
pictures I had seen.

"His name is William Marvin. The Marvin is for my
adopted father, but we call him Billy, which is a little
bit odd, because it was Sarah's husband's name—Bill.
He is autistic, which is ultimately what broke up my
marriage—his father couldn't handle a less-than-
perfect child. But he is very sweet and is doing quite
well."

I asked about that first trip to meet Sarah.

"You both stayed here in her house?"

"Yes, for those two days Jim was sleeping on the
sofa. That's why I took the quilt and pillow to the attic,
though I guess it wasn't necessary."

"Sarah had kept track of you all your life, Jamie," I
told her. "Mildred Scott, your next-door neighbor sent
her pictures and letters about you."

"I know," she said, looking a little embarrassed. "We

found them in a hidden basement room. Jim had to kick open the door to get in."

"Oh, good. I was afraid it was Ed and, since they wouldn't fit his version of things, he probably would have destroyed them. Don't worry about the door. It's your house, after all."

"I guess it *will be*," she said, remembering.

I had told them about Sarah's last changes to the will, seeing no reason to keep it a secret.

"Family money aside, Sarah left Jamie the house, but nothing specifically to you," I said to Jim.

"She knew I don't need it and Jamie does," he told me. "Billy's needs are more than she can handle on her own, and I have a good job that brings me a good living for my family."

"You have children?"

"Two and a half," he grinned. "Twin boys—rascals, both—and my wife's about to have another—a girl this time. I think we'll name her Sarah."

"It would please her." As it pleased me.

Jamie had the letter that Ed had stolen from my bag and I had given Jim the one I had accidentally kept safe in Sarah's secret space in the bookcase. It was what they had been searching for in the house.

"She told us she was leaving letters, but as far as we knew they were never found. We didn't know you had them."

We would never know what Sarah wrote to Ed in her letter, though we could pretty much guess what was in Alan's. I doubted that Ed would have believed anything she told him anyway, and now his rejection of it didn't matter. Alan would not be unhappy to know that he was right and Ed was—as Alan always claimed—*"not my father."*

Before the two of them left, I suddenly remembered

Sarah's jewelry, so, taking them upstairs to her bedroom, I showed Jamie the moveable molding in the closet and explained to her how the tradition of secret hiding places had started when Sarah and I were in college together.

"Clever!" Jim said, echoing my own thoughts.

Jamie was overwhelmed by the jewelry.

"I've never had anything so nice. I'd be afraid to wear these."

"Don't be. Sarah didn't believe in having things she couldn't wear. I remember her wearing each of these, and often. She would want you to wear them."

When Jamie came to the child-sized locket on its small gold chain, she looked at it for a minute and handed the box to Jim.

"You must have this for your new Sarah," she told him.

"I'll give it to her and tell her all about her grandmother when she's old enough," he promised.

"Will you come to live here?" I asked Jamie, as Stretch and I walked them to their car.

"I don't know," she said thoughtfully. "It's appealing, but Jim is the only family I have now and I think I want to be in the same community. Maybe I'll rent it, so I can have time to make up my mind."

"Not a bad idea."

But I couldn't help wondering what Sarah would have thought about breaking the four-generation line of people to live in the house.

It's only a house, Maxine, I heard her whisper, and knew that she would have approved of whatever Jamie decided to do with the old Victorian.

If yesterday's gathering had been a line I crossed, then Sarah must have crossed it with me, for there she was, reminding me of things.

I watched her children drive away and knew neither of them would be lost again.

"Not if I have anything to say about it," I promised Sarah aloud, and went back to the Winnebago, where I slept very well, thank you very much.

CHAPTER TWENTY-SIX

TWO DAYS LATER, OVER SEVENTY MILES SOUTH OF Grand Junction, I had parked the Winnebago, walked to a lookout point on the south rim, and stood feeling the breeze in my hair and clutching a guardrail to look down at the tiny thread of a river 2,250 feet below in the Black Canyon of the Gunnison.

I had left early to drive in the cool of the morning, so I could have the windows open as long as possible, and reached Montrose about an hour later, where I took a few miles detour east in order to take a look at this new national park. I was glad I had, for it was, not as I expected, similar to the Colorado Plateau, but remarkably different.

Instead of red sandstone, dark rock made up the walls that for two million years had been carved by the Gunnison River. They were what geologists call "basement rock," part of the metamorphic foundation of the earth's crust that had been subjected to and altered by unimaginable heat and pressure. At more than 1.7 billion years, they were some of the oldest on earth and included schist that shone with polishing and glittered with mica and garnets, and grayer gneiss that held chunks of pale quartz.

From where I stood, I could look directly across to the famous Painted Wall, its sheer cliff of dark rock marbled with streaks of pink granite like a road map, and hear the calls of the fearless acrobatic swallows in the air. There was plenty of time to appreciate this spectacular side trip, for I had decided on an easy day's drive with Durango as a destination, just over a hundred miles farther toward New Mexico.

Being able to freely follow my interests was a relief from the restrictions of the last few days. That I was once again on my own and pleasing no one but myself was satisfying, but I knew that, without Sarah to draw me there, I probably wouldn't go back to Grand Junction for some time to come.

I had left Stretch in the motor home, so I soon turned and went back to resume the trip that would be a more leisurely one than my drive from Alaska to Colorado.

Before leaving Grand Junction, Don Westover had assured me that all was well with the processing of Sarah's will—that Alan had accepted sharing and would not contest it.

"I finally convinced him that he would never win in a fight over it."

So I was free until, and unless, I was needed later, but I had left him with power of attorney, so he could probably handle anything that arose.

What would happen to Ed, I had no desire to know, but Officer Bellamy had assured me a conviction was inevitable.

* * *

Doris Chapman had waved me off, after insisting that I accept a plastic container of brownies. "For the road."

She had been joined by Jamie and Jim, who were about to head back to Salt Lake. We would keep in touch, as Sarah would have wanted and which contented me.

Opening the door of the Winnebago, I had let Stretch climb aboard, tail wagging, ready for another adventure. Before stepping in myself, I had suddenly caught a hint of honeysuckle that floated in from somewhere on the morning breeze and turned to take one last look at Sarah's house and yard, missing my friend, as I knew I always would.

That I wasn't sure exactly where in New Mexico I was headed didn't matter. I had no definite timetable and there was all of the Four Corners canyon country temptingly close.

Like Indian paintbrush, I can grow almost anywhere, and I've always liked journeys as much as destinations.

Besides—an open door always has a question in it.

Jessie Arnold and Alex Jensen return in

MURDER AT
FIVE FINGER LIGHT

a Jessie Arnold mystery from Suc Henry, coming
in April 2005 from New American Library.
Turn the page for an exciting preview. . . .

SHORTLY AFTER MIDNIGHT IN THE DARKEST HOURS OF an early morning in mid-September, the grumble of a marine engine slowly and cautiously approaching a tiny three-acre island was little more than a mutter within the insistent pulse of the incoming tide that splashed and gurgled ceaselessly against the sharp stones, the dying result of a windy rainstorm that had swept through the area the previous evening.

In the northern reaches of Frederick Sound, midway up the Alaskan length of the Inside Passage, the island was the largest of five narrow ridges of jagged rock that had come to be known as the Five Fingers, for seamen contended that they resembled a grasping hand. A treacherous four of these barely broke the surface, but the fifth and largest was unique for rising some fifty feet above the salt waters of the sound, and for the light-house that had been placed there and operated for just over one hundred years as a warning to mariners to travel farther to the west and avoid the risk of foundering upon the lurking fingers that were dangerously concealed at high tide, in darkness, or in rough weather.

The growling powerboat approached gingerly and without running lights, the operator well aware that, without an available dock or landing, caution must be taken to avoid being caught by the surf and bashing the hull against the ragged natural stone ramp rising up from the sea to the level of a wide concrete platform below the lighthouse. Between this rough ramp and a support wall below the platform lay a narrow but deep that provided partial protection from the insistent waves. Using the boat's two heavy Mercury outboard engines off the transom, the operator carefully maneuvered the twenty-six-foot Kingfisher into this semiprotected space. A second figure hopped on and helped to rig a pair of opposing lines that would hold the craft off both the rocks and the wall but close enough for unloading the small but valuable cargo.

High over their heads in the cupola of the tower, the automatic solar-powered light revolved steadily, sweeping the line of its powerful beam across the underside of a low-hanging layer of cloud that threatened more rain and reflected just enough light to make the area visible to eyes already accustomed to the dark. It would probably rain again, but the accompanying wind had died and the waters of the sound calmed their thrashing to mild whitecaps and lacy foam.

The boat tied off safely with two lines, the operator cut the engines and stepped out onto the aft deck, opened a hatch and removed two carefully waterproofed packages about eighteen inches square.

"You're sure there's no one here?"

"Yeah, sure. They won't show till around noon next Sunday."

"It better be like you say. I'm not up for any surprises on this one."

"It's fine. We've got plenty of time to stash this stuff and head for Petersburg. They'll never know we were here. It's like I told you—perfect cover."

"It better be. Here, take this. I'll bring the other one."

"Bring a flashlight. We'll need it."

"No inside lights?"

"Not unless we start a generator, and we don't want to do that, do we?"

Each warily carrying one of the packages, the two figures, one shorter and huskier than the other but both mere shadows in the dark, carefully climbed the uneven, slippery stones of the ramp to the platform and crossed to a pair of double doors that led into the lower floor beneath the lighthouse that towered over them.

"Got the key?"

Balancing the package on one arm to free a hand to dig into a jacket pocket, the answer came with a nod. "Yeah—same one I used last time I was here."

"Hey—be careful you don't drop that. Just open the damn door. Let's get this done and be gone."

Swinging the doors wide, the pair vanished into the blackness of the basement, returning empty-handed in a few minutes to lock the door behind them.

In less than ten minutes they were gone and the island was once again left to the enduring isolation of its automated duty.

Far across the wide waters of Frederick Sound, the pilot of a fishing boat took comfort in recognizing its familiar beam and in knowing that he was finally nearing his home port, little more than an hour south. Briefly he wondered about the people from Juneau who now owned Five Finger Light and the whale-watching station that rumor had it they intended to locate there.

Shrugging, he took another swig of rapidly cooling coffee and focused on achieving the most direct route across the sound to Petersburg.

COMING SOON IN HARDCOVER

Murder at Five Finger Light
A Jessie Arnold Mystery
by
Sue Henry

Jessie's friends, Laurie and Jim, have acquired their dream—an old lighthouse on the Alaskan Inside Passage—and invited everyone they know for a party. This is a weekend Jessie won't soon forget—especially when one of the guests ends up dead.

At first the death seems accidental. But when someone cuts the telephone and the radio connections, Jessie realizes there's a killer loose on the island.

0-451-21397-1

NAL5

More exciting mystery from

DANA STABENOW

"An accomplished writer...Stabenow places you right in
this lonely, breathtaking country...so beautifully evoked it
serves as another character." —*Publishers Weekly*

BETTER TO REST
0-451-20960-5
Just when his personal life starts to heat up, Liam
Campbell must put it on hold...after the grisly discovery of
a dismembered hand leads him to a crashed World War II
Army plane frozen precariously in a glacier.

NOTHING GOLD CAN STAY
0-451-20230-9
Shocked by a series of brutal, unexplainable murders,
Alaska State Trooper Liam Campbell embarks on a
desperate journey into the heart of the Alaskan Bush
country—in search of the terrible, earth-shattering truth.

SO SURE OF DEATH
0-451-19944-8
Liam Campbell has lost more than most men lose in a
lifetime: his wife and young son are dead; his budding
career is in a deep freeze ever since five people died on his
Anchorage watch. Demoted from sergeant to trooper, he
lives on a leaky gillnetter moored in Bristol Bay, brooding
on how to put down roots on dry land again and rekindle
his relationship with bush pilot Wyanet Chouinard, who
won his heart long ago, and then broke it.

SIGNET   (0451)

FROM THE MYSTERY SERIES
MURDER,
SHE WROTE
by Jessica Fletcher & Donald Bain

Based on the Universal television series
Created by Peter S. Fischer, Richard Levinson & William Link

Available wherever books are sold or at
www.penguin.com